Three ... kn...

50p

Edmund de Graves
Revered, powerful, golden

Rafe Bracton
Worldly, charming, dangerous

Sir Alaine of Darby
Handsome, gallant, noble

*miraculously find brides –
just in time for*

Yuletide Weddings

Yuletide Weddings

Jo Beverley

Margaret Moore

Shari Anton

M&B

*M&B™ and M&B™ with the Rose Device
are trademarks of the publisher.*

*First published in Great Britain 2006
by Harlequin Mills & Boon Limited, Eton House,
18-24 Paradise Road, Richmond, Surrey TW9 1SR*

YULETIDE WEDDINGS © by Harlequin Books S.A. 2006

The publisher acknowledges the copyright holders of the
individual works as follows:

The Wise Virgin © Jo Beverley Publications, Inc. 1999
The Vagabond Knight © Margaret Wilkins 1999
Christmas at Wayfarer Inn © Sharon Antoniewicz 2001

*ISBN 13: 978 0 263 85505 0
ISBN 10: 0 263 85505 8*

28-1206

*Printed and bound in Spain
by Litografia Rosés S.A., Barcelona*

CONTENTS

JO BEVERLEY, was born, raised and educated in England, and holds a degree in English history, so it comes naturally to write historical romances set in her native land in her three chosen periods: Medieval, Georgian and Regency. Her twenty novels have gained her numerous awards, including four RITA®s from the Romance Writers of America and two Career Achievement awards from *Romantic Times Magazine*. She is a member of the Romance Writers of America Hall of Fame.

In a review of her first book, *Rave Reviews* declared, "The sky's the limit for this extraordinary talent!" and the reviewer has been proved correct. Her novel *Forbidden Magic* spent five weeks on the *USA TODAY* bestsellers list, and appeared on the extended *New York Times* bestsellers list. In a review of her later medieval release, *Lord of Midnight*, *Publishers Weekly* described her as "arguably today's most skilful writer of intelligent historical romance."

Jo lives in British Columbia, Canada, with her husband and two sons.

Jo enjoys receiving letters from readers. Please write to her c/o The Alice Orr Agency, 305 Madison Avenue, Suite 1166, New York, NY 10165, USA. A self-addressed envelope with return postage is appreciated for a reply.

The Wise Virgin

Jo Beverley

Prologue

"THEY'VE STOLEN THE Blessed Virgin Mary!"

The serfs of Woldingham gaped after the horsemen thundering away down the road into the winter woods, their captive's cries fading on the frosty night breeze. Then, like a flock of starlings in the field, they scattered. Most ran for their simple thatch-roof houses, hoping not to be connected with the disaster. The really cautious gathered their families and took to the woods themselves.

After all, who else but the de Graves would commit such a crime? And when the Lord of Woldingham clashed with his old enemy, no one was overcareful where the arrows and even the sword blades fell.

Soon only the village priest and headman were left on the moonlit road leading up to the castle, if one didn't count the abandoned donkey stolidly waiting, head down. Even Joseph had thrown off his borrowed cloak and scuttled away. The two men looked at each other in silent commiseration, then they set off at a run toward the castle that loomed nearby. Despite narrow hall windows blazing with festive light, and bonfires in the bailey, it was an ominous shadow against the starry sky.

Someone had to tell Henry de Montelan, Lord of Woldingham, that his daughter had been seized by his bitterest enemy.

At Christmastide, too.

The gates stood open, waiting for the traditional procession to bring the holy couple up to the castle seeking shelter on Christmas Eve. Unlike the wickedness shown in the Bible, the Lord of Woldingham would offer the shelter of his keep to Mary and Joseph, leading them into the luxury of his solar chamber. The play was a tradition dating back generations, to the last de Montelan to go on Crusade, a tradition closely linked to the blood feud between Woldingham and the nearby castle of Mountgrave.

The two guards stared at the hurrying men, then peered behind for sight of the procession. The priest, Father Hubert, and the headman, Cob Williamson, told of the disaster as they rushed through. The guards came to full alert.

Trouble.

And at Christmastide, too.

The two men threaded their way through the

crowded bailey, calling their news but not stopping to answer alarmed questions. Tipsy cooks stopped basting the carcasses roasting on spits, and the sweating baker cursed, then called his assistants to clear tables of bread into baskets and out of the way.

There'd be armed men and horses through here soon.

And at Christmastide, too.

The noisy celebration in the great hall spilled golden light out of the arrow slits and billowed jollity from the open, expectant door of the keep. The two men labored up the outer stairs then stopped to catch their breath. Within the hall, huge fires leaped to drive away the winter chill, spraying sparks as logs settled, blending smoke with the torches flaming on the walls. Around the room, the ladies and gentleman of Woldingham made merry along with guests, household knights and senior servants. A tumult of children—striplings to babes—romped under and around the tables, tangled with a pack of dogs.

Slowly they were noticed, and an expectant silence settled.

Lord Henry de Montelan rose, massive, gracious and rosy with good cheer. "Here at last, eh? Well, say your piece!"

The headman looked at the Father Hubert and the priest accepted his role. He stepped forward. "Lord Henry, a terrible thing has happened."

The silence darkened. "What?" demanded Lord Henry, coming down off the dais toward them. His four stalwart sons rose, dazed but alert. A hound growled.

"What has happened? Where is the holy couple? Where is my daughter?"

The priest fell to his knees. "The de Graves have stolen her, my lord."

After a deadly moment a man howled. Sir Gamel, fiercest of Lord Henry's sons, leaped over the table in front of him in one bound, his teeth bared. "My sword! My sword! I'll gut them all. To horse! Revenge!" He stormed toward the door, brothers not far behind.

Lord Henry stopped him with a hand, perhaps the only man in England able to do it. Though Lord Henry's color stayed high, it was not a sign of good cheer anymore. "Aye, my son, we'll have revenge, and blood and guts aplenty, but we'll not run into a trap. Horses!" he bellowed, and the men in the hall burst into action. "Armor! Weapons! Gamel, Lambert, and Reyner—you hunt them down and bring Nicolette home safe. *Safe,* remember. Harry," he said to his eldest son, "you and I will stay here. In case."

Stalwart Harry agreed, but with a scowl of disappointment.

"At Christmastide?" young Reyner asked, sixteen but nearly as big as his brothers. "They'd steal the Virgin on Christmas Eve?"

"Nothing," growled his father, "is too wicked for the de Graves."

In moments the noise of the castle changed to martial tone, and the lord, his oldest son, and his master-at-arms were huddled in military conference. Father Hubert and Cob silently congratulated themselves on coming out of it whole and slipped away down the steps. Since no one seemed to be in a mood for feasting, a hunk of roast pork and some loaves went with them. A bit of a feast for the poor villagers.

"A fine state of affairs," mumbled Cob around a piece of juicy meat.

"At Christmastide. At a holy pageant! Godless men. Godless!"

"It's to be hoped the poor Lady Nicolette comes to no harm, Father. For everyone's sakes."

"Indeed, indeed." Then the priest slid a look at his friend. "But do you know, Cob, I could have sworn I saw Lady Nicolette up in the gallery over the hall, peeping out."

The headman stopped. "What? Nay, Father, you must be mistaken. How could that be?"

"Well now, what if some other gentle lady played the part of the Virgin? I thought it a little strange that Lady Nicolette did not speak to me and kept herself so huddled in her cloak."

Cob swallowed the meat in one gulp. "But it's *tradition*, Father. A holy tradition. The youngest virgin of marriageable years in the lord's family plays the part of the Blessed Virgin. And by—"

"—being welcomed into the hall of Woldingham, instead of turned away to lie in a stable, brings God's blessings to everyone in the coming year. Yes, yes. It makes you think, doesn't it?"

"It makes you bloody afeard, it does! What's to become of us all with the tradition mucked about like that?"

"And what's to become of those involved when it all comes out?" the priest muttered.

He wasn't thinking about the peasants, or even the feuding men, but about the young women involved in this perilous deception.

And the possible reasons for it.

Father Hubert crossed himself and started to pray.

Chapter One

THE HUGE PADDED BELLY finally had a benefit, Joan of Hawes decided as she bounced across the horse, face down, in front of her captor. It cushioned the worst of this. She'd given up screaming and yelling. All that had achieved was a sore throat. Her captor was treating her as if she were a roll of fleeces, ignoring her—other than one strong hand in her belt that stopped her falling off, accidentally or on purpose.

Despite fury and fear, she was grateful for that firm grip. They were racing down a woodland track at a gallop, and she'd no mind to die over this. But who had snatched her off the donkey, and why? And why now, when it would cause such terrible trouble?

Suddenly the rider pulled the horse to a head-tossing, stamping stop, and hoisted her up just like a bundle. Before she could shriek, he turned her, and put her down sitting sideways in front of him on the horse. By the time her dizzy head had settled, they were off again and she'd only caught a glimpse of a dark-hooded form. Now, however, she could see other riders around. Strange riders, flowing dark, fast and fiendishly quiet through the winter-bare, frosty wood.

Earlier, they'd swooped down on the village in silence, like black hawks from the sky….

"Sweet Mary, save me," she whispered. Had she been seized by the forces of darkness?

She twisted to try to see if her captor had a human face, but saw only darkness. A shiver of unholy terror passed through her, but then common sense returned. He was hot like a man, and smelled like a man—sweat, wool and horse. Now she saw that his hood hung forward to shadow his face, and his skin was darkened in some way. A common raider of some sort.

Then she understood more. This galloping horse had no saddle, and the man she was squashed against wore no mail. The bridle and reins were rope. Not un-earthly devils, then, but men without jingle of bell, harness or mail. All the horses were dark, too. No wonder they'd appeared as if out of nowhere.

It was—it had to be—the de Graves, her uncle's bit-terest enemies, taking this opportunity to ruin the de Montelan's most sacred ceremony. All the same, she couldn't help admiring the planning and execution. She did so love a job well done.

But why, oh why, did they have to choose *this* year to make mischief, when it was going to cause such terrible trouble? Her cousin Nicolette had been supposed to play the Virgin, and no one must know that she and Joan had changed places.

Perhaps they'd let her go soon. They'd succeeded in disrupting the ceremony, and had no need to keep her. If so, could she get back to the castle before Nicolette was discovered there? Probably. If he put her down now.

"Sirrah," she said.

When he ignored her, she shouted it. "Sirrah!"

He paid no attention, intent on the dark road and speed. Speed taking them farther and farther from Woldingham. Joan eased her arm forward and jabbed back as hard as she could with her elbow.

The horse misstepped, and her captor grunted slightly, but he only said, "Stop that."

Then they were off again, and she knew—knowing men—that there'd be no stopping until he decided it was right to stop. May the devil rot his toes. She thought of throwing herself off the horse, but wasn't feeling suicidal. Just frightened and irritated.

What foolish mischief this was. But then, the whole bloodthirsty feud between the de Graves and the de Montelans was foolish. It had cost lives over the generations, and disrupted the whole countryside hereabouts, and all because of a piece of cloth carried to Jerusalem back in the First Crusade.

In the weeks since Joan had arrived at Woldingham to be companion to her cousin Nicolette, she'd learned all about the wicked, dishonorable de Graves family. They were supposedly guilty of everything from stealing that banner to putting the evil eye on the Woldingham sheep last August. The stories might be true, but she wasn't convinced, mainly because of the current head of the de Graves family.

Not that she'd met the famous Edmund de Graves, of course, but all England had heard of the Golden Lion—beautiful as Saint Michael, brave as Saint George, protector of the weak, defender of the right, dire vengeance on all who did evil…. Legends were told of him, and troubadours sung his praises.

The Golden Lion was son of the famous Silver Lion—Remi de Graves, mighty warrior and advisor to the king. Lord Edmund had been trained from boyhood by the best tutors and warriors, including the almost mythical Almar de Font, a renowned hero in his own right. At sixteen, the Golden Lion had carried the prize at a glittering tourney. At seventeen he had fought brilliantly in the war against France. At eighteen he had singlehandedly cleared out a nest of outlaws, who were terrorizing the area around one of his estates.

It was possibly true that generations ago a de Graves had cheated a de Montelan out of the banner, but the Golden Lion could have nothing to do with wicked rivalry and revenge today.

Could he?

So, was she *not* in the hands of the de Graves?

The horse was pulled to a halt again, pressing her even harder against her captor. Whoever he was, he was a superb rider. This was a fiery destrier, heat and muscles seething beneath her, and her captor was controlling the beast with just legs and a piece of rope.

"Husha, husha, Thor," her captor murmured, leaning forward to pat and soothe the horse's arched neck. His massive chest almost crushed Joan and she squeaked a protest.

He straightened. "My apologies, Lady."

"Now, sirrah," she said, ready to argue for release, but he told her to wait and turned to the other dark riders gathering around, breath puffing white in the cold air.

To her irritation, Joan found herself waiting. She studied the half-dozen hooded men, seeking a clue as to where they came from. They wore no badge, and were almost silent shadows against the moon-silvered woodland, with horse-breathing and hoof-shuffling as the only sounds.

"All's well," her captor said, and without comment the others spun to ride off, scattering.

They really scattered, too, going in different directions, avoiding paths and melting into the woodland. This efficiency did hint at the hand of the great Lord Edmund, but she wouldn't believe he would stoop to something so petty.

It must be some of his men indulging in a prank. She'd heard that the men-at-arms and retainers of the two families were the ones most keen to make trouble. The main point here was to get free and get back to Woldingham.

"You are from the de Graves?" she whispered, as he turned his horse into the woods, in a different direction again to that taken by the others.

He leaned over her again, but this time to protect her from the prickly holly branch he pushed aside. "Of course. You are safe, Lady, never fear."

Safe. It seemed a strange thing to say, and he was wrong. Joan had never felt less safe in her life, and it had nothing to do with him. She and Nicolette had planned to switch back once the Holy Family was in the castle, but the more time that passed, the more likely it was that Nicolette would be found. Uncle Henry would think they had played a childish trick, and would be furious. If he found out *why*, though…. Joan couldn't even imagine the rage and violence that would result then.

She had to get back.

"Let me go," she said urgently. "You've achieved your purpose."

"Have I?"

"Of course—"

He put a large, callused hand over her mouth, and she heard what he'd heard—the distant howls of her uncle's hounds.

"Sounds carry on still winter air," he breathed into her ear. "Don't try to speak."

He removed his hand and they moved on, the pace slow now because of the unpredictable ground. *Don't speak?* How was she to hammer sense into his head if she couldn't speak? All the same, Joan sagged into silence. *What point in arguing?* How was she to get back to her uncle's castle undetected with hounds on their trail?

The thought of Nicolette; however, made her try again. Perhaps the hounds wouldn't be interested in her trail. "Put me down," she whispered, "Then you can get away."

"We are getting away," he whispered back, with a hint of humor.

"You're alone. You can't fight them. And the hounds—"

"Have many tracks to follow. You find it hard to hold your tongue, don't you, Lady Nicolette?"

Before Joan could decide whether to tell him she

wasn't Nicolette, he said, "And here is the well-planned water, to hide our trail."

It was a shallow stream, gurgling noisily over rocks. The horse splashed into and along it, guided by its rider with only subtle shifts of his muscular body.

Clever yet again. "What do you want with me?" she whispered. "Why are you keeping me?"

"Can't you imagine?"

Imagine? Their plan was to disrupt the ceremony. What else?

Then a horrible thought occurred to her.

What if the plan went further than that? What if the plan was to stir the smoldering feud into a hellish fire? There were some at Woldingham who wanted all out war, including her cousin Gamel. What if there were similar men at Mountgrave Castle? Men who wanted to pour oil in the fire.

Disrupting the pageant would be a mere splash of oil. Kidnapping only a cupful. But rape…rape of Lord Henry's only daughter would be a whole barrelful. It would start a conflagration quenched only by the blood of a whole family.

And if only Cousin Joan was available, well, a jug of oil would make a violent enough flame.

Joan sent an urgent, silent prayer to Mary, protector of all virgins, and tried desperately to think of a way to escape.

Fight him off? Ridiculous.

Jump off the horse and run? She'd be caught in a moment.

Push him off the horse and escape on it?

A trained war horse wouldn't be taken, and she might as well try to push the hills alongside the stream as push this man off this horse!

Helplessness started an uncontrollable shivering, and a whirling panic in her mind.

"Cold?" he said. "We'll be in a shelter soon."

"Where? What? Where are you taking me?" Her voice turned shrill, and with a curse, he clasped his hand over her mouth again.

"To a cave," he said, sounding irritated. "It's prepared for a lady's comfort. Now, stay silent until we reach there, woman."

Since he kept his hand over her mouth, she didn't have a choice. However, Joan's fear shrank a little. Thrown back against him as the horse picked its way up what was probably a sheep track of some sort, she considered his irritated tone. Could a man intent on rape and murder really speak like that?

How could she know? With a bundle of brothers, she knew men quite well, but she knew nothing of how they behaved in war, or in a bloody feud. At the thought of her brothers and her family, tears smarted in her eyes.

In trouble again. That's what they'd say if she lived to face them. Her brothers would rush to kill her defiler, but that wouldn't do much good after the fact. They'd all think it was her own fault, and as usual, they'd be right.

WHEN JOAN HAD ARRIVED at Woldingham, wrapped in furs and hoping for new adventures, she'd found her cousin Nicolette a feeble, weepy sort of person. She'd been summoned, apparently, because of that—to be a companion and raise her spirits. Her aunt Ellen had informed her that Nicolette suffered from a case of a lovesickness—that she was even having to be guarded from running away with the man. She was not to be encouraged in her folly.

"Your parents report you to be a young woman of sense, Joan, and not given to foolish fancies."

Joan had not been feeling particularly sensible at that moment as she was temporarily staggered by the opulence of Woldingham—by the size, the number of retainers and the glittering treasures everywhere she looked. She'd mumbled meek agreement—she had promised her mother she'd behave—but ventured a question. "Whom does Cousin Nicolette love, Aunt?"

"It doesn't matter. He is completely impossible. Completely."

Joan couldn't imagine how Nicolette could be so silly as to imagine herself in love with a landless knight or a troubadour, and she was happy to help her recover. She herself was firmly of the belief that love could be guided toward sensible, suitable targets.

Nicolette had seemed to welcome companionship and distraction, and soon became a lively, charming friend—even if she did sometimes relapse into sighing, unhappy moments. Joan had enjoyed the wealth and comfort of Woldingham, and the rich selection of handsome, eligible young men paying suit to Nicolette.

She'd already decided an older, sensible man would suit her better as a husband, but she had no objection to flattering flirtation with toothsome gallants.

Even though Nicolette was clearly not tempted by any of her gallant swains, Joan had expected the excitement of Christmas to banish all sighs for a while. The closer it drew; however, the more distracted and melancholy Nicolette became. Her loving parents fretted, but never gave the slightest sign of bending.

The man must truly be impossible.

Then one day, Nicolette fainted. After she'd been carried into the luxurious bedchamber they shared and left to rest, Joan gave her a piece of her mind. "Nicolette, this is foolish beyond measure. No man is worth starving and fainting over!"

"Yes, he is," her cousin said mutinously, but then tears glistened in her eyes. "But it's not that exactly…I'm so afraid…"

"Afraid? Of what?"

"The…the play."

"The Holy Family one? On Christmas Eve?"

Nicolette nodded.

"What is there about that to make you ill? You've played the Virgin for three years, haven't you?"

"Since I started my courses, yes. The youngest virgin of marriageable age…"

"So?"

Nicolette's eyes searched the private room as if someone might be lurking, then she whispered, "I'm not."

"Not what?"

"A *virgin*."

Joan gaped. It was so outrageous she'd not believed it.

Except that it instantly explained so much.

"What's worse," Nicolette added, covering her face with trembling hands, "I'm with child! What am I going to do?" She looked up, wild-eyed. "Don't tell Father and Mother!"

"Of course not." Joan, however, felt ready to lose her breakfast herself. "Why? How…? I assume," she snapped in outrage and terror, "you weren't visited by the Archangel Gabriel! Were you raped?" It seemed the only explanation.

Nicolette sat up. "Of course not. I love him!"

Joan stared. Mooning over Sir Nobody, or a charming troubadour was one thing. Giving her body to him…? "When?"

"At the Martinmas Fair. I didn't plan it. I swear it. It just happened. We stole a few moments. We were so unhappy, and…oh, if only Father would relent! But I never thought until recently that I might have conceived."

Would Uncle Henry soften when he learned of the child? She knew the answer without asking. Nicolette's parents doted on her, but that meant that if they'd refused the match so firmly the man must be truly unsuitable. A baby would change nothing.

Except that it changed everything.

She shuddered at the thought of the reaction when Nicolette had to confess. Would the baby save her from blows? From being thrown into the foulest dungeon? Would her parents' love survive the shock and shame?

Whatever the immediate reaction, Nicolette would end up in a convent until she bore her child, and it would be either strangled or given to serfs to raise. After that, she would either stay behind walls or be married off to whatever man would take money to overlook her flaw.

Joan gathered her weeping cousin into her arms, though she had no real comfort to offer. The growing child could not be hidden forever. It was all just a question of time.

When her cousin had collected herself a bit, Joan gave what little comfort she could. "Don't worry about the play. Nothing shows. No one will know."

Nicolette stared at her. "Joan, God will know! I can't represent the Blessed Virgin! It will bring a curse on us all."

"Your baby will bring a curse on all soon enough. What difference does a play make?"

"All the difference in the world!" Nicolette put her hands to her stomach. "I know I carry disaster, but that means I cannot add to it. Ever since the de Graves stole the Bethlehem Banner—" she hiccuped on new tears "—ever since then, Woldingham's well-being comes of the Holy Family play."

Joan hoped she was as good a Christian as any, but she had little belief in God paying attention to plays. The reenactment had a lot more to do with human rivalry than with piety.

The grand de Graves and de Montelan families had many estates and moved between them, but they both celebrated Christmastide here in the area. The de Graves displayed the banner that had been carried into Bethlehem during the Crusade. In direct reaction, the de Montelans welcomed the Holy Family into their home, proving their superiority to the rest of mankind.

Both families were thumbing their noses at one another rather than engaging in an act of piety.

"You're going to have to do it for me," Nicolette said, jerking Joan out of her thoughts.

"What?"

"Play the Virgin."

"I can't do that!"

"You have to. You *are* a virgin, aren't you?"

"Of course, I am!"

"Well then. I looked at the family records, and I think you are the youngest virgin of marriageable age anyway."

Joan considered what she knew. Her mother was Lord Henry's sister. Of three brothers, two were unmarried, and one had only sons. She had four older married sisters and five brothers. It did seem likely.

"But I can't pass as you."

"Yes, you can. To preserve the illusion of the Holy Family, you'll slip out of the castle secretly."

"With no guards?"

"The guards will just see you down to the village, then return. They won't notice anything. You'll be enveloped in a head-cloth and cloak, with a big cushion for the pregnancy. Besides, it's not their place to speak with you. And remember, when you appear in the hall no one here is supposed to recognize you, either, so you stay well swathed."

Joan had to admit that it seemed possible. "But

what of you? You can't be seen. And won't anyone notice that I'm not at the celebrations?"

Nicolette leaned back, frowning over it. "Your courses!" she suddenly said. "You suffer so much from them."

"That's true," Joan agreed. She always had terrible pains and, for at least one day a month, had to take to her bed with soothing potions and warm stones to hug.

"You'll have your pains on Christmas Eve."

"My courses are not due until a week later."

"I don't suppose anyone will be counting. And I'll pretend to be you."

"That won't work. Your mother fussed over me the last time."

"You'll make it clear you don't want fussing, and then she'll be so involved with the Christmas Eve festivities that she'll not have time. I'll huddle down in the bed and moan if anyone comes."

"I can see a hundred ways for this to go wrong!"

"So can I, but we have to try. Please, Joan. I won't commit sacrilege."

In the end, Joan had sighed and agreed. "But the problem still remains, Nicolette. What are you going to do?"

For a moment she thought her cousin wouldn't answer, but then she whispered, "I've been in touch with *him*. I've told him about the child. He's going to find a way."

It was a solution, but a terrible one. "Run away? Leave your family?"

"I have no choice."

"Oh, Nicolette!" Joan leaned forward to embrace her cousin, tears stinging her eyes. It was tempting to berate her again for the string of follies that had led to this suffering, but she knew her cousin must recognize every single one. Now, in this dire situation, what choice was there? It would be hard enough to evade the guard around Nicolette and steal her away. Then Nicolette would be cut off from her family forever, and everyone at Woldingham would be cast into misery. And for what? For that phantasm called love, that wildness called lust.

The best Joan could pray for was that in this dreadful situation, Lord Henry would bend and decide that accepting an unworthy husband was better than losing his daughter forever. After a month at Woldingham, she had doubts. Though just, Lord Henry was relentlessly stern. The innocent were not punished, but the guilty were not spared. He seemed to regard any flexibility or hesitation as if it were a deadly plague.

And, she thought, clasped in the enemy's arms, here she was. Guilty of deception, and possibly sacrilege.

What's more, Nicolette was stuck in the castle, presumably still huddling and groaning; the play and feast were both ruined; and the de Montelans were out in furious pursuit of the de Graves, murder on their minds.

Chapter Two

THE HORSE HALTED, and she glared up at the man. "You," she said, "have made a stupid mess of everything."

"This mess is none of my making," he said shortly, sliding off the horse. He reached up and lifted her down as if she weighed nothing, which certainly wasn't true. She was instantly reminded that she was the prisoner of a very strong and ruthless man who might have evil intentions.

"Come into the warm," he said, leading her toward an ominous opening in the hillside. "Perhaps it will improve your mood."

A curtain had been hung at the cave opening, probably to hide the light, for inside, the space was lit by three dish-shaped oil lamps. There must be an opening above, for the smoke wasn't choking them. It was a little warmer, but not much.

Hay and water stood ready for the horse, and he cared for the beast first. Joan hadn't been aware of how much warmth she'd drawn from his body during the ride, but now she shivered. Perhaps also with fear. A fire was laid ready, so she lit it from one of the lamps and held her hands to it as she looked around. Two fine wooden chests, three jugs and thick furs spread over a ledge of rock.

To make a bed? She swallowed, trying to decide if she were better off trying to pretend to be Nicolette. Then she shook her head. Even neighbors who were deep and ancient enemies couldn't help but meet. This man doubtless knew Nicolette by sight, and no one who knew them would confuse them.

Nicolette was slender, with fine hair the pale gold of rich cream. Joan was well-curved with curly hair closer in color to honey. The huge bolster that faked her ripe pregnancy was proving useful in hiding the shape difference, but that couldn't outweigh the rest when he had a chance to really look at her.

With a final pat of the horse's neck, he came over to her.

"Please, Lady Nicolette, take a seat," he said, gesturing to the furs.

Joan stayed facing the fire, putting off the moment. "Who are you, and what do you want with me?"

"I'm sorry," he said, sounding sincere. "I thought you truly would have guessed, Nicolette. Beneath dark cloth and grime lies Lord Edmund de Graves, and you are now safe in my care."

Joan turned slowly, dizzy with shock.

Golden hair, and beneath the soot on his skin, a face handsome enough for the Archangel Michael. His skill with the horse. The very quality of that horse. His effortless air of command.

The Golden Lion.

And he'd rescued Nicolette. Why?

Because, of course, he was her lover!

She took the few steps backward to the ledge and sat with a thump. What man would be attractive enough to turn her cousin's wits, and yet the most unsuitable husband in the world for Nicolette of Woldingham?

Lord Edmund de Graves.

"Don't be afraid," he said, pulling off his leather jerkin, revealing a rich green tunic beneath. "We're safe here. In a little while, the first hunt will have died down and we can make our way to Mountgrave."

He dipped a cloth into a bucket of water and scrubbed his face clean. Joan just sat there, stunned and bitterly disappointed. She supposed he was going to be as bitterly disappointed any minute now. Dense of him not to have realized he had the wrong lady, but after a lifetime with her dense brothers she wasn't completely surprised.

At least she needn't fear rape. Instead of pure relief, however, she ached with regrets. Regrets for a tarnished hero. Edmund de Grave—the sort of man to ruin a maid in some corner of the Martinmas fair.

He turned to her. "Please, my lady. We are safe. Make yourself more comfortable."

There was no point putting it off. Joan unwound the enveloping head-cloth.

The smile disappeared. "So. Who are you?"

"Joan of Hawes, cousin to Lady Nicolette."

He sank cross-legged beside the fire, in a breathtakingly elegant movement that seemed unconscious. "Then we have a problem, my lady."

Fighting tears, Joan stood and loosened the low girdle that held her paunch in place. With a wriggle, she made it fall to the ground so she could kick it away.

Well-shaped lips twitched. "Such a casual way with offspring."

"I'm sure many women wish pregnancies could be ended so easily."

"True enough. Why were you playing the part, Lady Joan?"

"You know that, my lord," Joan snapped, sitting down again, and gathering her cloak around her.

"Ah," he said, eyes widening slightly, "the virginity of the Blessed Mary. Truly, I should have thought of that."

"Indeed you should!"

His brows rose a little at her tone. They were lovely

brows—golden and smoothly curved. His hair was lovely, too, waving down to his shoulders.

What a deception.

What a waste.

What a temptation, even so.

This was doubtless a lesson planned by heaven to reinforce her belief that a woman who chose a husband by looks was a fool.

Suppressing a sigh at a bitter lesson learned, she rose. "Now will you return me to Woldingham before folly turns to tragedy?"

He didn't move. "If I had a magic wand, I doubtless would, Lady Joan. As it is, we still must evade the first fury of the hunt. We'll have to rest here for a while." He swiveled, reaching for a jug and two cups, then poured wine for them both. He held one out, and Joan took it, noting that the cup was heavy silver, richly worked. When she sipped, she found rich mead. Even as a fugitive in a cave, Edmund de Graves did not live simply.

That part of the myth was true. The splendor of Mountgrave was part of the myth.

And part of the bitterness between the families, since the de Montelans attributed the de Graves' extreme wealth to their possession of the banner.

Joan wanted to insist that they leave but knew he was right. This area would be full of Woldingham men by now, men who would kill first and think later. The Golden Lion was reputed to be a warrior of almost miraculous skill and strength, but even if that were true, he couldn't defeat ten or twenty—especially unarmed.

Then she saw his armor and sword in the corner near the horse, dull steel and glittering gold, glinting in the firelight. Even armored, however, he couldn't get her safely undetected back to Woldingham yet.

Which blew away any hope of returning before Nicolette was discovered and their actions were known to all.

With a sigh she leaned back on the luxurious makeshift bench.

"Where is Lady Nicolette?" he asked.

"In bed, pretending to be me and unwell."

"Can she remain there undetected for long?"

At least he was as clever as described. No need to lay it all out for him. "Perhaps for a while, my lord. If no one suspects."

"Lady Nicolette is deeply loved by her family. No one will visit her to make sure she is comfortable?"

"You forget. It's not Nicolette. It's me. I'm a mere cousin."

"But a guest. It seems neglectful."

She really didn't want to discuss her private matters with the Golden Lion, but she said, "I have very painful courses, my lord. I've had one bout since arriving at Woldingham. Lady Ellen knows there is nothing to do for me but leave me alone for a while. And she will be busy."

"Ah, and by great good fortune, your courses came now? You are bearing up bravely."

Heat rushed into her cheeks. "They are some days off yet, my lord. We could only hope that Lady Ellen is not paying close attention to such matters."

He shrugged and sipped his wine. "How could you have hoped to pull off the deception to the end?"

She told him of the concealment on the way to the village. "Then, if everything had gone as planned, Joseph and I would have been escorted to the solar, and the feast would have begun. We would have put aside our cloaks and slipped out to join in the celebration. Nicolette would have appeared, of course, not me. I'd have taken her place in the bed. The deception would not have had to last for long. In an hour or so, I was going to have a miraculous recovery and join the company." Rather wistfully, she added, "I was looking forward to it."

"Poor lady," he said, with a hint of a smile. "We had no choice, however. Other than tonight, Lord Henry has kept his daughter under close guard, and I want no more bloodshed between us."

She thought of the howling hounds and gave him a look.

"There's been no bloodshed yet, and will not be if I can help it," he said.

"That's another reason you won't try to get me back to Woldingham now."

"Exactly. If your family managed to kill me, it would not promote peace."

"This whole adventure will not promote peace!"

"I know it all too well. How long can Lady Nicolette maintain the deception?"

Joan abandoned any thought of making him see how stupid it had been to seduce Nicolette to begin with. "It's impossible to say, my lord. Will Lady Ellen be distracted by the seizure of her daughter, or will she think to come to me with the story? I hope the former. It is possible that I'll be ignored until tomorrow. Can you return me before then?"

"Perhaps. It was never part of the plan. What will happen to Lady Nicolette if she is discovered?"

Joan shrugged. "She can't reveal the real reason, so she'll have to claim it was a girlish trick. Lord Henry will punish her for sure."

"How severely? You have destroyed Lord Henry's holy play. Perhaps committed sacrilege, or even treason."

Joan didn't need the worst put into words. "Lord Henry loves his daughter deeply."

"But I don't suppose he loves you that deeply.

Perhaps it would be better not to return you to Woldingham at all."

"I will not leave Nicolette to face him alone." The noble statement was interrupted by a noisy rumble—from an empty stomach.

Lord Edmund's brows rose, but he stood to pick up a wooden box and put it open on the ledge beside her. "Pork, bread and a cake of dried fruits. Not a feast, but something."

He took none, and returned to his seat by the fire. Joan would have liked to match him in nobly ignoring the food, but she was famished. "Woldingham fasts on Christmas Eve," she said. "I've only had dry bread and water all day."

"Whereas I have eaten fish and other foods. Please, my lady, eat. It is for you. While you eat, we can decide what to do."

Joan tried to control her hunger in front of him, and took only dainty nibbles of pork and bread. "You have to return me to Woldingham, my lord, in case there's a chance to preserve the deception."

"If the deception has been discovered, however, it will go hard with you."

"I don't suppose he'll kill me. Or Nicolette," she added, suddenly struck by his lack of concern over his beloved. "Of course, when he finds out about the child…"

"I am aware of that danger, Lady Joan. This was all an attempt to bring Lady Nicolette to safety."

She opened her mouth to berate him for getting Nicolette with child, but she managed to control herself. "How long before we can attempt the return?"

He looked at the box. "With your appetite, not long."

With heating cheeks, she realized that, morsel by morsel, she'd eaten most of it. "I'm hungry."

"It's as well I'm not." Did his lips twitch again? Was he *laughing* at her? Joan was taking a hearty dislike to the Golden Lion.

Deliberately she picked up the last of the fruit and took a big bite. "*When* can we return me to Woldingham, Lord Edmund?"

"At dawn, perhaps. The serious hunt should have petered out by then. Your safe return will still leave Lady Nicolette imprisoned, however. Can you think of a way to help her reach Mountgrave?"

Joan was about to declare that she wouldn't do that even if she could, when logic intervened. This was the father of Nicolette's child, the man her cousin loved, and at last he seemed to be putting her welfare first. Nicolette would want to be with him, and would be infinitely safer with him than with her family once her belly started to show.

"Why should I help you?" she asked, hoping to

find out more about his intentions. Did he plan to marry her cousin? How could he, without the blessing of her family, with Lord Henry doubtless howling his outrage to the king?

He sipped from his cup. "Wouldn't she like to be reunited with her lover?"

"I'm not sure. It will cause such grief and trouble."

"The cursed feud has been causing grief and trouble for generations. Her belly will cause more. Will Lord Henry soften when he knows she's with child?"

He clearly knew the answer. Joan put down the fruit, her appetite truly gone. "This is such folly. Why must the enmity between you and Lord Henry run so deep?"

"It runs dry on my side, I assure you, despite the deaths over the years."

Joan remembered hearing that Lord Edmund had asked for a truce. "But he will not bend?"

"He's not completely inflexible. I think, deep inside, Lord Henry tires of this madness as much as I do. But this matter has turned it all back into chaos."

"As it was bound to!" Patience snapping, Joan leaped to her feet. "'Fore God, Lord Edmund, how could you have been so foolish?"

Ignoring his sharp movement, she carried on. "Seeing you, I can begin to understand why Nicolette was swept beyond wisdom, but you have more years and experience. You are the Golden Lion! You should have had strength for both." She turned to pace the confines of the cave, and her thoughts continued to spill out. "Ah, you men are impossible! You think with your—"

He grabbed her skirt and jerked her toward him. Short of toppling onto the fire, she had no choice but to go. "Stop that!" At the last moment, she fell down on her behind rather than go any closer, but he seized her waist and drew her implacably onto his lap.

"Seeing me?" he said, a strange glint in his angry eyes. "Lust after me yourself, do you, Lady Joan?"

May the clever man get warts, and she deserved them herself for revealing her folly.

Joan turned her face away. "I merely accept your appeal, my lord. To a susceptible young woman."

"And you, of course, though young, are not susceptible."

"Not at all." Hastily she added, "And please don't feel you need to prove otherwise—"

He cinched her closer, tight against his broad chest, forcing her to face him, to face teeth bared in a furious smile. "How well you know foolish men, Lady Joan. We can't resist a challenge, can we? Are you sure you were fit to play the Blessed Virgin?"

A hand slid up to settle beneath her breast. Only beneath. A subtle threat, but he could probably feel the frantic pounding of her heart. Why, oh, why hadn't she followed her mother's advice and learned to hold her tongue with men?

"My lord," she said, trying the soothing tone she'd use with a snarling dog, "you don't really have any interest in me, and you dishonor Nicolette by this behavior."

"But we men are impossible." Confining her with one strong arm, he seized her long plaits in the other hand. "And we think with our rods. That was what you were about to say, wasn't it, my foolish virgin?" He began to wrap her hair around his fist, drawing her head inexorably back, then back farther. She squeaked a protest, but it did no good. She ended up stretched like a bow, waiting helplessly for the attacking kiss.

Only then, his eyes on hers, did his lips slowly lower.

At the last moment, they slid away, down to her extended, vulnerable neck. A choked sound escaped her as he ran his hot lips up and down her throat, teasing skin, nerves, tendons and the pounding blood vessels beneath.

It was nothing.

It was terrifying.

"Don't. Please..." Her plea escaped as a whisper.

He ignored it and pressed his teeth into the side of her neck—not hurting, but showing ruthlessly how vulnerable she was. How he, like a ferocious animal, could sever skin and flesh to kill.

That wasn't, however, why she was so panicked. What terrified her was the ridiculous excitement bursting into flame within her. She'd never been handled like this by a man before—never. And her astonishing reaction was a breathless dizziness that was equal parts bizarre, irrational pleasure and blind terror at feeling this way.

He raised his head to look at her with dark, angry eyes. "Still think you are a good judge of men, Lady Joan?"

She could only stare, knowing her eyes must be white around the edges, feeling her heart thunder close to bursting.

"You thought me safe, and I am not. You thought I would take your sharp tongue without retaliation, which I will not. And then you thought worse. You impugned my honor."

With a sharp tug on her trapped hair, he said, "This has not been my idea of a perfect Christmas Eve. This enterprise was embarrassing to think about, tedious to arrange, and dangerous to carry through. It springs from stupidity, weakness and rigid minds. And now, by the thorns, it was all for nothing. I have the wrong woman, and she's a sharp-tongued bitch who wants to lecture me about wisdom and strength. Don't believe the legend of the Golden Lion, Lady Joan. I'm just a man, with all the faults of men. Perhaps I raped Nicolette. She is after all, the precious daughter of my enemy."

Joan found the power to shake her head as far as she was able.

"No? As I said, don't believe the legend."

Consciously or not, he'd relaxed his grip a little. Swallowing, she said, "Nicolette said it wasn't rape. She wouldn't lie about it."

"Will she stick to that story when her family's fury falls on her head?"

"She won't lie."

"Even though she has been such a foolish virgin?"

His cynical disdain was stinging places that had no right to care. "She was clearly a very foolish virgin to give herself to you."

Anger flashed and his teeth showed like fangs, but then, like light shifting, it became a true grin, and his expression gentled. "Ah, Joan, but you're beautiful when you're angry."

Before Joan could react to that ridiculous statement, his lips descended on hers at last, his strong arm holding her close against him, too close for struggle or escape. She tried to writhe, but even that was scarcely possible, and her bound hair meant she could not free her lips from the overwhelming assault.

She must have stopped struggling, because his left

hand was now stroking her side. He started to rock a little, and his lips freed hers to murmur, "My honey, my pretty one, my sweet, fiery Joan. Give me your lips, give me your soft sighs. Melt to me. I'll never hurt you."

He kissed her again, and she couldn't stop her lips softening a little, soothed by his gentle, foolish murmurs.

Foolish.

Scarce believable. But...

Edmund de Graves. And her...

He kissed her cheeks, her eyelids, then her lips again. "Open to me, sweetheart. Let me taste you fully."

She wanted to taste him, just this once. She let the Golden Lion meld their lips, let him taste her mouth. Tasted his heat, felt his hand on her breast, rubbing the astonishingly sensitive peak.

Her head swirled as with a fever, but she knew this was madness. She must stop him. This was what he'd done to Nicolette, and look at where that had led!

Just a little more, though? A little more before fighting him off...

He suddenly lay back, their lips still joined, so she sprawled on top. Both hands seized her thighs, spreading them over him. He set her lips free, but stayed close, breath warm against her cheek. "I hunger for you, Joan. Let me feel more of you, just a little more."

He was big and hot, as if power glowed out of him and into her. She hungered, too. Dazed by him, by her effect on him, she cradled his strong face in her hands, loving that intimate contact. "A little, then…"

She wouldn't go too far, but she could enjoy a little more.

He pulled her skirts free so she was naked against his tunic. Murmuring soothing nothings, he eased up his own clothes. She stiffened then. No, she mustn't.

But it was only his belly he exposed to her. Her skin lay against his hot, hard flesh, so she felt each of his deep breaths in her most intimate place. Poised for flight, she still thought, *Not yet. Not quite yet. This is too extraordinary, too wonderful.*

He slid his powerful, callused hands up her legs, beneath her skirts, to grip her hips, to hold her pressed to him. "So hot and wet against me." He shifted his torso, moving under her, against her. "Beautiful lady. Give yourself to me."

Joan swayed, fevered, feeling almost as if she breathed through her secret places, breathed in him— his heat, his power, his vibrant essence. His eyes trapped her wits, gazing at her, into her, dark with desire.

For her.

No.

It was *Nicolette* he loved. Nicolette!

"No." She clawed first at one confining hand, then

the other, making no impression through the cloth of her garments. "We can't! Let me *go!*"

His hands swooped free to ruthlessly trap her wrists. Oh, what a foolish maiden she had been. And yet, even then, she wanted. Perhaps, even, she wanted him to force her, to override her sense and honor and force her into pleasure.

If not for Nicolette.

Poor Nicolette, betrayed…

Helpless, Joan went still, tears escaping. "Don't," she whispered.

Suddenly Lord Edmund let her go, flinging her hands away. Thrusting off, she toppled free and scrabbled away from him, away to the far side of the cave. When she looked, he was rearranging his clothes.

He met her eyes calmly. "Let that be a lesson, Lady Joan, not to be so disdainful of weak, susceptible women."

After a shocked, agonized moment, she picked up a rock and hurled it at him.

He ducked, and it cracked against the far wall. "Don't do that again." It wasn't a request.

"You're vile! How could you do that when you love Nicolette?"

"I don't give a hen's hoof for Nicolette of Woldingham."

"But—oh!" She wished she had the courage to

throw another rock at the heartless brute. "She loves you!"

"No, she doesn't. She loves my brother Gerald. I look forward to introducing you two. He, at least, deserves the sharp edge of your tongue."

"Your—" She let out a shriek of pure frustration. "You should have told me!"

"You should not have impugned my honor with your vile assumptions."

Joan covered her trembling lips with her hands as she finally accepted what a fool he'd made of her. Deliberately. Effortlessly. And she'd crumpled.

And even now, under shock and anguished embarrassment, under the certainty that she would hate Edmund de Graves till the day she died, a little glow warmed her at the thought that at least he wasn't Nicolette's lover.

Fool, she told herself. Fool. Even if free, he was not for Joan of Hawes, and she wouldn't have him if presented on a golden platter by a choir of six-winged angels!

He'd found his cup and was filling it with more mead. "I hope you've learned your lesson, Saint Joan. Seduction's an easy enough matter, especially for a man with a pleasing form. You women," he added, glancing at her, "are all too possible."

Joan actually curled her fingers around another

loose rock, a lovely fist-sized one, but she knew when a threat was real. This was a man who'd take instant retaliation. She miserably accepted that she was frightened of him as she'd previously been of no man—that she'd met a will and an edge equal to her own. She'd rather die, however, than let him know. She turned her back in frosty disapproval.

He chuckled and moved. Her skin prickled with wariness, but the next she knew, he was through the curtain and out of the cave.

First came relief, then fear. Would he abandon her here?

His horse was still here, however, placidly munching hay. Despite his lesson, she did know men quite well. She had five brothers. No man would leave such a horse for long, nor his armor.

Private for a moment, she hugged herself and even let a few tears escape. Some of them came from fear about this whole situation, but mostly they came from shame. She hated him, but she hated herself more for being such easy prey, for that foolish, newly found part of herself that had wanted to believe his trickster lies.

That she was beautiful when she was angry.

That she could stir instant passion in a man like Edmund de Graves.

More than anything, however, the tears were a sign

of her frustrated fury. Oh, but she wanted the last little while back, and a chance to behave differently. To win. Now she could think of all kinds of clever ways she could have turned the tables and made him look the fool.

She rubbed tears away. She couldn't turn back time, and a wise woman learned lessons so generously offered. Aye, she thought, sitting up and straightening her garments, she'd even be grateful to him for it. No man in the future would cozen her like that, and it did indeed make her more sympathetic toward her cousin. No wonder Nicolette had succumbed—and she had also been in love.

But not with him, a silly gleeful part of her noted. With his brother!

There, it was a warning against love, too! Joan had already decided that love was a folly, and that young men—especially handsome ones—were more trouble than they were worth. She planned to marry an older man, a placid one who would be happy to have a managing wife and who wouldn't want too much attention in bed.

Recent memories flared, saying that bed attention might not be all bad, but she stamped them out. It had been a lesson. Nothing more than a lesson.

She rested her chin on her raised knees and contemplated the glowing fire, trying to settle her mind to serious matters. How could everyone get out of this with a whole skin?

By sweet Saint Margaret, mother of the Virgin, it would be hard. Despite the dangers, she had to get back into Woldingham, and quickly. If Nicolette had not been discovered, and if Joan could sneak back in undetected, they could pretend that Nicolette had been the victim all along and had escaped.

That wouldn't solve Nicolette's true problem, but it would get them through Christmastide.

Lord Edmund didn't want to try to return her to Woldingham now, and Joan could see his reasons, but she felt they must try, and soon. In fact, it would be easier and safer if she attempted it alone. The worst that could happen would be that she'd be "rescued" by the men of Woldingham.

Despite the excellent sense of it, she knew Lord Edmund would not agree. It would offend his manly honor to let her go off alone. Perhaps if she put to him sweetly and gently…

She sighed. She wasn't sure she was able to be sweet and gentle, even under this dire need. For the first time it stung a little. She knew she was too fond of speaking her own mind and making her own decisions. Her parents had seized on the invitation to Woldingham with glee, and not just because it was an honor to visit their grand relations. They'd hoped that Lord Henry's firm rule and Lady Ellen's gracious elegance might teach her better ways, ways more likely to find her a husband.

They had also hoped she would benefit from the example of the sweet-natured, soft-spoken Nicolette.

Lord Edmund was right. Despite liking her cousin, she had looked down on her for her gentle ways, and for letting a man trick her into giving him her maidenhead, no matter how much she might love.

Love. A weakness, not an inevitable part of human existence.

Lust, she admitted, was a part of God's plan, designed for procreation, and she'd just been given a short, sharp lesson in the power of lust. She really should thank him. She'd be forewarned and forearmed another time.

Another time.

With Lord Edmund?

She suddenly blew out a breath. What kind of thoughts were these? They were certainly unsuited to the moment. If she didn't find a way out of this predicament, she'd likely end up in a convent as punishment, with lust a matter that need no longer trouble her.

What was needed here was a sound plan, and she had it. All she had to do was convince the ever-noble Golden Lion to let her make her way through the winter woods alone.

She sat up straight. If he'd gone any distance, perhaps she could just slip away. Before she lost courage, she stood, gathered her cloak around her, and went to ease out through the curtain.

Chapter Three

SHE ALMOST WALKED INTO HIM, a dark silhouette against a starry sky. He turned at a sound. No chance at all of slipping away. Why had she expected it?

So, she had to persuade him, but Joan paused, caught by the scene before her eyes.

From their hillside, the land lay before them like a black cloth embroidered with fire. To her right and in the distance glowed Mountgrave. To her left, and closer, lay Woldingham, with lights in the keep and bailey. Perhaps they were continuing some semblance of the feast. People had to eat.

Between the two castles, the dark was scattered with smaller lights from peasant cottages in tiny hamlets, and in the middle, a bonfire of some sort. Above, like a high arched roof, the sky flickered with silver stars, God's protective mantle, with the Christmas star the most brilliant of all.

The star of the Prince of Peace.

"A wonder of God's work, is it not?" the man said quietly from beside her.

"God's beauty above, man's folly below. What of the lives of all the ordinary people down there, my lord, disrupted by a quarrel?"

She heard what might be a growl. "It is more than a quarrel, Lady Joan, and is no fault of the de Graves. We want only peace."

"Have you offered to return the Bethlehem Banner?"

"Return?" He turned to her, stiff with outrage, and they faced each other in the dim light like the warring castles. "The Bethlehem Banner never belonged to the de Montelans."

"They tell another story. They say a de Montelan carried it into Bethlehem. But does it matter?" She spread her hands, gesturing at the scene below. "Lord Edmund, someone is going to have to bend."

"Lady Joan, you are naive. To bend is to be defeated."

At that moment, the bell at the monastery of Colthorpe began to ring, counting the hour of terce. Midnight.

Joan sighed. "So Christ is born again to bring peace and brotherly love to the world. It is as well," she added pointedly, "that God's patience is infinite."

"It is not becoming of a lady to preach."

"It is not becoming of a Christian to refuse to turn the other cheek. Or to refuse to forgive your enemies."

He stabbed a furious finger toward Woldingham. "Go preach to your uncle, woman!"

"I tried!"

"And you still have your skin? You cannot have preached very hard."

Joan gave a wry smile, though Lord Edmund probably couldn't see it in the dark. "It was in the days before Christmas. Lord Henry takes the season seriously."

"But not seriously enough to end a pointless feud."

"How, when you will not bend? I'd hoped, from your reputation, that you were a better man—" She caught herself, scolding like a shrew again.

She'd become used to thinking of herself as honest and forthright, someone who did not dress up her opinions in silk, and who would not be intimidated. Now, here, talking of Christian forbearance and humility, she began to think that perhaps her mother was right about more than tactics. Perhaps it simply wasn't very Christian to be so blunt.

"I'm sorry," she said carefully. "The feud is no concern of mine, except that it explains why the de Montelans will never allow Nicolette to marry your brother. For now, we had better discuss what to do next."

"Apart from beat you?" But then he shook his head. "Lady Joan, you are an unnatural, undisciplined woman, but I'll leave you to your uncle. He deserves such a cross to bear. As for our actions, I have decided that at dawn I will take you to safety in Mountgrave."

"*Mountgrave!*" She paused and moderated her tone. "My lord, for Nicolette's sake, you must return me to Woldingham."

"The possibility of her remaining undetected, and my returning you undetected, is just too small. The area still crawls with your uncle's men." He gestured, and she saw tiny, moving lights here and there. Parties from Woldingham, still hunting.

"I see lights near Mountgrave, too. Will they be your men?"

"No. My men have instructions to stay safely within the walls. I am trying to accomplish this without bloodshed. Just before dawn, my forces will ride out to clear a way to Mountgrave, so we should be safe."

"But you're casting Nicolette to the wolves! If I went alone, now, to Woldingham, I might make it in time."

He turned to her. "You jest!"

"About such a serious matter? Lord Edmund, I know it offends—" She bit that off. "I know it would be hard for you to let me make my way there unescorted, but it is the way most likely to bring everyone off safe."

"Impossible. By stealing you away, Lady Joan, I

have made myself responsible for your safety. I cannot allow you to take such risks."

"I don't see why you have any right to prevent me!"

"Because you are a woman, and I am a man."

"Very well! If you insist on being so noble, my lord, escort me to Woldingham at dawn instead of to Mountgrave."

"I cannot risk making myself another martyr, and stirring deeper enmity. Your uncle's men will be forced back from Mountgrave, but they will keep both watch and search near Woldingham. Also, my men can come to our aid on my land, but not on Lord Henry's."

Joan tucked her chilly hands up the sleeves of her gown. "But what of Nicolette?"

"And what of you, in the end?" he said. "You tried to help your cousin, Lady Joan, and do not deserve to suffer from it." He suddenly moved, turning toward the cave and putting a hand to her back to steer her in that direction. "Come into the warmth and let us see if we can find a miracle."

Joan went, hoping he hadn't noticed her start at his touch. This power he had over women was most unfair.

As they sat on the ground, safely separated by the low fire, she raised a question that had been scratching at the back of her mind. "Tell me something, Lord Edmund. Where is your brother? Should he not be here with Nicolette rather than you?"

"Indeed, he should." He put another piece of wood on the fire, and it crackled into flame. Concern in his eyes, he said, "I don't know where he is.

"He was supposed to be in this role," he continued, "but he disappeared yesterday. Out on some business that went against my orders. I chose to go through with my plan. I pray he's returned to Mountgrave by now, and is keeping his hot head."

She suddenly had a terrible suspicion. "Did you tell him what you were arranging?"

He jerked to look at her. "Are you a witch, woman?"

"Are you a fool? Why didn't you *tell* him?"

"I do not need to tell my younger brother everything I plan. And he deserved to sweat for his stupidity!" He suddenly leaned forward, almost too close to the flames. "How did you guess? What do you know?"

Her mouth dried, but not from fear. Because she had bad news for him. "Lord Edmund, I'm very much afraid that Lord Henry has your brother in his dungeon."

"What?" He surged to his feet, and for a moment, she almost feared for her neck, but then he controlled himself and sank down again across the fire from her, not relaxed at all. "Speak."

Joan took a breath. "This morning, in the midst of all the preparations for the feast, some guards brought a prisoner to Woldingham. I didn't get a clear look at him. Perhaps it isn't your brother. And yet, he didn't look like a peasant, despite simple clothes. My uncle had him put into the dungeon, saying that he'd have no unpleasantness at Christmastide, but he seemed extraordinarily pleased about something, and he doubled the guards. I didn't think much about it, being more concerned with my own problems, but now, I fear it is your brother, caught while attempting some rescue of Nicolette."

"May the imps of hell torment him," Lord Edmund said.

"Lord Henry?"

"My brother."

"You should have told him. Of course he thought you didn't care—"

"A stick will do, Lady Joan. There is no need for the flail." He rested his head for a moment on tense hands. "So, we have two to get out now."

"And me to return." She held chilled hands to the fire, wondering whether Lord Henry's resolve about the peace of Christmas would hold when he thought his daughter was in the hands of his prisoner's family. Gerald de Graves might be under torture even now.

She looked at Lord Edmund. Despite arrogance, he clearly loved his brother, and was also one to take the burdens of the world on his shoulders.

"If I could return secretly, my lord, perhaps I could free your brother. Then he could escape and maybe even take Nicolette, as well."

"I thought you said that Lord Henry had him under double guard?"

"But it is Christmastide."

"If even one of my guards could be tricked or overcome by a woman, Christmastide or not, I'd have his neck. And unless I underestimate Lord Henry, he will have put his best men to guard a de Graves. He finally has the key."

"Oh." She felt stupid for not seeing it. "He'll offer your brother's life for the Bethlehem Banner?"

"And if you did manage to steal that chance for victory, your life wouldn't be worth a pin."

"He couldn't know."

"Once considered, who else?"

After a moment, she said, "Nicolette. If I managed to return undetected, Lord Henry would think Nicolette had been the Virgin, not me. If she then disappeared with your brother, he'd think she'd returned to free him. If they got away, all would be well."

It sounded hopeful to her, but he shook his head. "First, no one woman—or even two—is going to free a de Graves from Lord Henry's dungeon, especially without being recognized. Are you willing to kill the guards? Second, from what I know of Lady Nicolette, even her doting father would not believe her capable of attempting it. No, I'm sure he'd have to realize that you are the key to the whole thing."

Joan couldn't help but feel rather flattered by that.

"If I keep you," he continued, "I have an equal piece to offer for my brother's life."

"I'm not Lord Henry's beloved daughter."

"You're a relative under his protection. He could hardly refuse."

He was right. "That saves your brother *and* your precious banner, but leaves Nicolette and me exposed! You have to let me try to get back into Woldingham. Now, in fact. I promise to try to get your brother and Nicolette out."

"It's impossible."

"Lord Edmund, you are the most inflexible man I have ever met!"

"You are hardly bending in the wind of reason, Lady Joan."

"Because I'm right."

He leaned forward. "I cannot risk the banner my family has protected for generations."

"I will not risk my cousin's skin, without at least trying!" She'd doubtless have thrust her chin right up to him if not for the fire. As it was, the heat was flaring at her jaw.

"You are my hostage, Lady Joan, my means to save

my brother. You will remain with me. If the two of you had not engaged in a foolish deception, all would have been well."

"No, it wouldn't, because my uncle would still have your foolish brother. And if you'd told him—"

"Stop flaying me! I have a family disaster on my hands, which is now going to make a feud I have been trying to end even deeper. I asked for none of this."

"Nor did I ask to be tossed over a horse, dragged to a cave, and…and assaulted!"

His tense face suddenly relaxed. "Yes, you did."

"What?" she spluttered.

"Ask to be assaulted. At least you asked for more. Begged, in fact."

She reached for a rock but then restrained herself. "Very wise."

He smirked. It was definitely a smirk.

She picked up the fist-sized rock and threw it. Since she was daring the devil, she did her best to hit him with it, and throwing things hard and accurately was one of her skills. If he hadn't flung up an arm to defend his head, she might have knocked him out. Then she could have escaped.

At contact, he hissed with pain, but he was already lunging for her.

The fire was between them, but it didn't stop him. Probably he was through it so fast it had no chance to catch him. She scuttled back but had no escape. And anyway, mad impulse past, she was fixed in terrified paralysis.

He seized her around the waist and swung her over his raised knee. Through three layers of sturdy cloth, his strong hand stung, but she thanked heaven for those three layers of cloth.

He stopped much sooner than she'd dared to hope, and straightened her to face him, kneeling.

"No screams?" he asked.

"Over that?" she asked, with a bit of bravado, for she'd felt the swats. "You're not howling and you'll have a bruise."

"Did you not consider," he asked, looking as if he'd like to spank her some more, "the wisdom of injuring the weapon arm of a man who might be your protector?"

"I was aiming for your head. You probably don't need that to—"

The flare of rage in his eyes silenced her. "I'm sorry," she said quickly, and meant it, though she did hope he didn't think his hand had cowed her. "But if you're going to beat me for my unruly tongue, Lord Edmund, your hand will wear out."

"I might consider it a noble sacrifice for mankind. And, Lady Joan, I punished you not for saucy words but for a dangerous physical attack."

"You shouldn't have taunted me!"

"You can't return word attack in kind?"

That halted her for a moment, but then she said, "Your original attack was physical."

He let her go and stood. "Ah yes, I suppose it was."

His look suggested that he understood how devastating his original physical attack had been, and how that had led to this. All she could do was meet his eyes as if he were a man who stirred not a single lustful thought in her.

As if he weren't as beautiful as a warrior angel.

As if his rare smiles didn't make her want to be foolish.

As if her innards didn't tremble every time he touched her.

Her eyes almost stung with the effort of staring blankly at him, but she did it.

After a moment he shook his head as if she were a mystery to him. Good. Very good. "Lady Joan, why are you at Woldingham?"

She was still kneeling as if at a shrine. She hastily scrambled to her feet, taking the opportunity to straighten her clothes, the excuse to look down. "To change my ways and find a husband," she admitted.

"The men being driven away by your daggerlike tongue?"

She couldn't help but smile at him. "Is it as lethal as that?"

He burst out laughing. "Lord save the world. I think your father should put you in a convent that has a vow of silence."

"I'd break out. I'm not just a tongue, you know."

"No, you have a brain behind it, which is why your tongue is lethal. Tell me, why do you attack when you must know you'll be punished?"

She'd never really considered that before. "I can't seem to resist it. People are so infuriatingly stupid sometimes."

He smiled, turning away as if trying to hide it. "Yes, they are, aren't they?" He looked back at her and a connection of some sort made her heart do a silly little somersault. Immediately she guarded herself. Oh no, my lord, that won't work twice.

"Very well," he said, sober again. "Truce. We're engaged in matters too serious for this. Don't throw any more rocks when I offend you, and I won't retaliate for the things you say to me."

"Are you sure that's wise?" she asked. "I'm not sure I've ever unleashed my tongue."

"I think I can bear it. The question is, what can you bear? You were right to point out that if I use you as hostage for my brother, Lord Henry will have to know about the deception. You will suffer for it."

"So will Nicolette."

"She deserves some punishment. Perhaps I should

return you to your own home, though you'll doubtless face punishment there, too."

Did he perhaps care about her safety? That tempted Joan to smile. "My parents wearied of punishing me years ago."

"It would have been better if they had persisted."

She cast him a reproachful glance and his lips twitched. "Unprovoked attack. I do beg your pardon, my lady."

"They will be disappointed," she admitted. "They continue to hope, you see, as if time might turn me sweet and pliant, make my hair silky and my figure willowy."

This time it was a definite smile. Lord save her, he had dimples. "Lady Joan, there is nothing at all wrong with your figure."

"Lord Edmund," she said, her thumping heart betraying her words, "I am immune to that sort of attack now."

"It's simple truth, Lady. Men's tastes vary as much as women's, and I like a woman of substance, one I'm not afraid of breaking."

"Oh." She realized she was running her hands over her generously curved body, and his eyes were following her hand.

More acting?

She told herself so. Whichever, she stilled her hands and clasped them modestly before her. "I think I must balance the scales by complimenting you back. You doubtless know it all too well, but you are a very handsome man."

"More curse than blessing. Women make fools of themselves over me, and if they are married women, they create enemies."

Make fools of themselves. Oh, if there were words to armor a maiden to a man's charms—even this feast of a man—those were they. Whether given deliberately or not, she silently thanked him.

"Now we are equal again," she said, turning to pace as she spoke, and glad to break the taut connection between them. "Can we return to plans? Returning me to Hawes would ensure my safety, but Nicolette and your brother would still be in peril. Nicolette has no safe explanation for the switch, and your brother will die unless you return the banner to Wol—"

"Not return," he interrupted sharply. "It was never theirs."

Joan flung up her hands. "How can an apparently reasonable man be so…so unreasoned! Sir Remi de Graves and Sir Henry de Montelan—I'm surprised you aren't called Remi, my lord—"

"My older brother, who died when twelve."

Joan rolled her eyes. Two families trapped in an ancient quarrel. "Sir Remi and Sir Henry went on crusade together, cousins and brothers in arms. They carried with them a banner they hoped to bear victoriously into Jerusalem and into the place of Christ's birth in Bethlehem."

"A banner made by my ancestor's mother and sisters!"

"But carried by both, yes?" When he didn't deny it, she went on, "Unless the de Montelans lie, Sir Remi was wounded in the taking of Jerusalem, and Sir Henry alone rode with it to Bethlehem to complete their vow."

"Remi was wounded in saving Sir Henry's life. His blood stains the banner to this day!"

"No one denies that. But why do not the de Montelans have a right to the banner half the year, as they claim?"

"Because, Lady Joan, they would not return it."

"Are you not judging them by yourselves?"

She watched his hands clench into fists then, with effort, relax. "Are you saying," he asked grimly, "that if I gave the banner to Lord Henry now, he'd return it in a six-month?"

"No. But he has many a six-month to make up for. Lord Edmund, someone has to bend!"

"It will not be me. I will not betray the generations that have gone before."

"I see. You're afraid of them, and of what people will say."

His fists clenched again. "Take back those words, Lady Joan. I fear only God."

Joan wished she hadn't said it, largely because she could see it hurt him in ways she'd not expected or intended. She was past the point of return now, however. "I cannot take them back, my lord, unless you prove them not to be true."

He whirled away, looking up. "What sins have I committed, Lord, that you punish me with this woman? Her tongue flays me, yet my honor says I cannot strike back! My body burns—"

Though trembling with physical fear, Joan caught those chopped-short words.

Oh.

My body burns. One thing was sure—that had come deep from within. It had been no trick.

Of course, she told herself, there was nothing deep and meaningful about it. But it was undeniably satisfying to think that at this moment, the Golden Lion burned for her.

He turned to look at her, almost sheepishly. "Lust," he said.

She nodded. "You're probably used to it. It's new to me."

"You've never lusted?"

"Not like this."

He ran a hand through his hair, looking away. "We should not even be aware of these things at such a time. When so many important matters hang in the balance."

"It's not easy to stop, though, is it?"

His eyes rested darkly on hers. Flickered over her. Back. "No, it's not easy to stop."

What would happen if she touched him? She'd probably end up like Nicolette. At the moment, it didn't seem to matter. "Does your lust make it hard for you to think straight?"

"I would have thought that was obvious!" He turned abruptly to seize the jug of mead and fill the two cups. Some splashed on the floor. He passed one to her and unsteady hands brushed, sending sparks up her. Their eyes held as they drank.

Broke free.

She wanted to ask many questions, the main one being, did this happen to him all the time with woman after woman, or was there anything special about it? Just a little bit special? Something about her?

Another one was, if she tried really hard, tried to become more gentle and sweet natured, to guard her tongue, would there be any hope…?

Oh, indeed, she was a foolish virgin. He wasn't trying to trick her again, but she was doing it all by herself!

"The first idea was better," he said, sitting on the rocky shelf covered with furs, as far as possible from her and the heat of the fire. "You will be my hostage to bargain for Gerald."

Matching his cool tone, Joan said, "I think it

would be better for me to attempt to return to Woldingham, now."

"The woods will still be crawling with men."

"I'm one small woman."

"And hounds."

She'd forgotten the hounds.

"If I use you as hostage, I can make it clear that the
raid was simply to gain a prisoner to balance my brother.
Yes, Lord Henry will be angry at you and Nicolette for
switching places, but if he does not punish during Christmastide, perhaps his rage will fade. If not, we still have
twelve days to think of some other solution."

The thought of Lord Henry's massive hounds on the
hunt had definitely sapped Joan's courage for a lonely
trek, but she said, "Your plan means Nicolette will
have to face them alone. She'll be so afraid."

"Unlike you?"

"I'm with you, and she's with Uncle Henry."

His brows rose. "As you've seen, I have no scruples
about meting out punishment at Christmastide."

She almost said that she didn't fear him, but he'd
probably take it the wrong way. She would mean that
she didn't fear terrible punishment from him unless she
did something truly terrible, in which case she'd
deserve it.

What if he did something terrible?

"What are you thinking now, you wretched

woman?" But the smile in his eyes took any offense from it.

She surrendered to honesty. "I was wondering whether you'd let me punish you if you did something stupid or wrong."

"No."

"Why not?"

"Why should I?"

"Strength," she complained with a huffed-out breath. "It's most unfair."

"Woman was put on the earth to be governed by men, and man was given the strength necessary for the task."

"So," she mused in deliberate wickedness, "if you were weakened by injury…"

"I'd stay well out of your reach! Very well, Lady Joan," he said, "I take your point and will make you another bargain. If ever, during our brief adventure, I give in to temptation and strike you again, I will let you pay me back in even measure." Before she could quibble, he added, "And you may compensate for strength and size by using a tool—stick, rock, what you will."

"Even your sword?" she asked, eyeing the magnificently scabbarded weapon lying near his mail.

"If you think that just."

She pulled a face at him. "I have to be just? That takes the fun out of it."

He laughed, a natural open laugh despite the perilous nature of their problems.

Something deeper stirred inside her. Here was the first man she'd found that she could talk to without watching every word, who seemed able—after a fashion—to accept her blunt speech, and even give as good as he got.

Sad that it would only be a "brief adventure."

Enough of that. She resolutely turned her mind back to plans. "If you exchange me for your brother, nothing will have changed."

"True. It will be worse, in fact. I'll still have to rescue Lady Nicolette or Gerald will rush into danger again. And all hope of peace will be over."

He sighed and leaned back against the wall. "The irony is that Lord Henry was moving a little. I've been negotiating with him for nearly a year, with only moderate success, but recently he became much more open to suggestions. Two things happened simultaneously, just weeks ago. Gerald confessed his folly and told me Lady Nicolette was carrying his child, and Lord Henry proposed peace, sealed by a marriage, the matter of the banner to be sorted out later. It was almost complete capitulation."

"Nicolette and Gerald? But then—"

"Of course not," he said, looking at her. "Nicolette and me."

"Oh." Joan could see what a disaster that had been, but she was struggling with the thought that even Lord Henry had tried to bend. He surely couldn't have known which de Graves Nicolette loved, so he'd assumed the most likely and tried to obtain him for his daughter.

"Without Gerald's news, I would have accepted. As it was, all I could do was propose a marriage to my brother, which Lord Henry quite rightly took as an insult. If I'd been given any time to plan at all," he added with irritation, "I would have married again myself and thus been unavailable."

"You've been married?" Ridiculous to be hurt.

He looked at her strangely. "I'm twenty-five years old and destined to be Lord of Mountgrave since I was ten. Of course I've been married. It was arranged when I was thirteen. An excellent alliance, but my wife died of a flux two years ago."

"I'm sorry."

He shrugged. "I've been busy with warfare and attendance on the king since I was sixteen, so I never saw her for more than a week in a six-month. I'd say 'poor Catherine,' except that she was perfectly content in the situation."

"I can understand that," Joan said, struck by the charms of such an arrangement. Her parents, and the neighboring families she knew well, did not spend much time apart. With grand families, however…

Then she looked at him, blushing. "I wasn't referring to you, my lord!" Then she wished she'd not even hinted at marriage between them.

"You think you could tolerate my presence for a little longer than that?"

"Of course! I mean…" She collected herself from the embarrassing mire. "I merely thought that I might seek out a similar husband. One much engaged with national affairs."

"A husband who will leave you in sovereignty over your world?"

"You have to see, Lord Edmund, how ill suited I am to day-by-day compliance."

He leaned back, studying her. "But—and remember you agreed not to throw rocks at me—you seemed to enjoy a man's physical attentions."

Her blush was an answer. "But I doubt many men could make them as pleasant to me as you did."

He smiled, and looked away for a moment almost bashfully. Truly, at times, Lord Edmund was a tantalizing mystery, and it was his faults and frailties that fascinated her more than his obvious charms.

If only…

Don't be foolish, Joan.

He patted the fur beside him. "Come sit over here. It doesn't suit me to talk across the cave like warring factions." When she hesitated, he added, "You have my word. I won't hurt you."

Chapter Four

"I KNOW," SHE SAID, walking over. "You seem to have forgotten that I might have reason not to want to sit."

"I didn't think I'd been so harsh."

"You weren't," she admitted as she sat. She looked at his arm, hidden by his sleeve. "What of you?"

He pushed up the sleeve and, with a wince, she saw a dark red bruise near his elbow.

"Nothing that will impede my fighting," he assured her, flexing the muscular arm. But then he held it out to her. "Perhaps you should kiss it better."

She looked him in the eye. "Oh no. Then you might think you should kiss *my* hurts better."

Dimples flickered. "If you wish, my lady."

She stared into his eyes. "Don't."

As if he understood, his expression turned wry and he lowered his arm, leaning back against the wall. "So, my wise virgin, what are we to do?"

She grasped the assumption that they were talking

about the feud, Nicolette and his brother. "I do admire your desire for peace."

"Even if I cannot bring myself to do what is necessary to create it, and surrender the banner?" His brows rose. "Silence? I pray I haven't cowed you."

"I'm practicing tact and tongue control, since I fear this will all end with me imprisoned in a convent."

"A terrible waste."

"Perhaps in time I'll become an abbess, able to flay the male world with impunity."

"A waste."

"My cleverness and administrative abilities would be put to full use."

"A waste," he insisted.

"A waste of what, my lord?"

"Of a great deal of heat and fire." He held out a hand. "Come here."

Though her body longed to leap at him, Joan made herself eye that tempting hand. "I've learned my lessons well."

"I have more to teach."

Joan swallowed. "I don't deny you have an effect on me, Lord Edmund, but two Woldingham maids carrying de Graves babies will hardly improve matters."

"I won't get you with child."

"Many a man says that."

That anger sparked in his eyes again, anger because she was doubting his honor. She didn't. Truly. And yet, she didn't trust any man in matters like this.

"Swear it to me," she demanded.

Frostily, totally without dimples, he said, "I swear on my immortal soul, Joan of Hawes, that I will not get you with child this night."

"Good." But she sighed. By obtaining the oath, she'd destroyed any chance of needing it.

But then his hand stretched out again, and her pulse started a nervous beat. "This is hardly the time—"

"This might be the only time. The feud is now likely to be cast in iron. Would even your tolerant parents allow marriage between us, to the great offense of Lord Henry?"

"*Marriage?* You can't expect me to fall for a trick like—"

"Joan!"

She covered her unruly mouth with her hand. "Oh, I'm sorry. I truly didn't mean... But—" she hardly dared put it into words "—are you saying you might want to *marry me?* Why?"

He captured her hand and tugged her closer. "Poor Joan. Have you been so unvalued?"

"N-no. I've had men interested, but none who interested me. But you..."

Dimples flickered. "Awed by the great Edmund de

Graves? I'd have thought you'd learned better by now."

"I've learned nothing but good of you."

She was against his broad, warm chest.

"You see my faults as virtues. What more can any man want?" A hand slid beneath her plaits, rough hot against her neck. "I like you, Joan, as I've liked no woman before. I like your courage and your calm head. Now I've grown accustomed, I even like your sharp tongue, for it is wielded by a clever brain." He tilted her head up toward him. "Can you imagine how wearying it is to be surrounded by people who reverence every word I say. I'd welcome a truth sayer." His other hand found her thigh and stroked upward, over cloth. "And my body likes your body—very well, indeed."

"My body likes yours very well, too. But is this wise? We have plans to make."

"The plans are made. I'll bring you through this unscathed if I can, so at dawn I will take you safely to Woldingham."

Complete reversal. "But—"

He slid her off the bench, to stand between his legs. "We have a night to pass before dawn, and I have plans for that, too."

"But your brother!"

"I'll find some other way." He pulled her close and his head came to rest between her breasts.

She held him off. "What of the danger to you?"

"It is nothing beside the danger to you."

"This is folly. Take me to Mountgrave and bargain me for your brother. At least Nicolette and I will not lose our lives."

"Trapped in a convent? Close to death for you, Joan. Let me prove it. Prove that it would be a waste." His hands merely flexed on her hips, but she swayed, and her body, her inner body, ached.

"All women feel this way, but many become nuns, and happily so."

"All women do not feel this way. Some, though excellent wives and mothers, are cool. My Catherine was. She was a dutiful bed partner, but if she could have started a child with a hug she would have preferred it."

Joan found that impossible to believe. Her hands rested on his shoulders, close to his bare neck. With her thumbs, she tilted his chin up. "Are you sure of that?"

"Yes, for we spoke of it. Though not as sharp as you, Catherine didn't hesitate to speak her mind. She was some years older than I, and experienced. Twenty when we finally wed, and two years a widow. I was just fifteen. She knew her needs and how to demand them, and did not mind if I took other women for more vigorous sex-play."

Joan frowned, and his brows rose as he continued, "Are you saying that when you wed your busy man, you will expect him to be virtuous when he's away?"

"I'd hoped he would not be much interested in sex at all."

"That would be a waste of another kind. Even if your matings are few, Joan, you should want them to be fiery." He pulled her closer. "Do you deny the fire in you?"

Hot almost to sweating, she could only shake her head.

"And I burn. Do you think I burn for every lovely young woman I meet?"

"Yes."

He laughed. "Very well. A little, yes. But not like this, Joan. On my honor."

He looked completely honest, but her stern common sense was not dead. "It's only the night, and the cave, and the fear."

"I'm not afraid."

"You're probably never afraid."

"Any man fears when there is reason to. He does not let it rule him. But I do not borrow fear, and nor should you. What tomorrow brings, we will deal with tomorrow. Now is now and, yes, it's the night and the cave. But it's also you." He rubbed his face against her, and his mouth brushed—once, twice—across her nipples. "I never thought I'd like a woman with a sharp tongue, still less one who hurled rocks at my head. But you are like pepper to my senses—burning but delicious."

Looking down, she could see her brazen nipples pushing at the cloth. She watched as he repeated, "Delicious," and put teeth gently to first one, then the other.

Conquered, she let her weak knees give way so she knelt, supported by her arms on his thighs. "You shouldn't encourage me. I'm sure my tongue can get worse and worse."

"Then I will teach it other tricks." He captured her head and kissed her, engaging her tongue in another kind of battle.

When it ended, she clung to him, dazed. "You could blunt a tongue entirely that way."

He smiled, stroking her hair. "That's what I thought. But there are other ways." Sitting straighter, he dragged his tunic and shirt over his head, presenting a stunning, firelit torso, a sculpture of muscle. "Explore me with your clever tongue, Joan."

She reached for him, but he captured her hands, holding them on his thighs. "Just your tongue."

Her tongue stirred hungrily in her mouth as she studied him, already savoring the warmth, texture and taste. Broad chest, small, flat nipples, a trace of hair low down the middle, around his navel and lower…

His navel, just above the drawstring of his braies.

Slowly she leaned forward to circle it with her tongue, closing her eyes the better to savor the heat, the taste of sweat and salt, the texture of smooth skin and ticklish hair. She dipped her tongue into it and felt his ridged belly muscles shudder.

Oh, she liked that.

Deep inside, her body pulsed insistently in response.

She wavered for a moment, fearful of her own hunger. Of conquest and consequences. But then she remembered his oath, and she knew the Golden Lion would keep it.

Putting her mouth to his navel, she kissed it, feeling his hands tighten on hers, feeling her own hands clench on his thighs. She took her mouth away to blow on his wet skin, smiling at his shiver. Glancing up, she saw that he was leaning back, his eyes shut, lost in sensations she was creating.

Smile widening, she trailed her tongue lower, easing beneath the tied top of his braies. She felt him move and looked up a little nervously, wondering if she'd gone too far.

His eyes were open, meeting hers, heavy lidded. "If I wasn't feeling kind, I'd dare you to go further."

"I'm sure you know I can't resist a dare."

"I thought you were a very sensible virgin."

"You swore an oath, and I'm a very curious virgin.

I've never seen…" To her annoyance, words escaped her then. "I can feel that you are… I mean…"

"Yes, I am." He released her hands and untied the cord that held his woolen garment up, then leaned back, leaving her to do as she wished.

With a bubble of excited anticipation and a wave of hot embarrassment, Joan lowered his braies.

Oh, my. She'd heard enough jokes and whispered stories to know what to expect, but she supposed most women saw this coming at them with intent. Presented to her like this, he was beautiful and she wanted to taste him.

"Tell me if I hurt you," she whispered, before touching her tongue to the tip of his rigid shaft.

She thought he laughed, though it might have been a groan. He was hard as rock, but like a rock warmed by the fireside then covered in silk. A musky smell teased at her, warm, comforting in some way….

Reason said other men were made much the same way, but she couldn't imagine feeling like this about another man.

He'd been right when he'd said her family would never permit such a marriage, even to the great Edmund de Graves. It would offend family loyalty too deeply.

What was to become of her?

Fighting away tears, she ran her tongue up and

down him. When she brushed the ridge near the tip he jerked. She noted that and returned to tease.

"Does doing this disqualify me from the convent?" she wondered, contemplating the glistening, vulnerable tip.

"You don't have to tell them." He did sound breathless.

Arms resting on his tense thighs, she looked up. "What's going to happen if I keep doing this?"

"I'll spill my seed. You won't get pregnant unless I spill it in you."

"Do you like what I'm doing?"

His eyes crinkled. "No. But I liked what you were doing."

With a laugh, she said, "Tell me what you'd like even more. Give my sharp tongue power over you, Edmund de Graves."

"Don't say sharp to a man at a moment like this!" But he was teasing, and he suggested things. With a smile, she did them, aware with dazzled astonishment of him falling apart, exquisitely, trustingly vulnerable here at this moment with her.

When his breathing steadied and he opened his eyes, she said, "You're right. I'm not suited to a convent. This is too much power to give up."

He laughed and pulled her up for a ravishing kiss. Before she knew it, his hand was under her skirts, his mouth was at her cloth-covered breasts. When she arched and cried out, astonished by building sensations, he stilled his clever fingers and raised his skillful mouth. "The power goes both ways, Joan. Do you want me to stop now, before you turn to mindless wax in my hands?"

She shook her head. "Serve me. Give me what I want."

He laughed at her parry and obeyed, and who was to say who was the victor, who the vanquished at the end?

They lay together on the fur-covered ledge, and for Joan, at least, it was a time of strange adjustment. He'd taught her a lesson earlier about lust, but this had been a more potent one. The lesson she had learned here was that lust had a beauty of its own, and that she didn't want to live without it.

She wasn't prepared to say that she could only experience the beauty with this man, but she felt quite sure such harmony of desire was rare.

Yet to have him was almost impossible.

Their marriage was no more impossible than Nicolette and his brother, a part of her argued, and that would have to be, despite the enmity.

She couldn't give him up.

She couldn't!

She rose up on her elbow to trace his lips with her finger. "I want to marry you."

Those lips twitched. "I'm good, aren't I?"

She punched him on the shoulder for cocky arrogance. Justified, though.

He turned serious and caressed her face, brushing wild escaping curls off her cheeks. "I'd like to marry you, too, but I don't see how. Duty comes first. I'm determined to end this feud. At the very least, I cannot make matters worse and steal you away, too."

"If your brother and Nicolette are to be together—"

He laid fingers on her lips. "Gerald is not me. He is not the Lord of Mountgrave. He can move to one of my other estates and be out of sight. He won't have to constantly deal with Lord Henry over local and national matters."

"Lord Henry will never forget or forgive the loss of his beloved daughter, even if they move to Spain!"

He closed his eyes. "I know it. But our marriage would be daily salt in the wounds."

Joan straightened, frowning. "Then there's only one way. We have to end the feud."

"Willingly. Point the way."

"There's always a way."

"I wish I had your faith." He captured her and drew her down to him. "As it is, all we have is now."

She didn't give up—there generally was a way if a person was determined enough—but certainly going around and around it now would be a waste of time.

Of precious time.

She slid out of his hands and off the ledge to remove his loose braies, taking deep pleasure in his long, muscular legs, only realizing then that she was down to her linen shift.

Yes, he was good.

When he was naked, she said, "Turn over. I want to explore your back."

He merely lay there. "Make me."

The resulting fight was a different kind of education to Joan, and equally enjoyable. She was like a child next to his strength, but he managed his power with control and was surprisingly vulnerable to tickles, so she ended up straddling his back, massaging his muscles, each flex of her spread thighs against him stirring her aching hunger.

Oh yes, she was hungry for him.

Famished.

Thank heavens, his oath could be trusted.

And curse it.

She thought he'd fallen asleep, but when she carefully eased off him, he turned and snared her, to stroke and suckle her into wild pleasure again. In fairness, she could only do the same for him, when they lay together talking, but carefully—not of anything connected to their troubles—till at last, they slept.

When she awoke, a glimmer of light around the

curtain warning of dawn, she felt more starving than sated.

If he'd planned to teach her that she was a lusty woman, he had undoubtedly succeeded. She leaned up to feast upon him with tear-stinging eyes. Two of the lamps had spluttered out during the night, but by the dying flame of the third she could see bristles on his square chin. She ran her fingers tenderly over the roughness.

His eyes flicked open, smiling, but she thought she detected the same sadness behind them as ached in her. "We must return you to Woldingham, Joan."

"What of your brother?"

"Lord Henry won't murder him. I'll negotiate something."

"You'll exchange the banner for him?" With sudden hope, she realized that would end the feud.

He rolled on his back, arm over eyes. "How can I?"

"It's a piece of cloth. He's your *brother!*"

The concealing arm fell away. "It's my family's honor through four generations. Blood has been lost over it many times."

"And clearly more will be." She was determined not to scream at him, especially about things he must know perfectly well.

"I swore an oath," he said. "All the men of our

family do at the time they become knights. An oath never to give up the banner to the de Montelans."

She shook her head. "And *they* swear an oath never to cease the fight to regain it. What madness it all is. All the same, when I'm back in Woldingham, I'll set your brother free. Somehow."

He gripped her shoulder. "I forbid it."

"If Uncle Henry won't kill your brother, he won't kill me."

His hand tightened. "He might not stop much short. Joan, for my sake, take no risks. The thought of you suffering weakens me."

She pulled free of his hand and stood. "The thought of you suffering weakens me, but I don't suppose it will stop you from fighting."

He sat straight up. "You are an unnatural woman!"

"So? I thought you liked that about me."

A wry smile chased away his frown. "My training is to control and protect you, Joan. It is the way of the world for men to fight and women to stay safe."

"Then why are you worried about what Uncle Henry will do to me?"

"It is also the way of the world for men to punish. You will not," he said, "try to rescue my brother."

"I'll not take unnecessary risks."

He gripped her arm. "You will take *no* risks!"

"And if your brother escapes," she continued,

despite a scurrying heart, "he'd better take Nicolette with him."

"Joan!"

Though quivering, she met his angry eyes. "You can't control me, Edmund. I will do what I think best."

"You will put your foolish head in a noose."

"*Why* do you assume you are cleverer and more sensible than I am?" She tore free again and put distance between them. "I assure you, I no more want to be caught by Uncle Henry than you want that. I'll take no foolish risks. But if I see a chance to get them away safely, I will take it."

He pressed his hands to his face, then lowered them. "Promise me one thing."

"What?" she asked warily.

"If you get Gerald and Nicolette out of Woldingham, go with them. Do not stay to face your uncle's wrath. I'll see you safe back to your family."

"I'll try."

"Promise!"

"I promise to try!"

He glared at her. "If it's you or her, you'll stay to face the punishment."

"Isn't that what you would do?"

"That has nothing to do with it." Edmund stood to pull on his braies and knot the cord. He turned his back to do it.

Joan began to dress, too, not nearly as miserable as she ought to be. She'd enjoyed that battle of wills as much as she'd enjoyed their wrestling earlier, and she loved his obvious concern.

He was right. She was an unnatural woman.

She'd kept her shift through the night, but her other clothes were strewn around. As she collected them and put them on, she watched him dress, savoring his beauty.

He was hers. Deep inside, she knew it, even though she knew their happiness might be impossible. Such a little time for so strong a bond, and yet it was there, tugging at her, already like a painful scar.

She knew he felt the same. That's why he was going to try to return her to Woldingham. It would put him in danger, and, even successful, would leave him in a weak position. *He* might have faith that Uncle Henry wouldn't torture his brother to death, but she wasn't entirely sure.

Joan pulled her tunic down over her head. "I think you should take me back to Mountgrave and arrange the exchange."

He turned to look at her. "That wasn't your plan."

"I've changed my mind. Your brother risks death."

"If it comes to that, I'll doubtless give up the banner for him. For his safety, and his marriage to Nicolette."

Joan should have felt enormous relief at that tidy solution to everything, but his anguish over it was obvious.

"Break your oath?" she whispered.

He sat to pull on low boots. "If he starts sending me my brother in pieces, what choice do I have?"

Joan put her hand to her mouth, sickeningly certain her uncle was capable of it. "But then—"

"Don't argue," he said curtly. "You'll waste time and tongue." He suddenly strode over and seized her, kissed her, putting her tongue to alternate use.

When he released her, she staggered, watching him go toward his armor, go toward becoming the Golden Lion, who was not for her. To the man who would risk his word and honor to give her the greatest chance of safety.

"This doesn't make sense!" she exclaimed.

He whirled. "Joan, you are the only innocent in all of this!"

"Innocent?"

"Gerald and Nicolette have committed sins both of stupidity and immorality. I pushed through this plan without truly thinking things through, and without involving my brother fully in it. This disaster is my fault."

Joan opened her mouth to argue, but he swept on. "You tried to help your cousin, and your plan was sound. If I'd not interfered, you'd be in no danger. Therefore you, at least, should come off safe. My honor demands it."

And there, she saw she was up against a wall as high and strong as those around both castles.

She went to help him into his armor, another thing she'd done for her brothers now and then. "My honor demands that I try to help you and my cousin."

He ignored her, and did without her help as much as possible.

As he put on iron embellished with gold, the change was completed. Her midnight friend and lover transformed into the Golden Lion, a creature of myth and glory—of another sphere.

Marriage? Had that really been whispered in the night? It just proved how foolish nighttime whispers were. Even if there was no enmity between their families, such a great lord was not for her. He might as well be the Archangel Michael as far as she was concerned.

It had, after all, just been the night and the cave, but she wouldn't have missed it for her chance of heaven.

And she still thought they ought to go to Mountgrave and exchange her for his brother.

Chapter Five

As MISTY GRAY HERALDED DAWN, they made their way down the steep hill toward flatter, more fertile ground. She was perched up behind Edmund on his big horse this time, hand in his belt. He only had padded cloth between himself and the horse, and the rope bridle, so they still moved quietly, except for the subdued rattle of armor. His sword was in its scabbard, but he carried his big shield on his arm, since he couldn't sling it on his back and had no saddle to hook it to. She couldn't help worrying that the weight must tire even him over time. She worried, too, that his right arm might have stiffened by now from her wound.

She smiled at her own ridiculous tendency to fuss over him like a mother with a delicate child. This was the Golden Lion, undefeated in tourney for many years.

For a while they moved through a misty world still silent as night, but then pink touched the sky and the first bird began to call. As the pearly light spread in the sky, Joan kept her ears alert for sounds of danger, as she was sure he was doing, but it was as if the hunt had ceased.

Here, at least.

She didn't know this countryside well, but she assumed that the deer paths he chose led to Wolding-ham, and if there were enemies about, that's where they'd be found.

Foolish man.

As when she'd been first captured, she thought of slipping off the horse to escape. It would be easier now since she rode behind him, but just as pointless. He'd capture her in seconds. Instead, she wrapped her arms around his mailed chest, hating the harshness between her and his flesh.

In the end, danger came abruptly, catching them in the worst possible place. Thor had just scrambled up the steep bank of a stream when four horsemen galloped along a nearby path.

Edmund immediately stilled the horse, and the men almost missed them. Then one glanced to the side and hauled his horse up, crying the alert.

To run was hopeless. To stand was surely to die!

"Get off and head for Woldingham. To our left and as the crow flies." Edmund dropped the reins and drew his sword.

"No—"

"Obey me, Joan."

The Golden Lion had spoken, and after a heartbreaking moment, Joan slid off the horse. He couldn't fight with her on his back—but she wasn't running away.

She ducked into the cover of some evergreen growth and wove as quickly and silently as possible to somewhere else. Anywhere else. Yells and the clash of metal made her jump, and she peeped out from behind a big tree, to see a mess of men, horses and swords.

They'd kill him!

She only just stopped herself from running out in a futile effort to help.

Then Thor kicked backward and a horse went down, squealing, the rider tossed off and, at least, dazed. Immediately, he reared, startling another horse into shying away. Praise heaven, none of the attackers was on a warhorse. A mighty swipe of Edmund's sword unseated another rider.

Joan expected blood to gush, and when it didn't she realized the Golden Lion was trying not to kill. "Noble fool," she muttered, but she understood. Any new death would widen the rift between the families.

The two remaining horsemen were hovering, not quite so keen to get close. The one who'd been thrown was staggering up, however, sword in hand. Edmund could probably ride away, but he was trying to guard her flight. Should she go?

Then one of the horsemen turned to where she'd run into the bushes and called, "Lady Nicolette! Come out! It's safe."

A strange definition of safe, but she was thrilled that they still thought Nicolette was the stolen Virgin. If she sneaked back into Woldingham...

Then it occurred to her that these men could have been out all night. If Nicolette had been discovered, they would not know.

She hovered, uncertain, her mind momentarily wiped of all ability to make decisions, and before her, the men seemed motionless, too, no one knowing quite what to do.

Then, the man on the ground charged, his sword pointed. "He's murdered her! He's murdered the Lady Nicolette!"

As if goaded, the other two charged, and Edmund whirled in the middle, miraculously countering three blades, but blood suddenly gushed from his right arm. He still swung the sword, but for how long? She could not possibly run away and abandon him.

Urgent breath burning her throat, she ran back to the stream, heedless now of noise or secrecy, and gathered half a dozen fist-sized stones in her folded-up tunic. Then, with them bouncing bruisingly against her thighs, she ran back as close to the fight as she dared.

Just two on one now, and only one mounted, but

Edmund was weakening, and the man on foot was creeping up on him. She fished out a rock, prayed, and hurled it as hard as she could at his helmeted head. The clang must have been enough to deafen him, and he wavered, then turned instinctively to face the new enemy.

Joan was behind another tree by then, watching Edmund ignore a perfect opportunity to run the man through. The moment let him wound the other man in the sword arm, however, disarming him. Then Edmund kicked him out of his saddle to the ground.

She hurled another rock at the man looking for her. She missed his head but by luck caught him on the sword hand. He howled and dropped the weapon. *Concentrate. Concentrate.* Her next rock found its exact mark in the middle of his forehead, and down he went.

The unseated man had remounted, but held his horse back, seeming not to like the odds anymore, but the first thrown one was staggering back to his feet. Joan hurled a rock at his legs. By luck, it took him on the knee, and with a howl, he collapsed down, hugging it.

When she looked back, the other man was unseated again, and when Thor reared up over him, he took to his heels. Edmund seized the nearest available horse. "Come on, my disorderly lady."

He was right. She was here in the open, hurling stones at her rescuers. She'd ruined all chance of a sneaky return. She scrambled up onto the big, nervous horse, and as soon as she was in the saddle, they raced off, one other loose horse driven before them. Edmund called, "Grip the mane!" and kept hold of her reins.

She obeyed, but screamed, "I can ride!"

He slowed for a moment, looking at her, then tossed her the reins. Side by side, they hurtled down a cart track, the free horse charging ahead. She dearly hoped they went in the right direction.

She *could* ride, but she'd never done that much flat-out galloping and the stirrups were far too long for her feet. She gripped as best she could with her legs, giving thanks that the saddle was high front and back, and took a firm hold of the pommel, as well.

She said a silent prayer of thanks, however, when Edmund slowed their pace, for she needed to catch her breath. Not for long, though, for their attackers might have regrouped, or the fleeing one might have found reinforcements.

When the warhorse came to a dead halt, she glanced a query at Edmund and saw him sway and almost fall. Bright blood poured from his leg. Thor must have stopped on his own, sensing his rider's weakness.

How much blood had he lost? How long could he keep conscious?

"Edmund!" she said sharply. "Look at me!"

His head turned, but she wasn't sure his eyes were focused.

Joan crossed herself. "Blessed Mary, help us." Careful ears caught no hint of pursuit, but she couldn't trust to a smooth journey. She wasn't even sure they were going in the right direction.

"Edmund, is this the right way?"

He shook his head slightly and looked around. "Yes. Not far now to Mountgrave." A spark of anger lit his eyes. "You should have done as you were told, and gone to Woldingham. You heard what that man said. Called you Nicolette."

She tersely made her point about them being out of touch. "And anyway, it's an issue no longer. They saw me. You might as well use me as a hostage. If you can stay on long enough to get home. Can you get on this horse? The saddle will help."

He eyed it, and shook his head. "Better to stay on Thor. You get up behind to help."

Joan much preferred a saddle, and she wasn't quite sure how to get up on the big horse without Edmund lifting her there, but she slid off her mount. With relief, she saw a hump of ground ahead and led Thor there. Blood still flowed down Edmund's leg, so she used her head-cloth to make a hasty bandage. More seemed to be coming from higher, though, from under his mail. No time to find that wound, or to treat his right arm.

From the hillock, and with some wincing help from Edmund's left arm, she managed to scramble up astride and behind. She heard him murmuring to the big horse, and having seen Thor in battle, she could only be grateful.

She could feel the horse's tension, however, a kind of seething need to act, probably because of the smell of blood. She looked down and saw too much of it on the earth and grass below.

They had to get to safety.

She kicked the horse's sides—far higher than it was accustomed to, she was sure, for her short legs were spread over the top of his mighty back. Nothing happened.

She glanced frantically behind. "Edmund, get him to move!"

Edmund jerked as if he'd been slipping into unconsciousness, but he said something and shifted his body slightly, and Thor began to walk. She wanted to scream for speed, but that would toss them off.

She twisted to stare down the road behind. All was quiet. As they made their way slowly, she strained for sounds. Then she heard it. Pounding hooves. Out of sight as yet.

"They're coming. We have to go faster!"

He was clutching the mane, half-collapsed forward

now. He couldn't stay on at any speed. If he didn't, she couldn't. She virtually perched on top of the huge beast and wasn't used to riding bareback, even at the best of times.

"I'll get off," she said, but he said, "No!"

He collapsed down, arms around Thor's neck. "Mount me, and take the reins."

Spurred by a raucous cry that meant their pursuers had caught sight of them, she scrambled forward so she was astride his waist. He choked a cry, and she almost retreated, but she looked back and saw the enemy. Five men with death on their minds.

She leaned forward to grab the reins, and screamed, "Go, Thor! Go!"

By a miracle, the mighty horse lunged into action, iron-shod hooves chipping frosty ground beneath, each pounding beat rattling her bones and threatening to shake both riders free. But it was almost as if the horse worked to keep his riders on, and she had only to grip with her legs and try to keep everything balanced.

Then she felt Edmund begin to slide. His left leg must have been painful or even numb, and his right arm hung useless. She shifted, trying to counter his slide. Thor stumbled, out of balance. An arrow whistled past, making her yelp in fear. A few inches left and it would have been in her back!

Perhaps that was why it was the only one.

Then Thor squealed and bucked. The whistle seemed to come later, so Joan only realized the horse had been hit by an arrow as she and Edmund began to slide off. She grabbed for the mane and fought it, and the brave horse stilled, shuddering, trying to help.

The hunting cries were almost at their back now.

They were taken.

Then, ahead, a true hunting horn.

Precariously balanced, she looked up and saw Mountgrave on its hill and an army pouring out. Too far. Too late.

But when she risked a twisting glance, she saw the five men behind had halted, staring at the rescuing force in frustration. One had a bow, and he nocked another arrow, aiming right for her. Another man pushed the arrow to one side, but he looked into Joan's eyes and promised retribution.

The men whirled and raced away down the path, back to safety, back to Woldingham with a tale of treachery.

Joan eased off Edmund's unconscious body and burst into tears.

The next little while passed in a daze, as release from immediate terror turned her almost faint. She was lifted onto another horse and carried back to the castle at a walk, faintly aware of somber concern all around, and not for her.

A reverent, whispering concern for Edmund de Graves. Dear Blessed Mary, was he *dying?* What terrible wound had caused all that blood? What harm had she done by sitting on top of him?

When they clattered into the castle, they were swarmed by another small army, this time of servants, some quick to help, others there to stare at their lord with distraught eyes. Joan, still carried in her rider's arms, saw Edmund being carefully eased off Thor's back.

He was silent and immediately submerged in a sea of caring bodies. He could be nobly suppressing pain. Or still unconscious. Or dead.

No, not dead. They'd be wailing if he were dead.

"Lord Edmund," she said to the man holding her. Older, with intelligent, experienced eyes. "I must go to him."

Did those eyes see too much? "No need, Lady. He will be well cared for."

"But…" Joan forced herself into silence. Her feeling that she should be by his side was nonsense.

"I am Almar de Font, Lady. And you, I think, are *not* Lady Nicolette de Montelan."

"Joan of Hawes. Lady Nicolette's cousin." Then she added helplessly, "*The* Almar de Font?"

His lips twitched. "If there were another, my lady, I'd be forced to fight him for possession of the name."

He turned and called something to the people around, and in moments she was carefully handed down and assisted, with fussing care, to stand.

He swung off and stood beside her. "All a man truly owns, my lady, is his honorable name."

Joan looked around at the massive, mighty walls and keep, at hordes of prosperous servants, dozens of fine horses, a small army of well-trained men. Edmund owned a great deal more than his name, but she wondered how much pleasure he gained from it.

She let herself be guided into the keep, feeling as if she'd arrived in a mythical land. Almar de Font was perhaps more famous than the Golden Lion.

He had enjoyed many heroic adventures of his own, but fifteen years ago, he had settled to being the mentor and trainer of his friend and lord's two remaining sons. The name Almar de Font *meant* honor, honor to the death, and she was bitterly sure that he would never let his lord and student bend his honor enough to give the banner to the de Montelans.

Not even to save Sir Gerald's life.

"Lady Joan!" She suddenly found herself enveloped in silk and perfumes, all part of a babbling woman. In a moment it began to make sense.

"So brave! So saintly! Come. Come."

Joan was given no choice, but carried on silk and perfume to a small but exquisite chamber hung with tapestries and warmed by two extravagant braziers. By then she had sorted out that her captor was Lady Letitia, Edmund's sister, and that the army was a bevy of maidservants, each one dressed more finely than Joan.

Joan was still wearing the costume of the Blessed Virgin, the simple clothes of a carpenter's wife. But even if she'd been wearing her festive best, Joan knew she would not have matched Lady Letitia's ladies, never mind the lady herself.

It didn't matter, since they immediately stripped her down to her skin and placed her tenderly in a huge perfumed, linen-lined bathtub. Despite feeble protests, soon every part of her body was being lovingly attended to by someone. She lay back and stared up at Lady Letitia, who was orchestrating this.

Edmund's sister lacked his spectacular beauty. Medium height, medium hair somewhere on the brown side of blond, medium figure. It was confidence and a fortune in silks and jewels that made her seem like a goddess.

"What's happening?" Joan asked.

Lady Letitia smiled, a full and joyous smile. "My brother will recover," she said, as if that answered the question.

"God be praised. But I meant, why am I being treated like—" she couldn't think what she was being treating like, except that it had never happened before "—an honored guest," she ended limply.

"But you are!" Letitia exclaimed, and sank to her knees to take the comb from a servant and work it gently through Joan's tangled hair. "You saved Edmund."

Joan hadn't even realized that her hair had come free from her plaits and must be a tangled mess. She suspected that despite Joan's status as heroic maiden, Lady Letitia would not be pleased to learn that her brother had created most of the destruction. She was tempted to laugh, or cry, or both.

If marriage between them wasn't impossible because of their families, she saw now that it was impossible in every other way. She'd felt like a poor relation at Woldingham. Here, she felt like an intrusive pig-girl.

She surrendered and let them wash her, dry her, lay her on a bed and massage her with perfumed oils. As she drifted off to sleep, she thought idly that it was not the treatment given an honored guest. It was more like the special care given a lamb destined for the Easter feast.

A sacrifice. Which is exactly what she was to be.

The next step was to hand her over to Uncle Henry in exchange for Gerald de Graves, and then the slaughter would begin.

Chapter Six

JOAN WAS AWOKEN by a gentle hand shaking her, and for a moment a strange softness and perfume confused her. Where was she? Then, reality rushed back, and she sat up straight, ready to face her fate.

She winced. She was sore and stiff in many places, some of which she would never admit to. Despite a hovering maidservant, she closed her eyes and tried to recapture a moment of the cave, a trace of her and Edmund, but it was like a dream, evading her conscious thoughts.

She opened her eyes and looked at the middle-aged woman. "Is it time?" Time to be handed over.

"Aye, Lady, it is. Come rise and let us dress you."

Joan saw two other servants, one older, one younger, and a spread of fine clothes. "Oh, that's not necessary." Perhaps if she was returned as the bedraggled Virgin, it would temper her uncle's fury. "What I came in will serve."

The woman pulled a face. "I'm sorry, Lady, but that's all been tossed in the rag pile. Nothing special to begin with, and soiled with mud and blood."

Joan looked at the glowing fabrics again. She didn't even know what some of the garments were, but it was all silk, much of it wondrously embroidered. "Then perhaps something simpler?"

All three were staring at her. "For the feast?" the woman asked.

"Feast?" For an insane moment, Joan imagined herself the chief dish, dressed for slaughter.

The woman laid a hand on her hair, comfortingly. Perhaps her fear had shown. "'Tis Christmas Day, Lady Joan, and none here wishes you harm. Woldingham has agreed to return Lord Gerald safe tomorrow in exchange for you, so today we can celebrate. Soon all will be gathered in the hall."

Tomorrow.

What difference did a day make? And yet it did. She had a day before the ax fell, and why shouldn't she enjoy it? And if she was to feast with the de Graves, she welcomed the chance not to appear a pauper.

She rose from her bed and let them slip over her head a shift of linen so fine it felt like silk. The full length gown that followed *was* silk, a winter warmth of silk that puddled ungirdled at her feet like richest cream, for it was that color. By contrast, the tunic that they dropped on top was light as a feather and almost transparent, so finely woven it was, except where it was embroidered in jewel-colored flowers. Joan looked down and smoothed her hands over the shining pattern it made against the cream—like summer flowers against snow—and could have wept at the beauty of it.

For a moment she wanted to reject it as too fine, too fine for Joan of Hawes, but instead she gripped both layers of silk. Tomorrow would come. For today, she would dress in silk and feast in grandeur, and even let herself dream a little that this could be for her.

Next came fine woolen stockings and pretty cream leather shoes that fit. Then the plump maid, Mabelle, opened a chest and took out a glittering snake. The girdle of gold and pearls was clasped around her hips, yet still hung extravagantly down to her toes at the front. A fine veil was draped over her unbound hair and secured with a circlet as fine as the girdle. She wished she could see herself like this.

Had she, like ordinary Lady Letitia, been transformed into a grand lady for a while? Or, as she feared, did Joan of Hawes squat like a toad among flowers, unchanged and out of place?

She stiffened her spine. This was her chance to experience grandeur for a few brief hours. She would take it.

When she was ready, the maidservants escorted her

out past a reredos into a staggeringly noisy and brilliant great hall. Banners hung from the high beamed ceiling, among coils of smoke from flambeaux, braziers and one great fire. The aromas of perfumes, spices and rich foods roiled in the air. Richly dressed people crammed tables all around, and servants lined the walls.

Waiting.

Waiting for her?

Embarrassed, she searched for her place, and Mabelle pushed her gently toward the grand high table to her right, raised on a dais.

Lady Letitia was there, and an older, even grander woman. A middle-aged man. Sir Almar.

Then she saw Edmund. Healthy?

No. Not Edmund, but the Golden Lion, sitting in the great central chair, dressed in crimson, with jeweled bracelets and a gold circlet on his hair—shimmering like a figure of gilt and jewels, scarcely human at all.

He was staring at her, too. Darkly.

He saw the toad.

Before she could panic and run, he pushed himself to his feet with his left hand—she could tell the movement hurt. Sir Almar, close by, and two attendants behind him, put out hands as if to help. When standing, Edmund bowed.

"Lady Joan. Welcome to my hall. Come, sit at my right hand."

To her breath-stealing panic, with rustles and scrapes everyone in the hall rose, even those at the high table. The knights bowed and the ladies curtsied, and the servants all went to one knee.

Joan stood there frozen.

Sir Almar came quickly down from the dais to her side and escorted her, dazed, up the steps and to the plain seat—but still a chair not a bench—at Lord Edmund's right hand.

She sat, and Edmund eased back into his seat. She noted that he accepted Sir Almar's discreet hand beneath his elbow to do it and that sweat glistened on his brow. He should be in bed. The hall sprang back into motion, but too many eyes lingered on her.

"I wish you hadn't done that," she whispered, head bowed, for she didn't know where to look.

His hand raised her chin and turned it to his pale face. She caught the flash of a number of large jeweled rings. "We do you honor, Lady Joan, that is all."

Once she met his eyes, he took his hand away, and, looking past him at the cool-faced older woman, she could only be glad. That must be his mother, the famous Lady Blanche de Graves, a grand lady in her own right, before marriage to his father. She was held to be at least partly responsible for the family's rise in fame and fortune.

The sort of woman he would marry next.

"I did not do so very much, my lord," Joan said.

"You saved my life, Lady."

"Thor would have brought you home safe, and you wouldn't have been in danger without me."

"You wouldn't have been in danger without me, Lady Joan, or *still* be in danger because of me."

"Ah," she said, breaking the disturbing connection with his eyes to look out at the hall. "Honoring the sacrificial victim. I see, my lord."

Liveried pages presented food, and Edmund silently selected choice items for her silver plate. She drank from a jeweled cup and began to eat, for she was very hungry. She wasn't entirely sure it would stay down, however.

Minstrels were concealed somewhere, playing peaceful, beautiful music, which would doubtless have delighted her in other situations.

She felt him lean back in his huge, magnificent seat. "I have no choice now, Lady Joan, but to exchange you for my brother."

"I understand."

"It was your preferred course, if you remember." She could hear gritted teeth.

"But it's a shame I was forced to show my split allegiance so clearly."

"I didn't force you into anything. I ordered you to escape to Woldingham."

And it was clear he wished she'd done that. Perhaps

it would have been better. They both would have been captured, but Lord Henry wouldn't have killed Edmund. To ransom the Golden Lion and his brother, Mountgrave would have had to give up the banner and all this would have been over.

But that wasn't true. If the de Graves lost the banner, they'd start a war to get it back. Their oaths demanded it.

"Lady Joan." She was startled into looking at his guarded face. "Tell your uncle that you helped me in order to prevent my murder by his men, because you knew he would not wish it, and does not approve of bloodshed at Christmastide."

After a moment she admitted, "That's clever."

"I am, sometimes."

Eyes say things that lips cannot.

His mother broke the silent connection, leaning forward to speak around him. "You have my deepest gratitude, Lady Joan, for assisting my son." Her heavy-lidded eyes missed nothing, and her thin-lipped smile did not warm them at all.

"I would not wish anyone to die over a piece of cloth, my lady."

The woman's fine nostrils flared. "It is not merely a piece of cloth, girl."

"No," said Joan, meeting her eyes. "It has been forged into a shackle for the men of two families.

Doubtless in time, Lord Edmund will require a binding oath of his son that he never bend, never negotiate on the matter."

Edmund's right arm must be heavily bandaged, but even so, he managed to grip her wrist. "Joan, be silent."

Joan saw his mother's features pinch, and it wasn't at her words. It was at Edmund's plain use of her name, and the tone in which he'd spoken. It had been a firm warning, but the tone had been almost intimate.

She saw him realize it. He removed his hand and pointed with his left hand, pointed to the right of the high table, where a length of dull cloth—faded reds and browns with some sort of stitchery on it—hung on a huge carved and gilded stand. "There it is."

The Bethlehem Banner. It hung like a figure of Christ on a golden crucifix.

War banners were rarely glorious after use, but this one was particularly faded and torn. Which, in a way, gave it additional power to move. She could believe that it had been carried into Jerusalem generations ago, had been stained with blood, then laid on the ground where Jesus had been born.

Or perhaps it was the suffering and blood through the subsequent years that gave it power.

Then she noticed how all the servants bowed to it as they passed.

She turned back to him. "Does it live there all the time?"

He was frowning at her tone. Perhaps everyone was, but she was intent on him. "Of course not. We have a special and secure chapel in the keep where it is kept, except at Christmas."

"It is locked away?"

"Six monks live close by to pray before it night and day, Lady Joan."

To pray for forgiveness, or to pray for yet greater glory for the de Graves, she wanted to ask. Seeing the grandeur in which he lived, sensing the reverence in which he was regarded, she understood better why the de Montelans believed the banner carried mystical power. Why they wanted it for themselves.

But it was all wrong. She felt as if that banner was trapped on that cross, as much a prisoner of cold-hearted men as she would be tomorrow.

He touched her again with his right hand, gently. "Joan, what is it? No need to curb your tongue, you know that."

A hint of a smile in his eyes invited her to another place and time, but that was past. Done. His mother's watchful eyes told her that. She owed him some honesty, however. "If we can speak together before I leave, my lord—speak alone—I will tell you my thoughts on this."

After a moment, he nodded. "So be it. For now though, as a kindness to me, enjoy the feast."

Since there was nothing else to do, Joan obeyed, taking particular comfort in Sir Almar's presence to her right. Though a quiet man, he spoke easily on a number of simple subjects, and encouraged her enjoyment of tumblers, magicians and riddlers. From time to time, Lord Edmund claimed her attention, too, with some polite comment or question, or to ply her with yet more delicacies, but that was all. She knew why he gave her this limited attention. He was the center of his world, and always watched, so he must not seem too fond with her. However, it would raise suspicions if they were to ignore each other entirely.

He had no choice. She knew that. Even if he truly wished to, he couldn't marry her, and without the exchange, his brother would languish in prison, or perhaps face torture and death. She knew without assurance that Edmund would try to bargain for her safety, to mitigate any penalty, but he had to give her over to her uncle, and once Christmastide was over, Uncle Henry would not be merciful.

And Nicolette, of course, was likely confined on bread and water even now.

She wondered if any kind of feast was taking place at Woldingham.

She wondered if Nicolette had been forced to confess the true and greater sin.

All appetite fled, and Joan began to feel sick.

A warm hand covered hers again, concealed by the rich table coverings, but he said nothing. She glanced at him, and his eyes met hers briefly, full of the same knowledge that lay bitter within her. They were both powerless within a pattern of events created by others but made more tangled by themselves.

Then the music picked up pace and entertainers ran laughing from the center space to leave room for dancing.

"I wish I could lead you into a dance, Lady Joan." It was a polite nothing, but she hoped she read a touch of honest sadness in his expression. She needed to believe that his feelings had some truth to them, some lasting quality. That it had not just been the cave and the night.

"I am in no mood to dance, my lord."

Lady Blanche leaned forward again. "There are many men here who would be honored to be your partner, Lady Joan."

Joan smiled at her. "I would rather not, my lady."

Lady Blanche smiled back, but her eyes flashed a clear message. *Harbor no foolish thoughts, girl.*

Joan watched the dance start, then said, "I assume your wounds are not too serious, Lord Edmund."

"Just painful and awkward, Lady Joan. They might have been worse without your skill with a stone."

She couldn't help a fleeting grin at him, though she controlled it quickly. "It was a game my brothers and I played, my lord."

She allowed him to draw her into talking about her home, her brothers and sisters, and the rough-and-tumble years of growing up with parents too harried by ten children—all of whom miraculously survived— to be keeping close watch on any of them.

"Of course, the boys left to be trained in other households, but they were replaced by other men's sons. Not many, my lord," she added deliberately, "for Hawes is not a grand holding."

Mountgrave bubbled over with pages and squires who had won the privilege of serving the Golden Lion.

"And none of these hopeful young men courted you, Lady Joan?"

"A few did. They were not to my taste, however. Too young."

"Ah yes, I remember now that you favor a sober, older man."

With that, carelessly or deliberately, he summoned the memory of their night together, and as she had said that night, she whispered, "Don't."

His left hand lay on the rich cloth covering the table, and she saw it clench briefly. She also saw, made herself see, the three precious rings he wore, the worked gold bracelet around his wrist, and the heavy silk of his robe, embroidered red on red. He did not need to trumpet his wealth with gaudiness.

And then, she wondered suddenly how hard it was to be Edmund de Graves, the Golden Lion, at only twenty-five. She remembered him speaking of how wearying it was to be reverenced all the time.

Impulsively, irresistibly, she squeezed gently on the hand that still rested on her. He turned sharply to look at her, then carefully away. But beneath the cloths, his thumb gently, almost sadly, whispered against the back of her fingers.

After a moment, he eased his hand free and turned to his mother. "My lady, I fear I am too weary to preside over this feast any longer. May I beg you and Sir Almar to take my place?"

Lady Blanche put her hand to his face and kissed him. "Of course, dearest. You know I wished you to keep to your bed."

"I could not disappoint everyone." He turned to Joan. "Be free, my lady, to stay or retire. You share my sister's room for the night."

Joan colored. She'd not even thought of where she would sleep. "I don't like—"

"It is no imposition, is it, Letty?"

Lady Letitia, on the far side of Sir Almar, cheerfully agreed.

Lord Edmund raised her hand with his left, and

gently kissed it. "I wish you good rest, my lady. Be assured that I will do my best to assure your safety as you did mine."

Both kiss and words were suitable for a hundred pairs of eyes and ears, and yet Joan bit her lip to force back tears. She watched as he was assisted to his feet by two strong servants and helped to limp away, obviously in serious pain. Under the floor-length gown, there was no way to know how badly he was wounded, but she didn't think he put much weight on his left leg at all. Even so, before the banner, he paused to bow.

For a little while, last night, that body had been hers. Hers to play with. Hers to care for.

She caught Lady Blanche's thoughtful eyes on her.

"How seriously is he wounded, my lady?" Joan asked directly. No point in trying to pretend she didn't care.

"As Lord Edmund said, Lady Joan, painfully, but not seriously."

"I bandaged his calf, but there seemed to be blood from higher. There was no time to deal with that."

"A blade slid up beneath the mail," said Sir Almar, and Joan turned to him. "Not a trick anyone could pull off, one on one. He was lucky it didn't penetrate all the way or he could have spilled his guts instead of a barrelful of blood."

Joan remembered the man on foot who'd charged with his sword. So close to death.

"But he will suffer no permanent harm?"

"If God is kind, Lady."

Infection. The ever-hovering danger. "He should not have left his bed. Surely he will keep to it now."

"He insists on delivering you to your uncle, Lady, and seeing his brother safe. But do not feel it is your fault. It must be done in person, on the neutral territory between the two lands. And no one wishes to delay matters."

"Neutral territory? I thought the lands met."

"They do, but at the start of this mess someone had sense to set apart four acres where the opposing parties can meet, honor-sworn not to spill blood. It's hardly ever used for that purpose, so the local folk use it as a common. They call it the Bethlehem Field."

She remembered a dark landscape and a flaring bonfire. "Do they light a fire there on Christmas Eve, Sir Almar?"

"They do, my lady. Peasants from both sides."

She looked at the banner and wished someone would throw it into the neutral fire.

"No, my lady," the man said as if he could read her thoughts.

She rose. "If you will excuse me, my lady," she said to Edmund's mother, "I would prefer to retire."

"Of course, Lady Joan. I will send some maids to care for you."

"There is no need."

"We would not want to fail in any courtesy."

Joan found herself accompanied by three younger maids, who she was sure resented being taken from the festivities, but who all insisted on remaining and settling to sleep on straw mattresses on the floor.

Alone in the bed she'd share with Lady Letitia, Joan smothered a grim laugh. Lady Blanche was clearly making certain that Joan engaged in no tryst with her son. It was flattering to be thought worthy of such measures, but a dismal confirmation that she was, after all, merely a toad.

Chapter Seven

JOAN WAS AWAKENED the next morning by early sun slanting through shuttered windows. It was warm under the heavy covers beside the sleeping Letitia, but the air nipped at her nose.

Though she didn't look forward to the day, she'd get up if she thought she had any clothes. She could hardly wear the feasting finery when she was taken to her fate.

Very soon a servant popped in to wake the three maids, and as they quietly began to dress and put away their mattresses, folding blankets into a large chest, she asked one to find her something to wear.

As she waited, Joan slipped out of bed and wrapped herself in one of the blankets. Then she opened the shutters a little and looked out over the castle complex and across the countryside that lay between here and Woldingham. Her breath puffed white, but she welcomed the sense of space, for even in this luxurious room, she felt imprisoned.

Perhaps an awareness of future imprisonment.

What would her uncle do?

She'd not just switched places with Nicolette for the Christmas play. She'd attacked, perhaps seriously injured, some of his men to defend a de Graves, and very actively helped Lord Edmund to escape. What was worse, if she'd not allowed herself to be brought here, there would be no hostage to exchange for Gerald de Graves, except the banner.

She'd try Edmund's clever suggestion, but her faith in it was weak.

She hugged herself against a chill deeper than the frosty morning. Poor, poor Nicolette, whose situation grew worse with every twist of this tangled event.

The door opened and she turned. It was one of the maids with an armful of cloth. Clearly no silk, this time, and not too bright of color.

"Thank you," Joan whispered, and waved the woman away. She began to dress herself in a sensible brown wool gown and a heavy tunic of russet color. Practical. Warm.

Letitia stirred and opened her eyes, obviously taking a moment to remember who Joan was. "Oh." Then, in a different tone, she said, "Oh, I'm sure we can find something better than that for you, Lady Joan." She began to scramble out of bed, but Joan waved her back.

"These are fine. I'll be going out, so something warm is welcome."

Letitia huddled back under the blankets and furs. "If you're going out, you need more. I'll lend you my fur cloak. I insist."

Joan thought of arguing but didn't. It was a loan only. And she rather suspected Lady Blanche would prevent it.

She was tying the woven girdle when Letitia asked, "What happened between you and my brother?"

The question no one else had asked. "You know what happened."

Letitia shook her head. "He's in a strange mood over you."

Joan didn't want to create trouble here. "He considers me under his protection. He doesn't want to hand me back to my uncle."

Letitia pulled a face. "I'd hoped he might have fallen in love with you."

Joan gave a convincing laugh. "Hardly."

"Love has no logic. He looked at you once or twice last night, as if...well, as if."

Joan didn't want this conversation, but it seemed rude to leave. Instead, she posed her own question. "Are you not married, Lady Letitia?"

"I was betrothed, but he died of a festering wound."

Joan's heart missed a beat. It could happen to

anyone, great or small. "I'm sorry," she said, but she longed to run to see if Lord Edmund was still healthy.

"So am I. He was a lovely man. I've not met the like."

Caught by her sadness, Joan sat on the bed. "How long ago?"

Letitia rolled onto her back. "Two years. Mother parades rich and handsome men in front of me like prize bulls, but Edmund won't let her push me."

"She wants you happy again."

"She also wants me well married. She takes pride in having well-married offspring. She's not going to like her younger son being entangled with Nicolette de Montelan."

"There's no choice now."

"Is Lady Nicolette strong?"

Joan knew what she was being asked. "Not in that way, but Ed—Lord Edmund said they'd live away from here, at one of his lesser properties."

"And never return. That will be hard for her. And Gerald."

"They made their own fates," said Joan grimly.

Letitia considered her. "Does that mean there's no chance you'll have a similar fate?"

Joan felt her face heat and stood. "Absolutely none."

"Oh." Letitia sat up, huddling coverings around

her. "Are you saying that the Golden Lion doesn't attract you in the slightest? That makes you a very unnatural woman."

"That's what he said." Joan considered Lady Letitia's astonishment and laughed. "You're right. There are forces of nature that no one can withstand. Of course, I'm in love with your brother. But I harbor foolish hopes."

With that, she did make her escape.

The castle was strange to her, but she could hardly get lost. In the great hall she helped herself to some of the bread and cheese set out as a breakfast, and sourly regarded the Bethlehem Banner. Two armed guards stood beside it, and in front on his knees, a monk prayed. The passing servants still bowed.

She turned away, trying not to be bitter, but unable to forget that piece of cloth was the price of everything, and despite his fabulous wealth, it was the one price Edmund de Graves would not, could not, pay.

A young man appeared before her and bowed. A squire, she guessed, but close to knighthood, and with the gilded confidence of wealth and power. "My lady, Lord Edmund would speak with you, if you will."

Her foolish heart couldn't help a little flutter. "Where?"

"In his chamber, Lady."

She almost asked if it were proper, but the squire

was not the person to ask, and anyway, Lord Edmund's chamber would not be a private place. She let him lead her back behind the reredos to the private quarters and to a richly carved door. With some wryness, she thought it looked like the door to a shrine except that an armed guard stood outside.

Who, exactly, did they think might attack their lord within his own castle?

The door swung open and she took one step through before halting in amazement. She couldn't help it. She had never seen a room as magnificent as this.

What walls were not hung with brilliant tapestries were painted with flowers and animals. All the structural woodwork was carved and painted, as was every piece of furniture. Two windows lit the room, glazed in plain and colored glass and, between them, a roaring fire was set in the wall. Uncle Henry had a fireplace set into the wall of his chamber, but it easily belched smoke. This one had a hood that stuck out into the room—a hood of plaster, she thought, for stone could not be so finely detailed—sweeping up to the ceiling. It seemed to ensure that all the smoke went up the chimney and outside so that the room was pleasantly warm without smoke at all.

And on the floor at her feet, halting her, lay a thick woven cloth in a rich design of red, blue and cream.

There were many people in the room in addition to Edmund, who was on his dais bed, and they were all looking at her. They were all also standing on the precious cloth. Swallowing, she walked onto it, too, and curtsied. "You wished to speak to me, my lord."

His bed was like the resting place of a precious relic, carved and decorated like everything else here and hung with heavy cloth woven in rich colors. Thick furs lay folded near the end, for show, no doubt. No one would ever need furs in a room this warm.

"If it please you, Lady Joan, sit." He indicated a chair by the side of his bed and the squire stepped forward to assist her to it.

As she brought her bedazzlement under control, she noted who was in the room. The squire, two man-servants, a rosy-cheeked page, a monk at a desk writing on a long sheet of parchment and a black-robed figure who might be a doctor.

A chair, she thought, as she settled into it. And padded, too. Before coming here she had never sat on anything but a bench or stool. Was it as great an honor as it seemed, or just part of the astonishing luxury of Mountgrave?

Uncomfortably aware of an audience, she said, "I hope you are well, my lord."

"Healing wounds hurt, Lady Joan, but it appears I am healing, so I have no complaint."

"It might injure you to ride today."

"Dr. Hildebrand has sewn me up quite firmly and thinks I will not split again."

She could imagine the pain, past, present, and future, but supposed that even great wealth had not spared him from it in his life. And despite the pain awaiting her, she did want this over. This place was too rich, too grand, for her, and Edmund was too great a temptation. Even now, she wanted to lean toward him, to touch his hair, to soothe his hurts, to be touched, to be soothed....

She sat straight, hands in lap. "You had something you wished to say to me, my lord?"

"Last night, you said you had something you wished to say to me, Lady Joan."

Her heart sank. In the sillier parts of her mind she'd been thinking he had summoned her because he needed to, because, despite hopelessness, he wanted to see her one more time. Instead, he was just courteously granting her request for audience.

She glanced around. These were doubtless his trusted people, and he must carry on his private business in front of them all the time, but she said, "I request privacy, my lord."

A mere gesture of his hand, and everyone bowed out of the room. Joan watched the door close, then looked back at him. "It must get very wearying."

He laughed shortly. "And yet it is all I know."

He was reclining against full pillows and wearing a red robe under the covers. His thick golden hair waved down to his broad shoulders, and seeing him leisurely for the first time in daylight, Joan discovered that his eyes were not the clear blue she'd imagined, but a blue muted by gray and perhaps even by green. Softer, subtler, and somehow comforting.

"What are you thinking?" he asked.

"I think I heard an unspoken 'you wretched woman' after that, my lord." As his lips twitched, she said, "I was thinking that the Golden Lion should have piercing blue eyes. I like your eyes better."

She sat to his left, so when he extended a hand to her it was without pain. Knowing it was unwise, she put her hand into his, and at first contact, at the gentle curl of his fingers around hers, something inside cracked and melted.

That wasn't good. It melted into threatened tears.

"Don't," she said, and pulled her hand free. "Don't."

"Not even a touch?"

"If I'm any judge, your lady mother will be here as soon as she learns that we're alone. I would not like to distress her."

After a frowning moment, he leaned back. "As you wish, my wise and foolish virgin. What did you want to say to me? Something about the banner, I assume."

She saw him brace to refuse, to refuse to bend, to break his oath, and she almost held back her words. He would never understand.

"Tell me, Joan. At the very least, give me your honest tongue."

That made her color flare embarrassingly, but she met his eyes. "I know this will seem a madness to you, but when I looked at the banner hanging in the hall, it seemed to me like Christ hanging on the Cross."

He frowned. "The frame is supposed to suggest the Cross. It contains fragments of the true Cross."

She shook her head. "That's not what I mean. It seemed...it seemed trapped there. Hung there. Tortured." She stopped, hearing her words sound crazier by the moment.

"Joan, a banner is designed to be hung. It must be the strain of this—"

"And then you said that you lock it away," she continued, determined to spit it out and be done with it. "Like a prisoner in a dungeon."

"It's a *chapel*. It's more splendid than this room! It's a small monastery, with chambers beside for the monks who care for it and pray before it."

"And if you were locked away in here, my lord, would it be luxury or dungeon?"

He moved both hands, then winced and ran only one through his hair. "As you said yourself, Joan, it's a piece of cloth. What do you want me to do with it? Don't tell me. Burn it."

She sat resolutely silent.

"It has to be guarded. You must see that." After a moment he said, almost yelled, *"What do you want me to do?"*

The door opened and his mother glided in, trailing expensive sleeves, hems and veil. "Edmund? Is something the matter?"

Joan rose and curtsied, prepared to be thrown out.

"No, Mother, though I was speaking to Lady Joan privately." It was clearly a reproof, and the lady stiffened.

"I heard you shouting, my dear."

"Then I was shouting at Lady Joan privately." His lips had softened, however, and mother and son shared a loving acceptance of his ridiculous statement.

She walked to the right side of his bed and leaned to brush his forehead. Secretly checking for fever, Joan was sure, as she'd wished to do. He caught his mother's hand in his left and kissed it. "I am well, Mother." Then he added, "I would ask you to do something for me, however."

"Anything, my dear."

"Go to the hall and stand before the banner. Look at it for me."

She straightened, frowning. "I do not need to look

at the banner. I have seen it through Christmastide for thirty years."

"Yet that is what I wish you to do for me, Mother. Stand, or kneel if you choose, and look at it for me. For as long as it would take to say twenty Paternosters."

Clearly both puzzled and concerned, Lady Blanche looked at Joan with no kindness at all. "And Lady Joan?"

"Will stay with me."

"It is not proper, Edmund."

"I am in no condition to ravish her, and she is far too sensible to assist me to her ruin."

"Are you, indeed?" Lady Blanche asked Joan.

"I fear so, Lady Blanche."

After a startled moment, a touch of humor twitched at Lady Blanche's thin lips, and perhaps a prickle of womanly connection passed between them. But then she said, "I will do as you wish, Edmund, though it is folly," and swept out.

Joan and Edmund looked at each other, and for lack of alternative, she sat down again. She couldn't bear much more of his company, however. It was like starving at a feast.

"If times were right, would you be my wife?" he asked abruptly.

"We have not known each other long enough."

He didn't misunderstand. "Yet we have."

She gestured at his room. "I could not cope with this."

"You could cope with anything."

"You overestimate me, my lord."

"I don't think so. But if you wish, I would have it peeled back to wood and stone and whitewashed like a nun's cell."

She looked down at her clasped hands. "That would be a shame. Don't do this."

In silence she heard the fire crackle and the distant life of his bustling castle, and tried to estimate the length of time needed to say twenty Paternosters.

She looked up. "What do you expect your mother to say when she returns?"

"If I'd known, I would not have sent her."

"If you'll be able to ride shortly, you could have gone to the banner yourself."

"But I know what I want to see."

"I don't understand—"

They were interrupted by an autocratic child's voice beyond the door. "We wish to enter!"

The rumble was doubtless the guard. The response to whatever he said was, "But it's Christmastide!" and a wail that seemed to be a second voice.

Edmund pulled a face, but there was a smile in it. "If you please, Lady Joan, go and admit them."

Puzzled, she went to open the door to see the guard

confronted by two blond children—a firm-chinned girl of about seven, and a much younger child in a trailing gown, thumb in mouth. They both instantly ran past the guard toward the bed, crying, "Father!"

Joan whirled. "Don't leap on him!"

Children. Why had she never thought that he must have children from his first marriage?

The girl turned with haughty anger, but then flushed. "We weren't going to," she said, but it was clearly a lie.

"You can sit on the bed if you're careful," Edmund said. "It's my right arm and my left leg that are wounded. And no bouncing on top of me for a while."

The girl lifted the younger child up onto her father's left side, and the toddler snuggled against him, thumb in mouth. Secure. The girl sat more sedately on his right-hand side, but Joan sensed she wanted to cuddle, too.

Motherless children, but at least they had one parent they loved and trusted, and who loved them.

"I will go," she said, but he shook his head.

"Wait until my mother returns. Come and meet my children. Anna, give Lady Joan your best curtsy, for she saved my life. Remi, you may stay where you are, but say thank-you to her."

The little boy extracted his thumb and said, "Thank you, my lady," then shoved it back in again.

Anna, who strongly reminded Joan of Lady

Blanche, made a perfect curtsy. "We truly are most grateful to you, Lady Joan, and also that you will be the means to save Uncle Gerald from the wicked de Montelans."

Joan flicked one glance at Edmund, but then smiled at the girl. "I am happy to be able to prevent bloodshed, Lady Anna."

The girl returned to her seated study of her father, and, lacking an alternative, Joan went back to her chair. The boy's head turned, watching her curiously.

"The de Montelans are not wicked, Anna," Edmund said, though it sounded like a struggle.

Anna's straight spine straightened further. "Father, of course, they are!"

"But Lady Joan's mother is a de Montelan. And your Uncle Gerald is hoping to marry the Lady Nicolette de Montelan."

She frowned over that. "Then it is just the men of the de Montelan family who are wicked."

"Adults make a great mess of things sometimes, Anna. It is good to be faithful to your family's interests, but rarely is one group of people better or worse than another."

It was perhaps as well that Lady Blanche returned then, brow furrowed. She smiled at the sight of her grandchildren, however, and Anna went to hug her.

The wicked de Graves. A happy, loving family.

The wicked de Montelans. Even if Lord Henry was older and sterner, still it was a happy, loving family in its own way. She could even believe that he'd tried to bend to secure Nicolette's happiness.

How sad this all was.

"Well, Mother?" Edmund asked.

She sat in another chair, one closer to the fire than the bed, and Anna leaned against her. "What do you want me to say?"

"Whatever you wish. That is why I sent you with no guidance."

She sighed, staring into nowhere. "It is strange. I have never looked long and closely at the banner since I came here as a bride, and I do not recall what I thought then. But now…" She looked at her son. "At first I was impatient, thinking it a waste of time. Slowly, however, I began to really see it. It is a sorry piece of cloth by now, but that is not the point. It seems out of place on that huge, ornate holder. Perhaps we need to build it something smaller, more delicate…."

She looked at him, clearly searching for a hint whether she was saying the right things or not. Joan knew he was deliberately not giving any response. But what was the purpose of this? Even if his mother's reaction was the same as hers, what could he do other than give the banner a prettier frame and perhaps not lock it away from sight for most of the year.

"What's going on, Father?" Anna asked, standing straight, a slight edge of panic in her voice.

"It's all right," Edmund said. "Nothing terrible is happening. We are all just thinking about things long ignored. Mother, was there anything else?"

Lady Blanche frowned almost in exasperation. "It sounds foolish to say, Edmund, but the banner did not feel *happy*. I found myself wondering whether Christ Himself would like a holy relic that had touched the place of His birth being the cause of so much enmity. It wouldn't be the first time, however," she added. "The Crusades themselves have been fought over Christ's holy places."

"True, but this is our relic, and our responsibility."

"You cannot give it up," Lady Blanche stated.

"Father!" Anna exclaimed, but he raised his hand.

"Anna, this is not for you to debate. I must think on it."

"But *Father!*"

"No, Anna. You must take Remi now. I will spend more time with you later, after I have returned Lady Joan to her family."

Lady Blanche rose and shepherded the reluctant children away. She glanced once at Joan but did not herd her out, too.

Joan stood on her own. "I will leave you to think. I know there's nothing you can do, so I do regret putting this extra burden on you, my lord. I felt that I had to speak."

He nodded. "I understand." He held out his left hand again, and she put hers into it, letting him pull her closer so he could kiss it. "Joan of Hawes, whatever happens today and in the future, know that I am honored to have met you. Never let the world cow you into silence."

Surrendering to folly, she leaned forward and lightly kissed his lips. "I'll do my best. God guide and keep you, Edmund."

Then she fled the room.

She found the castle strangely unaffected by the turmoil she was experiencing, though she gathered some traditional outdoor games had been postponed because of the planned meeting with the de Montelans at Bethlehem Field. In the bailey horses were being groomed and prepared to make a magnificent show. A number of men were already in armor surcoated in the livery of the Golden Lion. They were eating and drinking festive food in high spirits, though one or two glanced at her with casual compassion.

They knew her fate.

She supposed it was like this when men had prepared to take the sacrificial virgin out to the dragon. In this case, Saint George was not going to ride to the rescue.

She was surprised when Lady Blanche found her and insisted she return to the hall and eat, but the woman didn't say anything of importance, either about her son or the banner. She didn't protest, however, when Lady Letitia insisted that Joan wear her fur cloak.

As Joan left the hall she turned to look one last time at the banner, surprised to find that pity for it had driven out anger. Both emotions were foolish, she told herself as she went down the stairs into the bailey. It was an inanimate object.

It was men who had made it what it was, and men—and women—who suffered.

Chapter Eight

A FINE DUN PALFREY had been prepared for her to ride, and Joan appreciated the quality of the horse, though she was surprised to be given one almost as big as Thor. The destrier waited beside, caparisoned magnificently and summoning a smile by the way he preened, knowing himself to be the center of attention.

Astride her tall mount, she watched Edmund emerge from the hall. When he let two men carry him down the stairs, she knew he was not recovered enough for the venture. He hobbled between the servants to Thor and she couldn't help but say, "You shouldn't be doing this."

"It has to be done, and I'll be better once I'm on the horse."

Getting him there, however, even with a mounting block was neither easy nor painless, and by the time he was in the saddle, he looked pallid.

"Edmund—"

"I do not need another woman to nag me about this!"

Joan literally bit her tongue to suppress words. At least this journey could be accomplished at a walk, and his saddle was a jousting saddle, high in the front and back and shaped to cradle his thighs. Even if he fainted, he'd probably stay on.

He wore no armor, but a magnificent crimson gown embroidered with gold thread. This, clearly, was not an occasion for subtlety. She realized she was the only person not glittering in the red and gold of the de Graves.

They moved out in procession, banner-carrying foot soldiers at the front, then herself and Edmund, side by side, with about two dozen armed squires and knights behind. She watched him anxiously. Perhaps he'd been right; his color slowly returned, and she sensed his pain lessened. He held Thor's reins in his left hand, however, and she suspected he'd rather his right was in a sling rather than resting on his thigh.

Needing to break the silence, she said, "Your children are delightful. Are there just the two?"

"My rare visits. Though Catherine was with child when she died."

"How sad."

He shrugged, and indeed, what was there to say about the hazards of life?

"Will your brother and Nicolette be able to marry?"

"It ought to be so, but first I must see Lord Henry and try to judge his mood. He and I have only met once since my father died." He glanced sideways at her. "You do not look comfortable."

"I could have wished for something smaller to ride."

"I didn't think you'd be happy bobbing along at my knee."

"No," she said. "No, I wouldn't. Thank you."

"No matter what happens today, Joan, I want you to know that I'm going to have the banner treated differently. And I will continue to work for peace between the families. Surely in time we can break the shackles we have put on each other."

"I will pray for it."

"And I promise you, Joan, that my sons will not have to swear an oath on the matter."

"I wish such an oath did not burden you."

"Oaths have their uses. Will you swear to me to try to make the richest use of your life, your courage and your wit?"

She quirked her brows at him. "I think my courage will be well used, and soon, but my wit is best kept in check."

He tightened his lips and looked away. Perhaps she shouldn't have said it, but there was no point hiding from unpleasant truths.

They rode the rest of the way in silence, except for jingling harness and falling hoof. The day was cold but lovely, with clear blue sky and sunshine gilding frosted furrows and bare trees. Crows cawed as they flew from their dark nests high in the trees, but no birds sang until a robin fluttered to a hawthorn branch and trilled at them.

The Bethlehem Field was outlined by a thick hedge all around with only two breaks, facing each other. When they arrived, the de Montelans were already on the other side, banners flying, ready to enter.

Edmund raised his left hand and made a gesture. His squire rode up alongside. "Lady Joan and I go in alone."

The squire wheeled to pass the message back, and Joan went alone with him into the large, open space. They were sworn to peace here, so she hoped all would be all right, though clearly in the past the whole parties had entered.

She saw some consternation among her uncle's people, but eventually, Uncle Henry rode in, every bit as magnificently dressed as Edmund, only in the de Montelan's blue and gold. He was leading another horse by the reins. Gerald de Graves' hands were tied in front of him and to the pommel of his saddle.

It had never occurred to Joan to try to escape. Would that be held against her, too?

They met in the center, and her uncle's glare made Joan shiver inside the thick fur. Noble sacrifice was all very well, but in the end it was real and frightening.

As the two lords greeted each other, she looked at Gerald de Graves. He was lighter built than his brother, but nearly as handsome, even dungeon-dirty and bruised. He met her eyes sympathetically but sadly. He gained his freedom here, but not what he truly wanted—Nicolette.

Lord Henry was holding out the horse's reins to Edmund, but Edmund said, "If you will, Lord Henry, I would speak with you."

The reins were pulled back out of reach. "You break your word?"

"Never. I wish to speak of more important things. The banner, for one."

A smile touched Lord Henry's lips. A hungry one. "The de Graves have come to their senses?"

"You know we swear an oath never to give the banner to the de Montelans."

"And we swear an oath never to rest while it remains in the hands of the de Graves."

Joan had to suppress a sigh.

The silence lingered so long that she thought it was all over, but then Edmund said, "Lord Henry, do you wish this feud to continue, generation after generation, poisoning this area with enmity, costing lives and happiness?"

"I do not. But I cannot accept the banner being in your unworthy hands."

Joan sensed Edmund taking a special breath. "What if it were in neither of our hands?"

"Edmund, no!" Sir Gerald exclaimed.

Lord Henry's horse stepped back, clearly stirred by some unwary movement. *"Destroy it?"*

"No. What I propose, Lord Henry, is that the de Graves and the de Montelans build a monastery here on Bethlehem Field, and house the banner in it. We would both swear to protect it, and to never try to move it from this place, and here it could be reverenced by any who wished to come."

Lord Henry looked around, frowning, and Joan bit her lip. It was a brilliant solution, but would her uncle agree? He'd never struck her as a quick-witted or flexible man, but he wasn't stupid, and she suspected he truly was as weary of the enmity as Edmund was. And he knew Nicolette loved Gerald de Graves.

The still moment was broken by pounding hooves, and everyone turned to see a horse galloping toward the field. The pale gold flying hair could only belong to Nicolette. The horse soared over the hedge and raced foaming right up to them. Joan had never suspected that her cousin was such a magnificent rider.

"Father!" she declared, "I must go with Gerald."

Joan saw a wince of exasperation on Edmund's

face, but was herself tempted to wild laughter. Would nothing about this go according to plan?

"I left you locked up, daughter, where you belong!"

"I will not be kept from this, because it concerns me, Father. You know I love Gerald. If you will not permit our marriage, I must still go with him." She raised her chin, though she'd turned deathly pale. "I am carrying his child."

Lord Henry turned fiery red and swung on the bound man, fist rising.

"Stop!" Edmund's authority halted the older man. "I cannot interfere without starting a bloody battle here, Lord Henry, but I will not let you strike my brother. Save for the feud, he and Nicolette would be happily married, and if you consent to my plan, they can still be so. Proof of better days."

Lord Henry glared around, clearly teetering on the edge of bloodshed for bloodshed's sake. Nicolette extended her hand to him. "Father, I love you, but I love Gerald, too. And now, because of my sin, I *must* go to him. Pray heaven, I do not have to lose you."

Lord Henry's lips wobbled through his glower. "Sin indeed, daughter," he said. Though he doubtless intended to growl, it sounded simply unhappy. "But at least you didn't soil our tradition by playing the Virgin."

Joan stared at him. She had never expected such instant understanding and approval.

"And you, Joan," he said, turning to her. "You did well. But not," he added, voice recovering, "in helping de Graves to escape!"

Joan swallowed and produced Edmund's clever explanation. "I believed your men would kill him, Uncle, and I knew you would not want that."

Lord Henry looked nothing so much as baffled. "I see, I see."

Edmund spoke. "My death or serious injury would certainly have made peace more difficult, Lord Henry. If we do not settle this now, however, such a death might happen, sealing us all in turmoil for yet more generations."

Lord Henry looked between Gerald and his daughter for a moment, and Joan could almost hear him muttering that this man was not worthy of her, but then he dragged Gerald's horse over to Nicolette and put the reins in her hands. "Here, daughter, have him." But he leaned to grasp the startled Gerald's tunic in his hand. "Harm her, neglect her, be unfaithful to her, lad, and there'll be violence that'll make this feud look like May Day."

"I love her, sir," Gerald said.

"Keep it so."

Lord Henry turned his horse. "What now, Lord Edmund?"

"You agree to my plan?"

Lord Henry nodded.

"Then the sooner the building starts, the sooner the banner can be moved. Perhaps by May Day."

Joan couldn't keep silent. "There could be a wooden chapel while the monastery builds. It could be up before the end of Christmastide."

Neither man looked pleased. She suspected Lord Henry glowered just because she had interrupted, but Edmund's frown could be because he'd rather delay the final step. But then he nodded. "It can be so. Lord Henry, will you lend men to help build?"

"To get the banner out of your hands? By Jerusalem, I will! In fact, I and my sons will help in this holy task."

To forestall Edmund stupidly making the same offer, Joan said, "Lord Edmund is wounded. But Sir Gerald will doubtless help. Perhaps he and Nicolette can be married—"

"Joan," said Edmund.

"Joan!" bellowed her uncle.

Her uncle continued, "Hold your tongue! I don't know what imp has invaded you, Niece, the way you speak out on men's matters!" He leaned forward and grabbed her reins by the bit, drawing her horse away from Thor. "Come. And you, too, Nicolette. Until you marry, you'll pretend to be a proper maid!"

Nicolette had untied Gerald, and they were both off

their horses, kissing and exploring each other's tear-damp faces in a way that brought an aching lump to Joan's throat.

There was no true barrier now between her and Edmund, but clearly he'd realized that she was unsuited to be the bride of the Golden Lion. He was quite right, too. She'd be miserable in such a situation.

As she was led away, however, he spoke one last time. "Lord Henry."

Her uncle looked back and Edmund continued, "Of your kindness, do not punish Lady Joan for her adventures."

Her uncle's look at her was sharp and questioning, but he said, "If she keeps her tongue mild and respectful, she'll have no hurt from me."

Chapter Nine

THE FIRST REACTION AT Woldingham was consternation, but soon happiness bubbled up, along with a subtle warmth and relaxation that showed how deeply the frost of enmity had cut. Though resentful at first, her male cousins took their father's point of view, and threw themselves enthusiastically into the building of the wooden chapel, seeing it as a victory over the de Graves.

Mountgrave would no longer have the banner!

She wondered how everyone was taking it there. She was sure some would see it as surrender, as weakness of some sort, but Edmund's status as the Golden Lion would likely carry him over that. As for herself, she worked hard at banishing folly. Despite an unexpected friendship, there was nothing lasting between her and Lord Edmund de Graves.

Lust, a part of her whispered. She had to accept that, yes, there was lust. That wasn't enough, however. She wasn't trained to be a great lady, and he was doubt-less wise not to tempt her with the notion.

The last thing she wanted was for anyone to guess at the foolish part of her mind, the part that would marry Edmund de Graves if asked and hope that a clever tongue could make it all work.

Meanwhile she tried hard to behave well, did her best to enjoy Christmas, and threw herself into her cousin's ecstatic preparations for her wedding. Gerald even visited, riding into Woldingham one day, unes-corted, testing the truce.

Though to begin with, the air boiled with tension, Nicolette's warm greeting and sensible Aunt Ellen's welcome brought it down to simmering point. Soon, though rather hesitantly, the castle moved again, ac-cepting the enemy in their midst.

Joan, however, had the task of chaperoning the two during the meeting. She sat in a corner, sewing and trying to ignore their soft murmurs and occasional laughter. At a silence she glanced over and saw them lost in a kiss she doubtless should not permit. But what harm in it?

Except to her.

She and Edmund had not kissed like that, a lei-surely kiss that promised aeons. There hadn't been any aeons to promise. She was dreading Twelfth Day, when the wedding would take place, and the banner would be brought at last to neutral territory. Could she survive it without making a fool of herself? After that, she would go home, for what was there to keep her here?

Eventually light faded and Gerald had to leave, though clearly he'd rather have stayed forever. He took Joan's hand and kissed it. "You are a most excellent chaperon, my lady."

"From a suitor's point of view," she said tartly. Golden as his brother, he was a handsome man who could doubtless charm birds to his hand, but beside Lord Edmund he would pale.

He smiled. "Of course. But if Lady Ellen had wanted more decorum, she would have stayed herself. It's a clever woman who knows when the horse has left the stable."

Joan gave him a severe look. "I'll have you know, Sir Gerald, that I consider you a scoundrel for seducing Nicolette into what could have been disaster."

He glanced at his beloved. "Is it always the man at fault?"

Nicolette blushed, but Joan said, "It is always the woman who pays the price."

Gerald looked at her, head cocked. "Edmund said you were a very sensible virgin. I see what he meant."

And then he left.

Nicolette said, "Joan? What's the matter?"

Joan laughed it off, but she could have wept. A sensible virgin. It was likely to be her epitaph, and she'd like to die soon if that was the sum of Lord Edmund de Graves' assessment of her.

IT SNOWED A LITTLE on the way to the wedding, but cleared to crisp gray by the time the de Montelan party approached the Bethlehem Field with its new wooden chapel to one side. The center of the field was left open for the monastery that would rise there soon.

The red and gold of the de Graves was approaching on the other side, but around, the ordinary folk hovered, keen to see this great day, and to see the Bethlehem Banner, but ready to flee at the slightest sign of trouble.

Joan didn't blame them. All around her, beneath handsome surcoats and cloaks, armor and weapons jingled. Most jaws were tense, most eyes watchful. No one truly believed that today could pass as planned, without violence. She hardly did herself.

This time both parties passed through the openings and into the field. The armed men formed opposing ranks, and the principal families rode to meet in the middle. Joan noticed Lady Ellen and Lady Blanche bow to each other with just as much caution as the men.

She scrupulously did not look at Edmund. She couldn't risk it.

Then the de Graves forces split, and through the middle passed the six monks, singing the Te Deum, the two front ones bearing the banner on a simple holder. Just in front of Joan, Lord Henry heaved himself off his horse and down on one knee. In the next moment, all his men followed, and then the men of de Graves.

Joan couldn't help but look at Edmund, but by then he was off and kneeling, and she couldn't tell what it had cost him.

The monks passed into the chapel, and the men rose. The ladies were helped down, and the two families followed. The air crackled with danger, and Joan saw that her male cousins all had their hands on their swords. Edmund and Gerald did not.

A good job had been done on the building. It was simple but straight and sturdy, and the main posts and beams had been carved with crosses. The walls were painted white, and ample long windows let in light. They let in cold, too, but that could not be helped. They also allowed those outside to glimpse events inside, which was doubtless wise.

On the end wall behind the altar, a frame had been prepared in which the banner could hang, with shutterlike doors that could be closed over it in harsh weather. The monks carefully placed it there and knelt before it.

Someone had clearly put together some kind of

ceremony, for now Lord Henry and Edmund walked forward and knelt behind the monks. Edmund still favored his leg, but didn't seem to be badly troubled by it.

One monk turned and held out a crucifix to them. Edmund first and then Lord Henry, they vowed to guard the banner here, to never try to remove it, and to cease the feud, putting all lingering hurts aside. They bound their families and their heirs to this cause.

When they stood, a silence settled, as if no one could quite believe that it had happened. But then tentative smiles broke, someone laughed and, outside, people began to cheer. Aunt Ellen and Lady Blanche shared a genuine smile.

Lord Henry's priest came forward then, and guided Gerald and Nicolette through their betrothal and wedding vows, blessing their union, though his brow twitched when he said the part about going forth to multiply. Nicolette blushed a fiery red.

When the couple ran out into the fresh air, however, hand in hand, clearly nothing clouded their happiness.

Despite everything, neither family had quite been willing to attend a wedding feast in the other's castle, so food was laid here on trestles, and barrels of ale stood ready. There was plenty for everyone.

Joan nibbled a piece of pork and looked around at

playing children and chatting adults content, despite her own unhappiness, with her work. There was lingering wariness, but the seeds of peace had been sown. She had created some of the seed, and it would be a worthy harvest.

As the ladies and gentlemen prepared to return home, leaving the remains of the feast to the peasants, she stepped into the chapel to contemplate the banner one last time. A monk was already in the first vigil there, and a number of simple people knelt in prayer. She stayed back so as to not disturb them. The cloth was still as timeworn and stained, but she fancied it did look more content in this simple place, a cause of harmony not strife.

She turned at last to leave—and came face to face with Edmund.

"Oh."

Dimples showed. "Is that your most eloquent commentary on this all?"

Her throat ached with tears, but she must not show it.

"You startled me. It went very well, didn't it?"

"Exceedingly. This is all your work, you know."

She wanted to escape, but he blocked the door. "You came up with this solution."

"But you lit the way." He captured her hand. "I was going to wait, but I sense that you are about to flee."

"You're blocking the door."

"I am clever, sometimes. But I mean I fear you plan to leave from this area."

She tugged her hand, but could not free it. "It is time. I came to be companion to Nicolette." She looked back at the people in prayer. "My lord, this is not the place…"

"It is exactly the place." He captured her other hand. She noted that his arm must be healing well. "Joan, I had to wait until this proved successful."

"Wait?" she queried, looking up at him.

"I want you to know that about me."

She felt as if her mind was hopelessly tangled. "Know what?"

"That I cannot always do what I most want to. That I have to put head before heart."

"Heart?" She heard herself sounding like a complete fool.

"When we left the castle to exchange you for Gerald I wanted to speak then. To tell you that I wanted a chance to win you as my wife. But I couldn't. If I couldn't make peace, we couldn't wed."

Joan just stared at him, trying not to breathe too hard and blow this all awry.

"I've fought over twelve days not to send you a message. I snarled at Gerald because he could risk visiting Woldingham and I could not. But now it seems as if this has worked. Incredibly, perhaps we have peace." He went to one knee.

"Oh, don't!" She'd seen him wince. She glanced behind and saw the peasants had turned to stare. A woman grinned at her.

"Joan," he said, drawing her attention back to him. "You are a wise virgin. I value the first, but very much wish to change the second."

A laugh escaped her. Someone behind chuckled, and he grinned unrepentantly. "Be my bride. My wife. My truth sayer."

She sank to her knees in front of him. "But not stone thrower?"

"Reserve the stones for our enemies." He let go of her hands and cradled her face, searching her eyes. "Do I have you?"

She covered his hands, part tenderness, part defense. "I don't know how to be Lady of Mountgrave."

"It needs your irreverent style, but my mother will teach you."

"Your mother doesn't like me!"

"My mother is waiting anxiously for me to tell her I haven't made a mess of this. She was only worried about yet more trouble with the de Montelans. Say yes, Joan. Please." He winced. "My leg feels tortured."

She leaped to her feet and helped him up, scolding.

"How could you be so foolish! There was no need to kneel to me."

He captured her and kissed her. "Yes, there was. But if I'd not thought you'd run away, that was another reason to wait a week or two."

"What did you think I was going to do? Go straight to a convent and take vows?"

"I would put nothing past you. Or you might have seized the first lazy old man you saw and married him."

She snuggled against his chest, dazzled, dazed—and slightly scratched by his gold embroidery. She pushed away.

He touched her face with a grimace. "As you see, I will not always be a comfortable husband. You haven't said yes. I cannot change much for you, Joan. I am the Golden Lion and the Lord of Mountgrave. Too many people depend on me."

"I don't want you to change." She reached up to touch his face. "I'm sure there'll be days when I wonder why I fell into this gilded trap, but you make me so happy, Edmund. And you seem happy with me. With *me*."

He turned his head and kissed her palm, then lowered to kiss her lips. "*You* are my most precious treasure, Joan of Hawes. You."

"You're going to make me cry," she said, rubbing her face against his chest—and scratching it again. She pulled free. "Take it off."

After a moment, he grinned, unfastened his belt and struggled out of the long, glittering gown to stand in a simple shirt and braies. "That, at least, I can do." He pulled her into a warm—and painless—embrace.

When they emerged from their kiss, cheers started, and Joan looked around to find every window crowded and a throng behind Edmund. She hid her burning face against his chest, and this time it didn't hurt.

Laughing, he swept up his rich garment and tossed it to his grinning squire, then led her out into the fresh air and smiling faces. His mother beamed, and brought his two children over to be the first to hear the news.

Before going to greet her new family, Joan turned at the last moment and curtsied to the silent banner. "Bless us all, Lord Jesus, de Montelan and de Graves, and all the simple people here. Bless us all forever."

Award-winning author **MARGARET MOORE** actually began her writing career at the age of eight, when she and a friend concocted stories featuring a lovely damsel and a handsome, misunderstood thief nicknamed The Red Sheikh.

Unknowingly pursuing her destiny, Margaret graduated with distinction from the University of Toronto with a Bachelor of Arts degree in English literature. She demonstrated a facility for language by winning the Winston Churchill silver medal for public speaking, as well as a place on an award-winning debating team. She now utilises this gift of the gab by giving workshops for various writing groups, including Romance Writers of America and the Canadian Authors Association.

A past president of the Toronto Romance Writers, Margaret lives in Toronto, Ontario, with her patient husband, two wonderful teenagers and two interesting cats.

The Vagabond Knight

Margaret Moore

To my parents, Clint and Donna Warren,
who give in so many ways.

Chapter One

SIR RAFE BRACTON blew a damp lock of hair from his forehead with a frustrated huff. The snow fell faster and heavier now, and night would soon be upon them. The chill wind penetrated his thin cloak, and his bare hands were red and chapped from the cold.

"Saint David in a dungeon, Cassius," Rafe muttered, addressing his sole companion as he again pounded his fist on the heavy wooden gates in front of him, "the place doesn't *look* deserted."

The huge black warhorse snorted, his breath like smoke in the frigid air.

They had been traveling for hours, and although they had passed a few poor hovels and huts on the road, Rafe had been certain they would find better accommodation if they kept moving. When he had seen the stone wall divided by a massive gate looming just off the main road, he had been pleased to find his opinion justified.

Until nobody came in answer to his hail and his knock. Perhaps the snow covered the desolation of an abandoned manor. Maybe the inhabitants had gone elsewhere to celebrate the twelve days of Christmas. Or it could be that all inside were dead of a fearsome disease....

A small panel in the gate slid open to reveal a wary, yet apparently healthy, pair of brown eyes peering out from beneath a snow-covered hood.

"Thank God," Rafe mumbled. He raised his voice to be heard above the wind. "I seek shelter from the storm!"

The eyes blinked stupidly.

"God's wounds, man, it's colder than a witch's teat," Rafe growled loudly, "and the storm is worsening. Be a good Christian and let me in!"

The man's eyes narrowed as Cassius snorted again, this time pawing his foot on the frozen ground as if as anxious as his master.

Then the gatekeeper glanced over his shoulder, appeared to listen a moment, nodded—and slammed the window shut.

A very colorful and remarkably obscene curse flew from Rafe's lips as he raised his fist to knock again. There was no other suitable shelter for miles around. He must and would gain entry here. He was a knight of the realm, by God, albeit poor and landless, and no one should—

The door slowly creaked open.

"That's better," Rafe mumbled as he grabbed Cassius's bridle and led him inside the small courtyard.

He looked at the short, rotund man who clutched

the gate's latch. No wonder the gatekeeper was loath to show himself, if he was the only defense. He appeared scarcely capable of protecting himself from a bee, let alone a hostile intruder.

Rafe surveyed the rest of the courtyard. The buildings were in excellent repair, very neat, well kept and prosperous looking. There was a hall, with a kitchen beside it, judging by the smoke rising from the louvered chimney. Outside the kitchen was a well and a tidy stack of firewood. On the other side of the hall was what he supposed were storerooms and a large building he took to be a stable because of the hay visible through a small window on the upper level. There was another smaller building near the gatehouse. Its long, narrow windows suggested a chapel.

Rafe sighed with satisfaction at finding so comfortable a refuge. He turned to the gatekeeper, prepared to be magnanimous.

"Now, then, my man," he said jovially, his deep voice echoing off the nearby walls, "where am I? Is this a small castle or a large manor?"

The gatekeeper glanced nervously toward the hall. "Sir, you had best tell me who you are, and I shall inform—"

"Your master? Of course, of course. I am Sir Rafe Bracton, knight. I shall not intrude upon your master's hospitality for the Christmas festivities, if that is what you fear—unless he wants me to, for I have been told

I am more entertaining than many a troubadour," he finished with a laugh.

"I do not think that will be likely," a woman's stern voice declared.

Startled by the tone as much as the words, Rafe stopped chuckling and looked in the direction of the hall.

A woman stood on the steps. She was tall and wore a black cloak, white wimple and black veil. That was all he could see through the falling snow.

"Good God, is this a convent?" Rafe demanded, turning to accuse the shivering gatekeeper. "Why didn't you say so?"

"'Tisn't, that's why," the man muttered defensively, "or I would have."

"This is my home, and I am sorry I cannot allow you to stay," the woman announced in a tone frosty as the air.

Emboldened by the knowledge that he hadn't inadvertently stumbled upon a convent, Rafe sauntered toward her. "What, no room at the inn and Christmas but two days away? Nay, Lady, say not so!"

When he approached the woman who stood as motionless as if she were carved from a block of ice, he noted that she might be quite beautiful if she weren't so haughty and unfriendly. As for her age, she could be anywhere between nineteen and thirty, for her pale complexion had few wrinkles and he could see nothing of her hair.

He also noted that she wore no wedding band on the ungloved left finger of the hand clasped so tightly over the right.

A spinster, then, or a widow. She certainly didn't strike him as the timid sort, but the lack of a male head of the household might explain why she would not be pleased to have a stranger enter her yard.

He hastened to put her at ease. "Allow me to introduce myself. I am Sir Rafe Bracton, lately in the service of Baron Etienne DeGuerre," he announced, bowing with a flourish.

What might have been the slightest hint of amusement appeared in the lady's eyes. "I am Lady Katherine DuMonde, in no one's service." She ran another rather scornful gaze over him. "It would appear you have been some days on the road, sir knight. Or were you robbed by brigands and stripped of all but your poorest garments?"

Rafe's usually merry expression disappeared.

"If you were staying, I would require some proof that you are more than a vagabond. However, since you are not staying—"

"Is this your idea of hospitality to a noble knight, to make sport of my garments and then send me away to be benighted in a snowstorm?" Rafe demanded as he gestured toward the rapidly darkening sky overhead.

"It is not snowing hard and you have time enough to reach the inn to the south."

"Even an imbecile can see that the weather's worsening. Besides, I'm heading north."

"Only a greater imbecile allows an armed stranger into her home."

"I am a knight and sworn to chivalry. I'm safe as safe can be, my lady," he assured her. "No need to fear I'll ravish you in your bed, unless you want me to."

The gatekeeper's horrified gasp was distinctly audible, even with the wind, and the lady's face turned scarlet.

"There is the gate, sir," she replied imperiously, pointing, "and all I want is for you to go out of it!"

She meant it, Rafe realized instantly. She would send him out, storm or no storm, twilight or not.

Simpleton! he silently chided, almost smiting himself on the forehead. "Forgive my impertinence, my lady," he said, giving her his most winning and contrite smile. "I have spent much of my life among rude soldiers. Sometimes I forget how to address a woman of quality."

"Please leave," she replied, not a whit mollified. "There is an inn a few miles down the road. If you hurry, you should reach it before the snow gets much worse."

Rafe took another step toward her and regarded her beseechingly. "My lady, my horse and I have been on the road some days, as you so rightly guessed. Cassius is weary and in need of rest and shelter. If you cannot think of me, I ask you to consider my poor horse."

She glanced past him to regard Cassius thoughtfully.

"My horse is not young," he continued when she

didn't respond, taking this for a hopeful sign. He made another little contrite grin. "Saint Hubert's hat, neither am I," he confessed. "I beg you to have mercy on us both. And the stable will do for us both, too, if it pleases you to give us refuge."

Whether it was because of Cassius or his offer to stay in the stable, Rafe wasn't sure, but at last the redoubtable lady before him regally inclined her head. "Very well. You may stay—in the stable, as you yourself suggest."

"Thank you, my lady. And Cassius, who has stood me in good stead these many years and in more melees than I care to count, thanks you, too."

The woman didn't even bat an eye. She simply turned on her heel and marched back inside the hall.

Rafe raised an eyebrow. "Not much of a welcome, but it will have to do, I think."

The wetness of the snow made the cobblestones slick and dangerous, so he walked carefully back toward Cassius and the gatekeeper, who was regarding him with wide-eyed awe. "What is it? Have I suddenly sprouted horns?"

"She's letting you stay," the man replied in a reverential whisper.

"I should hope so," Rafe replied with a shiver. He tugged his worn cloak around his broad shoulders, then took hold of his horse's bridle. "It's bloody freezing! Is that the stable over there?" he asked, gesturing with his head at the likely building.

"But you're a *man!*"

"I'm a knight."

"Ah!" the gatekeeper sighed, nodding with sudden comprehension. "That's it, of course. You're a knight, so she has to let you stay."

"If I were not a knight, would she really have made me leave?" Rafe said as they made their way toward the stable.

"In a heartbeat. Unless you was really poor and shiverin' and starvin'. Then she'd likely let you stay in the kitchen."

"I gather your mistress does not overflow with the milk of human kindness."

The gatekeeper barked a laugh, then looked guiltily around the courtyard.

"That does not fill me with hope for a bite of supper at her ladyship's table," Rafe remarked as they came to the door of the stable.

"I'll tell you, sir, if I was you, I'd praise God for softening her heart enough to let you into the stable. Lady Katherine DuMonde has no use for men, except as servants, and doesn't trust any of us."

"What, men or servants?"

"Both," the little man said decisively before he turned away from Rafe to slip and slide his way back over the cobbled courtyard toward the gatehouse.

With a frown, Rafe shoved open the door and entered the large stable, which seemed very commodious for the manor. He was at once surrounded by warmth and the familiar smell of hay and horse. When his eyes adjusted to the dim light, he realized that this building was as neatly kept as the courtyard. In fact, it was the neatest, least malodorous stable he had ever been in.

A man in servant's garb—the groom?—and a lad, possibly the stable boy, stood inside, regarding him with grave expressions. Their garments were neat and tidy, too, and their faces remarkably clean.

The lady of the manor obviously prized cleanliness and order. He glanced down at his own rather shabby and unmended garments. Perhaps that was why he had not seemed to pass muster with her. "I am Sir Rafe Bracton, and Lady Katherine—"

The man and boy were already nodding.

"You know I am to stay here tonight?"

"Aye, sir," the man said, his voice a gruff rumble. "We heard it all." He gestured at a stall. "That's for your horse and you can take the one beside."

"You are the groom?"

"I am, sir, Giles," the man replied, tugging his forelock. "Been in her ladyship's service since she come here as a bride, nigh on fifteen year."

The lad gazed at Rafe with undisguised awe. "You're really a knight?" he whispered loudly. "Where's your armor?"

The groom cuffed him lightly on the back of the head. "Egbert, mouth shut unless you're asked sommat! Besides, he can't be wearing it in the snow, can he? It'd rust." Giles gave Rafe an apologetic smile. "Forgive my son's impertinence, sir."

Rafe smiled kindly at the boy, who looked to be about twelve. A small sigh escaped him at the thought of the twenty years that had passed since he was twelve years old. "Indeed, I am a knight, and as your father wisely notes, snow is not good for armor. I keep it in that large leather bag when I am not wearing it," he explained, gesturing at the pouch strapped to Cassius's saddle.

Egbert grinned happily and rubbed the back of his sandy-haired head. "I want to be a knight someday."

"Egbert!" the man chided again as he began to remove the baggage.

"It's a fine thing to have dreams," Rafe replied as Egbert hurried to help his father.

Rafe picked up a wisp of straw from a manger and began to chew the end as he leaned back against one of the posts. "I seem to recall hearing of Lady Katherine's marriage," he lied.

In truth, he had never heard of the lady, but he was curious to know more about his reluctant benefactress. "She was quite young at the time, I think."

"Sixteen she was, and a beauty."

"She's not so ugly now."

He meant what he said. Despite her cold mien, her complexion was flawless, her hostile blue eyes large and bright, and her mouth…well, if she would stop pressing her lips together in a disapproving frown, he didn't doubt that she had lips worth kissing.

As the groom and his son began to rub Cassius down, Rafe remembered her lack of a wedding ring. "Unfortunate about her husband, of course."

"I heard he was a right glutton—" Egbert began eagerly, until a warning look from his father made him flush and fall silent.

So, she *was* a widow. "He was not the nicest of men, I recall."

His apparent acquaintance with the late lord achieved its anticipated result as Giles sniffed disdainfully. "That's one way to put it."

As tempted as he was to pry further, Rafe decided to take another tack. "He left her very well-off, I see."

The groom glanced at him over his shoulder. "He left her without a penny of ready money."

"She is an excellent manager of the estate, then."

"Estate?" That elicited a laugh from the groom. "There's no estate but what you can see outside. All the land she's got is encircled by yonder wall."

Rafe tossed aside the piece of straw. "But this place seems so prosperous."

"She's well paid for what she does, because she's the best at what she does," Giles replied.

"She's a whore?" Rafe asked, an idea that shocked him momentarily—but then again, she was not at all unattractive and he wouldn't be surprised if she proved to have a very shapely figure under that black cloak.

"God's holy heart, no!" the groom cried, turning around to stare at Rafe with outraged disbelief. "You should be stricken dumb for saying such a thing!"

"Well, my man, what else can a woman do? She does not look to be an alewife or a nursemaid."

"A nursemaid would be closer to it, if you would use the same term for the man who trained you in the skills of a knight," Giles said. "She teaches young ladies in the duties and arts that will be required of them when they marry."

"And for this she is paid?"

"Aye, and well paid, too," the groom said, returning to his task. "You ought to see the way the nobles line up in the spring. Half of 'em bring their daughters with 'em only to be turned away. She'll only take twenty."

Rafe realized he had an explanation for the commodious stable. "Then this *is* a kind of convent, and it's no wonder she didn't want a good-looking, virile man like me about the place."

Egbert, who was filling the trough for Cassius, tried to stifle a giggle at Rafe's wry, self-mocking words.

Even the groom chortled softly. "Well, you're handsomer than lots we've seen," he said. "Some of them got faces you couldn't make any uglier if you took an ax to 'em."

"I'm flattered."

Finished, Giles put down his brush. "But it wouldn't matter if you looked like an angel, because our lady don't have nothin' to do with men unless she can't help it."

"Now that's a pity."

Father and son both looked at him as if he'd suddenly declared an undying passion for their mistress.

"Even you must admit she is a beautiful woman, in that cold, Norman way," Rafe said. "And I daresay she'd warm up if the right man came along."

Rather unexpectedly, the groom grinned as he led Cassius into the stall. "That'd be you, I suppose, sir?"

"Perhaps."

"I'd sooner snuggle up to a boar," Giles muttered.

"All good knights enjoy a challenge. I believe I shall wash, then join Lady Katherine in her hall for the evening meal."

Clearing his throat, Giles came to stand beside his son. "Excuse me for asking, sir, but was you invited?"

Sir Rafe Bracton drew himself up. "I am a knight of the realm. I do not require a formal invitation, for courtesy demands that she offer me the hospitality of her table whether she wants to, or not."

Suddenly reminded that they were speaking to a titled, trained warrior and not a common man, the groom and stable boy flushed with embarrassment and shifted uncomfortably.

Just as suddenly, Rafe gave them a conspiratorial

grin. "Now, if I may have privacy, I must prepare myself to face the dragon in her den."

The boy grinned and his father chuckled as they went to the door.

Rafe watched while they hurried outside into the rapidly falling snow, the door blowing shut behind them. He wondered if the groom appreciated how fortunate he was to have such a fine lad for a son, and a comfortable place in which to live and work. From what he could see of the manor, Lady Katherine DuMonde's servants would not be wanting for the creature comforts any more than the lady herself.

They would never have to worry where their next meal was coming from, or hope that they could find a cheap, relatively vermin-free place in which to bed down for the night. Nor would they have to wonder if the tournament they were about to partake in would be their last because of death or serious injury, leaving them at the mercy of providence or the charity of the Church.

"I've still got plenty of time left to win a place in a lord's service and the estate that will go with it," Rafe muttered as he went to the leather bag containing all his worldly goods. "As long as I don't get drunk and feel called upon to list the faults of the next lord I serve at the top of my lungs."

He turned his wry gaze on to Cassius, placidly munching in his stall. "Well, old comrade, shall we see for ourselves if my lady really is as impervious to your master's considerable charm and good looks as she seems?"

The horse snorted.

"To speak the truth, I fear you may be right."

THE DOOR TO THE AUSTERE hall opened with such force it banged loudly against the wall. The noise made Katherine jump as if someone had come up behind her and struck her between the shoulders.

She half rose, then quickly sat again as Sir Rafe Bracton strode inside. He threw off his snowy cloak and proceeded to shake himself like a dog, giving her an opportunity to study her unwelcome guest.

Sir Rafe's unkempt black-and-gray hair badly needed a trim, for it brushed his broad shoulders. His chin was shaven but poorly, and his leather tunic unlaced, as was the somewhat dingy linen shirt beneath. His dark woolen breeches were obviously old and worn, and his boots no better.

She also couldn't help noticing that, for a man of middle years, he was rather remarkably muscular and his lithe movements seemed as youthful as his brightly shining hazel eyes and impudent grin. Unfortunately, these were not points in his favor.

Sir Rafe tossed his unlined cloak onto the nearest bench and arrogantly strolled down the hall past the central hearth as if he were a king expecting homage. He ignored the shocked stares of the servants as they sat at table, and the serving wenches as they stood openmouthed, their duties quite forgotten.

To be sure, the man was hard to ignore, with his handsome, mature face, muscular body and easy manner, but Katherine DuMonde was not so easily impressed. Men who thought she owed them deference or respect merely because of their rank were often surprised to discover that she was singularly unmoved by that alone.

Nor was she a woman to be swayed by good looks or a genial manner.

She was the mistress here, and she would not permit this man—or any man—to make her feel subservient, for any reason.

"Saint Simon in a smithy, I'm nearly soaked through!" Sir Rafe declared, his deep, rich voice filling the hall as he came to a halt in front of her table on the dais.

"Then you should have stayed in the stable," Katherine replied with icy calm.

As she spoke, his expression altered. He still smiled, but the friendliness in his eyes disappeared, to be replaced with a rather unexpected sternness. She suddenly realized that no matter how pleasant and unthreatening his general deportment, he was a man of rank and pride.

"Sir, won't you please join me at table?" she asked, her tone slightly more polite. As she spoke, she glanced at Hildegard, the maidservant closest to her, and then at the nearest chair. Hildegard hurried to set it beside Katherine's.

The fierceness in Sir Rafe's eyes ebbed and a merry twinkle took its place. "I shall be delighted, my lady," he said, coming around the table in a few athletic strides.

He nodded his thanks at the obviously impressed Hildegard, and then winked at the maidservant—as if her hall were a tavern! The middle-aged, unmarried, very thin, gap-toothed Hildegard hurried away, her face red as a holly berry.

Katherine was profoundly glad the last of her charges had returned to their homes for the Christmas celebrations. She shuddered to think of the disruption and tomfoolery the boisterous presence of a man like this vagabond might inspire among her girls. It was enough of a struggle to maintain order and discipline as it was.

"Something smells good, my lady," Sir Rafe noted, inhaling deeply. "I tell you, a good cook is worth his weight in gold," he went on, as if she must be interested in his culinary observations. "The Baron DeGuerre had a fine cook, and his men thanked him for it every day."

"I do not know the Baron DeGuerre."

The blushing Hildegard returned with a trencher, and another, equally ridiculously smiling maidservant brought a goblet of wine.

Sir Rafe winked again at the women.

It might have appeased Katherine somewhat if she

had known that Rafe winked more out of habit than any intention to cause trouble, and he was really far more interested in the spiced, mulled wine than the woman serving it.

"The baron's got quite a family, considering he married late in life," Sir Rafe observed. "Three sons and a daughter. Big, strapping fellows they're going to be, fierce as the devil, too, if they don't kill each other first."

"How fascinating," Katherine replied in a tone intended to tell him she was utterly bored by his gossip.

"Yes, and a pretty little thing Valeda is, too. Spoiled somewhat, although you'd never have thought the baron would be the kind to soften so, even for a daughter. Mind, she's a sweet-tempered girl, and the image of her lovely mother."

The rest of the meal arrived, and Katherine breathed a sigh of relief, for surely Sir Rafe would have to stop talking to eat. She didn't want to hear anything more he had to say in that robust voice of his.

Regrettably she soon discovered that his presence seemed to fill the room even when he was silent, and that a full mouth did not deter him from talking. "Where are your charges?" he demanded as he ripped the leg from a capon. "Do they not eat in the hall?"

"How do you know about them?" Katherine asked suspiciously.

"Giles told me."

"Oh." She would have to remind Giles of the necessity of holding one's tongue in the presence of strangers. "They have all gone to their families for Christmas."

"That will give you more room for your company," he said knowingly before he belched. He surveyed the hall. "And more time to decorate this room. A little holly and ivy must make a great deal of difference."

Katherine wrinkled her nose at his coarse manners and told herself she didn't care what he thought of her hall. "I do not have company at Christmas, except for the priest who comes to say mass in the chapel."

Sir Rafe's wine goblet halted on its way to his lips and he gave her an incredulous look. "Why not?" he demanded as if he had every right to know.

She stiffened, prepared to tell him that her personal affairs were none of his business, until she met his gaze.

It had been a long time since anyone had regarded her with anything but the utmost respect, as though she were not quite human but some sort of supernatural creature. To be sure, she had striven to make it so.

But Rafe Bracton's frank hazel eyes looked into hers as if he truly could not understand why she spent the festive season of Christmas without family or company of any kind, and her heart started to race and her face flush. She felt like a shy maiden having her first intimate conversation with a man not her relative. Suddenly every twinge of loneliness that had ever resulted from people's deference seemed to pile on her shoulders and weigh her down.

Why not tell him the truth? her heart urged. He would not be staying. What harm could there be in a small, personal revelation?

Chapter Two

"I HAVE NO FAMILY LIVING," Katherine replied.

"None at all?" Sir Rafe demanded. "No distant relatives to avail themselves of your delightful hospitality at Yuletide?"

"No."

"Neither have I," Sir Rafe unexpectedly confessed. "It saves a lot of trouble, doesn't it?"

Apparently unresponsiveness was no deterrent to Sir Rafe's inquisitiveness, and Katherine regretted revealing even that little about her past when he continued to interrogate her. "Surely you have friends who—"

"I have no special company at Christmas. I do not celebrate Christmas with a lot of extravagant waste. We have a special meal, and that is sufficient."

Sir Rafe could frown, at least with puzzlement. "Wasn't that a Yule log I spied at the side of the road some ways back?" he asked.

"No. A tree fell across the road earlier this year and will be cut into firewood when it is needed."

"Well, I don't celebrate Christmas with a lot of extravagant waste, either," he continued, unabashed, "but that's because I haven't got anything to waste. Mind you, I don't begrudge sharing what I do have with the people I'm with at a festive time of year."

"Perhaps that is why you have nothing to waste."

His grin did not diminish and a new expression came to his eyes, an intimately speculative one that made her blush, despite her efforts not to react to anything he said. "But I greatly enjoy the sharing."

"That I don't doubt," she retorted, "since you do not seem a prudent man. Otherwise, you would not have gotten caught in the storm."

"I will not contradict you," he said with a low chuckle that seemed as suggestive as his gaze.

"I can only wonder if you remember anything of your celebrating afterward."

He barked a boisterous laugh. "To speak the truth, I have woken up in more haystacks, gutters and strange beds than I care to count," he admitted without a hint of remorse or shame.

She didn't want to think about him in any kind of bed at all. Really, this man was too disgustingly disruptive, with his long, barbarous hair, broad shoulders, deep voice and roaring laugh.

"You don't sound at all sorry," she observed haughtily.

"I'm not."

She took a sip of the mulled wine spiced with cinnamon and reflected that she had never encountered a man so at ease with his shameful behavior.

"I've never done any harm when I've been drunk, except to myself and my prospects," he continued, just as jovially unrepentant. "Unless you count the time I spilled a full goblet of wine on a lord's fine new boots. That pretty much ruined them, of course. Not that I'm sorry for it. He was a vain idiot and dead drunk, so it was too good a chance to pass up. I tell you, Delamarch should be glad that's the only thing of his I ruined."

"Would it be Sir Frederick Delamarch of whom you speak?" she asked after a moment.

"You know him? If you've met him, you must agree he's the vainest creature in England," Rafe observed. "I doubt any of your young ladies could top him for vanity, which might be acceptable in a pretty girl, but is truly disgusting in a knight. I never saw a man so in love with himself. It was a wonder he could find the time to seduce maidservants." Sir Rafe laughed. "By Saint George's lance, you should have seen his face when his boots squelched from the wine."

Her head lowered, Katherine wiped her lips with a napkin. It occurred to her that it was going to be a chilly night. Perhaps she should allow him to sleep in the hall with the servants. After all, there were several of them, so he would never dare...

Her body flushed with unaccustomed warmth as her

196 THE VAGABOND KNIGHT

imagination conjured up visions of some things this bold, impertinent fellow might dare.

A clatter at the entrance to the kitchen made Katherine look at the red-faced Hildegard, who hastened to pick up the fallen platter.

"I suppose the young ladies make good company," Sir Rafe remarked.

"They do not come here because I desire companionship. They come here to learn."

"Oh, yes, to be sure."

Satisfied that she had made him understand she was not lonely or in need of any kind of companionship, and weary of his chatter, Katherine rose majestically.

"Good night, sir," she said.

"What, you are leaving me already?"

"I fear I must." She fastened a stern gaze upon him. "I would not take kindly to anything or anyone who disrupts my household in any way," she said with an accompanying glance at the still-flustered Hildegard.

"My lady, I assure you your maidservants are all perfectly safe. I have no lustful intentions," he replied as if mortally offended. However, his sparkling, merry eyes belied the seriousness of his tone.

And then his lips turned up in a slow, seductive smile that Katherine could well believe would bring many a foolish maiden to his bed.

Fortunately, she was not a foolish maiden, and so was impervious to his devilish charm.

She turned on her heel and swept out of the hall, then up the stone steps to her bedchamber at the top of the western tower.

If Katherine had deigned to look back, she would have seen Rafe and the servants watching her depart, a speculative look on his face and a wary one on theirs.

THE ARRIVAL OF A FLUSHED and flustered Hildegard bringing apples interrupted Rafe's study of the lady's retreating form. He instinctively smiled at the serving wench, who was not young and not pretty and in no way nearly as fascinating as her mistress. He grabbed an apple and bit into it so deeply the juice ran down his chin. Absently wiping it off, he leaned back in his chair and again surveyed the somewhat barren hall.

He had been in larger halls before, and ones more modern than this, with their large fireplaces in the wall. Still, this one was not uncomfortable, considering that it was of a more ancient design, with a central hearth. The dais upon which he currently sat seemed to be a newer addition. The plain furnishings, apparently made with only function in mind, appeared to be not many years old. Tapestries covered the walls, and since they were not yet sullied by years of exposure to smoke and dust, he could see enough to suspect that they were the handiwork of Lady Katherine's charges rather than the efforts of true artisans.

Despite the simplicity of the furniture and plainness

of the hall, the rushes beneath the table were fresh and sweet smelling and the meal had been the best he had had since leaving the baron a month ago.

Or rather, since having it pointed out that it would be wise to leave the baron's service, before he said something else to insult his overlord.

Rafe flicked his finger against the side of his now-empty goblet and the ensuing sound assured him that it was indeed made of silver.

So, Lady Katherine, who had no family, was most certainly well-to-do. She had money, she had servants, and she knew several nobles whose daughters she taught. She was frugal, perhaps, but judging by the food and wine, not a miser. And, if Rafe were any judge, she was lonely, despite the company of her charges and her servants.

Indeed, he was sure of the latter, for he had seen mirrored in her steadfast blue eyes—

Mirrored? No, for he was never lonely. He had a knack for making friends, and women vied for his attentions.

Not as much as they had when he was younger, of course, but even here, even tonight, that gap-toothed serving wench would probably come to his bed if he asked her.

Tomorrow night, he could have another wench warm his bed, and another the next, if there were any more worth having here. He wouldn't have to bother getting to know or care about them. Of course, they would never get to know or care about him, either, but that was good. As he had said about his deceased relatives, it saved a lot of trouble.

He had plenty of friends, too. He was always a welcome companion—until he said or did something foolish when he was in his cups.

But that didn't happen so very often.

Just often enough that he had yet to have a lord offer him a permanent place in his service, and an estate to go with it.

Rafe rose, straightening his shoulders. He still had much to offer a woman, at least temporarily, and especially one like Lady Katherine DuMonde. If not tonight, there was always tomorrow.

KATHERINE ENTERED HER bedchamber and firmly closed the door. No one, not even a maidservant, was allowed to enter there. It was her private place, maintained by her own capable hands, and probably far less luxurious than anyone suspected.

After her husband's death, she had been nearly penniless. She had tried to think of some way to earn money as she sold off her belongings one by one. Finally, after recalling certain noble visitors who had been complaining about their wives' woeful ignorance when it came to the duties and responsibilities of a chatelaine, she had decided to offer her services as a teacher to the daughters of the nobility. She had written to those nobles she knew had daughters of suitable age. Four had responded with interest. Determined to make a good impression upon them, she had used the last of her money to have good food, a comfortable hall and fine quarters for the girls when they arrived. That meant she herself had to do without, but it was worth it when the nobles agreed to leave their daughters in her care and pay for her expert guidance.

In the beginning, the financial straits of her daily existence had been another reason to send the girls home during a festive season that required special food and gifts.

As the years had progressed, Katherine had taken on more girls and improved the public areas of her home with an eye to impressing the noble parents. Her own comforts could wait.

They were still waiting, she reflected as she looked about her spartan quarters with suddenly dissatisfied eyes. She had but a plain wooden table, a stool and a rope bed bearing a straw mattress and covered with plain sheets and two coarse woolen blankets.

Katherine struck flint and steel to light the tinder in the brazier she had prepared before leaving her room that morning. When it was burning, she lit a candle—a rare extravagance here—then went to her chest and rooted about until she found the looking glass she had put there long ago. She should have sold it, perhaps, as she had sold the rest of her wedding gifts after her husband's death.

But some remnant of worldly vanity had compelled her to keep it for the last, so now she was able to look at her face. It was not so much changed as she had expected. There were wrinkles at the corners of her eyes and marking her brow, yet she did not look so very old. Setting the mirror down, she removed her cap and wimple and shook her hair free. The chestnut locks fell to her waist, thick and curling. Again she picked up the mirror, dispassionately noting the few strands of gray among the ruddy brown.

Then she frowned and hurried to return the mirror to its place.

She was no vain, silly girl on the threshold of womanhood to be examining her reflection. She was a mature, respected widow. She would not let the jolly prattling of a handsome man reduce her to acting like an immature, foolish female again.

Not after all she had suffered.

THE NEXT MORNING, Katherine awoke with a start at the sound of a feminine shriek coming from the courtyard. Scrambling from her bed, she wrapped herself in one of the rough woolen blankets and, regardless of her freezing feet, ran to the window.

The first thing she noticed was that it had stopped snowing. The ground was covered by a thick, white blanket and the damp stone walls surrounding the courtyard sparkled like diamonds in the dawning light.

Then her gaze caught a white object sailing through the air. The snowy missile came from the direction of the slightly open stable door and landed with a thud, audible even to her, square in the middle of the stout gatekeeper's back as he approached the kitchen.

Dawson bellowed with rage and ducked behind the well near the kitchen as Sir Rafe Bracton leaned out of the stable to fashion another snowball. At nearly the same moment, amid much female laughter, a large ball of snow went flying through the air from the kitchen toward the stable. She watched as it exploded when it hit the stable wall right above the knight's head.

Howling a battle cry, Sir Rafe rose and let fly his snowball in one surprisingly graceful and athletic movement, nearly catching Hildegard in the shoulder. Unfortunately for Sir Rafe, Dawson had been awaiting a chance for retaliation. He jumped up and threw, and his snowball struck Sir Rafe squarely in the cheek.

"Saint Simon's shadow!" the knight cried with what sounded like real pain as he staggered, holding his cheek. He took his hand away, and Katherine gasped when she saw blood.

There must have been a broken bit of a stone from the well in the ball, she thought with dismay as she dressed hurriedly. Swiftly tucking her hair in her wimple and affixing her cap, she grabbed her box of medicines, lifted her skirts and ran down the stairs, through the hall and to the door, where she met Sir Rafe and the others coming inside.

"Sit by the hearth," Katherine commanded, "and I shall examine your injury. The rest of you, be about your business."

Dawson and the others began to leave, warily glancing back over their shoulders as they obeyed.

Although he continued to hold his cheek, Sir Rafe waved his free hand dismissively and grinned at her, his eyes twinkling as though his injury were nothing more than a joke—but there was a very real trickle of blood on his cheek. "It's nothing. Merely a cut."

"I shall be the judge of that."

Sir Rafe frowned. "It was not your fault."

"I know that," she snapped. "I didn't initiate your game."

She pointed to a bench near the central hearth. "Sit here by the fire so I can see better. Hildegard," she commanded the maidservant, who still lingered in the kitchen entrance, "fetch warm water and some clean linen rags from the storeroom, and be quick about it."

Sir Rafe sat on the bench and Katherine set her medicine box beside him. "Lower your hand please."

He grudgingly did as she requested. Trying to keep any hint of her disgruntled thoughts concerning the childish behavior of men who should act with more dignity from her face, Katherine concentrated on examining the inch-long gash and surrounding bruise. To see better, she put her hand under his stubbled chin and turned his face toward the fire.

"You look flushed, my lady. I fear I have upset you."

"You are my guest, so of course I am upset that you are injured, no matter how it came about."

"I am very sorry to upset you, but I can never resist a battle," he replied, grinning, his flesh moving beneath her fingers.

Bearing a basin of steaming water and with some white rags over her arm, Hildegard sidled up to them. "My lady?" she said with extreme deference.

"Set them there."

"Your servants make too fine a target, too," Sir Rafe explained. He grinned at the maidservant, who giggled.

Until Katherine glanced at her. "Thank you, Hildegard," she said, her words an incontrovertible dismissal, which Hildegard quickly obeyed.

"My servants may be fine targets, but apparently they vanquished you," she noted as she dipped a rag into the basin.

"I must confess I was taken aback to discover they could throw with such accuracy, but they also behaved most unchivalrously."

Katherine gave him a cynical look before she started to clean the wound. "I was not aware the rules of chivalry applied to silly games."

His hazel eyes suddenly flashed a cautionary look, and she quickly drew back. "I'm sorry—did I hurt you?"

"I do not appreciate being called silly."

With a frown, she went back to gently wiping the wound. "What else would you call it when a man of your years throws snow?"

"My years?"

Katherine opened her medicine box and searched for the appropriate salve. "We are both past the first flush of youth, sir."

"We are not yet in the grave, either."

Katherine took the cloth coated with beeswax off the top of a small clay vessel. "Now keep still while I apply this."

"Saint Swithins in a swamp, that smells disgusting!"

Her lips twitched in what might have been a smile. "Yes, it does, but it will help your wound heal."

"Very well, I shall submit—but only because I enjoy having a beautiful woman caress my cheek."

Rafe kept the satisfied smile from his face as Lady Katherine flushed. He was enjoying himself immensely, and not in the least because he really did relish having a beautiful woman touch his face.

And no matter what the lady herself thought, she truly was beautiful, her proximity as she attended to him giving him ample opportunity to study her face.

To be sure, she was not wrong in saying they were both past the first flush of youth and, indeed, even the second, as his aching muscles reminded him every morning. Nevertheless, he was right, too. They were not yet in their graves, or past the age of feeling the thrilling excitement that could exist between a man and a woman, an excitement that was making his pulse beat with some rapidity right this very moment.

Try as she might to hide it, he was quite sure she was feeling something similar, too.

"There now," she said briskly, stepping back and reaching for one of the rags. "That should heal quickly."

"I hope it doesn't mar my handsomeness too much."

Lady Katherine's brow furrowed.

"While I don't consider myself ugly as an ogre, I was but jesting," he said, his own expression growing graver. "I must confess, my lady, I have never met a woman who takes things so seriously."

"I take serious things seriously."

"What of comical things?"

"I rarely encounter comical things," she muttered as she began to seal the jar of stinking ointment.

"Do you not? I encounter amusing things all the time."

She slid him a sidelong glance.

"I pity you if you cannot see the humor and whimsy around you."

"Perhaps if I were a nobleman with few responsibilities, I might."

"And if I had such a comfortable home as this, I would be smiling all day long."

Katherine regarded him stonily as she picked up her box of medicines. "I have a comfortable home because

I have worked for it. I have not had the leisure to enjoy what amusement the world might provide."

Rafe rose, meeting her steadfast gaze. "Forgive me, my lady, if I have offended you. It simply seems a pity that you do not smile more, for truly, I think you would look lovely if you did."

Katherine cursed herself for a ninny even while she felt a girlish blush steal over her features at his blatant, outrageous flattery. "Since the weather has cleared, you will be on your way shortly, will you not?"

"Aye, if I must."

"Yes, you must."

"Sir! Sir!"

They both turned to stare at Giles, who burst into the hall as if a horde of barbarians were storming the gates.

"What is it?" Katherine demanded as Sir Rafe drew his sword, a very determined look in his eye.

"It's your horse, sir," Giles replied anxiously. "It's sick, sir. Breathing all queer."

Rafe blanched but didn't say a word. He simply ran from the hall as if the horde of barbarians were now at his heels.

Katherine again snatched up her box of medicines and hurried after him.

"OH, CASSIUS!" Rafe murmured as he stared at his poor stallion, the horse's breathing labored and rough as he lay on the floor of the stable.

Rafe slowly knelt in the straw and ran a gentle hand over the animal's heaving side. "When did he lie down?" he asked the anxious boy hovering nearby.

"A little after you left," Egbert offered in a hushed whisper.

Rafe silently cursed himself. He had realized something wasn't right with Cassius this morning, but had ignored the altered sound of his horse's breathing to throw balls of snow at servants, then flirt with a woman cold as that same snow, and all the while his faithful horse was sickening.

In truth, Cassius should have been put out to honorable pasture years ago. He was far too old to be carrying an armored knight, and far, far too old to be carrying that same knight into melees at tournaments.

If only he had earned an estate, Cassius would be spending his days in comfortable retirement befitting a noble warhorse, and not carrying a man around the length and breadth of England seeking one more chance to prove himself.

Rafe glanced up as Lady Katherine came to stand beside him. "It's a thickening in his lungs," he explained. "I should never have ridden so far yesterday."

"You sound very sure of his trouble."

"I have spent years around horses, my lady, as well as knights. Indeed, more than one man who has met me in a tournament has suggested that I stop being a knight and become a dealer in horses, since I seem to know more about them than fighting."

However those thinly veiled insults had rankled at the time, he would forget them all if his skill could make Cassius better.

He took note of her box of medicines. "Do you have calamint?"

She made a little frown. "You would give calamint to a horse?"

"Why not? It loosens the congestion."

"I know, but I have never heard of dosing a horse with it. How much would you put in the water? How often should he drink it? Too much might be worse than none at all."

"I will judge by his weight, as if Cassius were a very large man."

"Ah! That might work," she said, truly impressed, not just by his opinion regarding the calamint, but by the alteration in his manner. Any sign of the jokester had disappeared, replaced by an intelligent, caring man who clearly knew what he was doing.

"I will dose him at the times you probably give it to your girls, sunrise, noon and sunset, more if his breathing gets very bad."

She nodded.

"I can pay whatever the calamint costs."

She stiffened slightly, disturbed that he would think she would begrudge his horse the medicine. "I would not withhold it when you are so desperate. Besides, it is nearly Christmas, a time good Christians should be generous."

His gaze faltered. "Forgive me, my lady. As you say, I am desperate. Is the calamint in there?" he asked, reaching for her medicine box.

She yanked it away. "Only I open this." Seeing his shocked countenance, she softened a little. "There are things in here that could make someone very ill if they were used incorrectly," she explained in a calmer tone.

"Poisons, eh?"

"No. I don't keep anything like that in here," she replied, setting the box on a nearby manger and opening it to take out the calamint. "It is only that I am used to the curiosity of girls, who are prone to meddle. I will go to the kitchen and prepare a draft at once."

He gave her the ghost of a grin. "You had better leave that to me. I am used to dosing animals."

"Then I will watch over your horse until you return."

"You do not have to do that. Egbert is here."

"I don't mind."

His expression altered ever so slightly. "Then I thank you. I am glad to have someone with some experience of nursing with him, if I cannot be, and since I have no page, I will use Egbert's help with the medicine."

Katherine made no sign that his heartfelt words pleased her out of all measure, while Egbert looked as if he had just been handed the keys to the kingdom.

Before Rafe departed, he took a moment to stroke

the stallion's neck and croon softly in the animal's ear as if the huge beast were a child.

Or his best friend.

After Rafe and Egbert departed, Katherine approached the horse somewhat warily, mindful of its huge hooves.

"*Are* you his best friend?" she whispered, reaching out to pet it.

As the beast shifted its head to regard her with its large brown eyes, she sighed softly. "At least he has you."

IT SEEMED TO TAKE a very long time before Rafe returned with the medicine, carrying it in a wineskin under his tunic to keep it warm. Egbert trotted at his side, obviously full of admiration for Rafe's unexpected and unusual knowledge.

"The servants didn't give you any trouble, I trust?" Katherine asked, voicing a concern that had arisen as she had waited.

"No. I took some time with the measure of calamint. I didn't want to make the potion too weak."

"How are you going to get your horse to drink it? The taste is not altogether pleasing. At least a person can understand that it is intended to make him feel better."

"That is why I put it in a wineskin."

He took out the stopper and went to kneel beside Cassius's head. Then he tilted it so that the horse could swallow the liquid as he slowly poured it into his mouth. Cassius's lips moved like a man tasting a beverage that wasn't entirely to his taste but not too terrible to finish.

"I have never seen a horse drink from a wineskin before."

She thought Rafe flushed, but it could have been from the effort of holding the wineskin aloft.

"I used to make wagers on this," the knight confessed. "But I wouldn't give him wine," he hastened to assure her. "Ale."

"You fed your valuable warhorse ale?"

"Not that much. Not enough to get him drunk. Besides, is that skill not invaluable now?" Although Rafe's smile was wry and self-deprecating, it was a smile of warmth and companionship, too.

She backed away. "I hope the calamint helps," she murmured as she departed.

Chapter Three

LATER THAT NIGHT, as Cassius lay wheezing in the straw, the stable door creaked open. Rafe raised his head, expecting either Giles or Egbert. He made no effort to hide his surprise as the pool of golden light from a handheld lantern widened and revealed Lady Katherine. In addition to the lamp, she had a basket over her arm from which toothsome smells emanated.

She wore a plain dark gray cloak, and that damned wimple and cap, but her cheeks were rosy from the cold—and the expression of genuine concern on her face made her even more lovely.

Although he knew he should stand upon a lady's entrance, he feared he was too stiff to do so without making that stiffness obvious. He wouldn't embarrass himself by struggling to his feet from his cross-legged position, so he merely nodded a greeting and turned back to his horse, hoping his worry over Cassius would excuse him.

Apparently it did, for her expression didn't alter as

she set the basket beside him and, placing the lamp on the ground at her side, sat on a stool on the other side of the stall. "Is he worse?" she asked softly.

"No, not worse. A little better, I am happy to say."

"You will need more calamint at sunrise. I will fetch my medicine box—"

He held up his hand to make her stay. "It will be some time before we need it. Sit with me awhile, won't you? I have had too many lonely vigils and would welcome your company."

She lowered herself back to the stool. "Very well." She looked at Cassius and sighed. "He is a very fine stallion."

"You should have seen him when he was younger." He grinned ruefully. "Saint Ninian's nose, I wish you had seen me when I was younger."

She didn't meet his gaze. "I have had lonely vigils, too. The girls sometimes get sick. I have often thought how welcome a little bread or cheese or wine would be at such times, so I brought you refreshment."

"I confess I suspected that's what was in your basket." He reached for it and pulled back the linen covering. "This is indeed very welcome." He took the small loaf of course brown bread and bit into it with relish.

"I suppose you have attended to sick horses many times."

"A few," he agreed.

"I daresay it is more difficult for a man like you to do so."

"A man like me?"

"A man who so obviously enjoys company."

"Well, sometimes even a man like me needs a little peace and quiet." He smiled ruefully. "That surprises you?"

"I must say you do not strike me as a person who would enjoy solitude."

"I do not *enjoy* it," he amended. "I said sometimes I need it. For instance, if I've just lost a bet and I'm ready to snarl at the next person who looks at me askance—then I like to be alone. Or if I'm tired. Or when I'm ill."

"I confess I enjoy being alone after spending a day with the girls. You would be amazed how much they can say about the simplest things! That is one reason no one is allowed into my sanctuary."

"Sanctuary?"

"My bedchamber," she admitted. "No one goes in there except me. I have heard the girls whispering their speculations as to the luxuries I have hoarded there, but it is really quite barren...."

Her words trailed off as she realized he was looking at her with an expression that made her feel outrageously warm.

She should not have come. She had debated sending Hildegard with refreshment for him, then decided it would probably be safer if she did. Otherwise, Hildegard might do something foolish that would bring shame to her household.

And if she were not careful, so would she.

She must remember that no matter how attractive this man was, she was the formidable, dignified Lady Katherine DuMonde. Despite that, she couldn't resist asking him another question. "Have you ever been married?"

"No. I never thought about it with any seriousness," he said lightly. "I was too busy trying to win prizes."

"With much success?"

"Some," he replied as if he were too modest to detail all the many and wonderful prizes he had captured over the years. "Cassius was one."

In truth, Cassius was the one and only prize of any great value he had ever won. He had never been first at anything. He had always missed the best prizes and rewards, sometimes by a little, often by more.

"You have traveled a great deal, too?"

"I have been to France, and London, of course. As far north as the Roman wall, and west to the coast of Wales."

"I have never been more than twenty miles from this place. My family lived that far away to the south, and I have not left here since they brought me to be married."

"I think that's a very good thing."

Her brow furrowed.

"If you had gone to London, your beauty would have thrown the entire court into an uproar."

"I am too old for flattery, Sir Rafe."

He shrugged and bit into the soft cheese. "Demure as you will, but it is the truth."

She ignored his comment. "I would like to hear about some of your travels."

His responses would, after all, be educational, she told herself, provided he spared her his ridiculous flattery.

Deciding it might be better to take refuge behind humor, Rafe grinned. "Since nothing pleases me more than talking about myself, and since you don't want to be flattered, I am delighted to do so."

As he continued to eat the bread and cheese and drink the wine, he told her of the sights he had seen and the people he had encountered. Usually he enjoyed regaling an audience with his tales, but tonight, with Katherine's steadfast gaze upon him, he began to wish he had accomplished more that could make him worthy of her respect and her admiration. Now every tournament seemed boringly similar to the next.

As for the places he had been, if she wanted a description of various taverns and brothels, he was her man. Instead, he stuck to the well-known attributes of famous buildings he had never actually seen, except from outside.

"I fear I am boring you, my lady," he finally said, wiping his wine-damp lips with the back of his hand.

"Not at all. I have never seen a tournament and have often wondered what they must be like."

"Well, I seem to have bored poor Cassius," he remarked wryly, nodding at the slumbering stallion. "Of course, he was there."

She looked at the horse. "He is breathing much easier, is he not?"

"Yes, and for that, I thank you and your medicine."

She smiled, and he saw that he had been right to suspect that her smile would make her the most beautiful woman he had ever seen.

If he had met her when they both were younger, when he was just beginning his life as a knight, full of vigor and pride and hope, what wouldn't he have done to make a woman of her beauty and intelligence like him? Saint Michael's miracles, what wouldn't he have done to make her love him?

But he was not young.

"You were the apothecary," she said. "All I did was provide the calamint."

"Without which, I don't know what we would have done. It is the best Christmas gift I have ever received," he said softly and sincerely. He leaned back against the stable wall. "Now tell me about your life."

A small wrinkle of displeasure appeared between her brows. "There is nothing to tell."

He doubted that very much, for surely there must be some good reason she had not remarried. However, he could see that it would be a mistake to press her for information she was not willing to impart. "If you do not want to talk about yourself, tell me about your pupils."

"I don't gossip."

He sighed and cocked his head. "You let me go on

about myself for a very long time. Now you must reciprocate, or I shall feel as vain and stupid as Frederick Delamarch."

She still looked unwilling.

"If you will not tell me about your charges, just tell me about the one you liked the best," he cajoled.

"I suppose that would not be amiss," she mused. A spark of pleasure appeared in Katherine's blue eyes, a glowing ember of vivacity that seemed to melt her frosty manner. "My best pupil was Elizabeth Perronet. She was one of the first, too. She was with me but a year, and then her family put her in a convent. While it is no shame to be pledged to God's service, I was sorry to lose her."

"Was she beautiful?"

Katherine frowned, looking as annoyed as if he had insulted the girl's memory. "No, not what most men would call beautiful, I suppose. Nor did she make much of an impression at first, not like her cousin, who came to me much later. Genevieve had more spirit and she let everyone know it. Elizabeth was different. She was an intelligent girl, yet humble and quiet, too—so humble and quiet it was easy to forget she was there, I confess.

"Then one day, when she had been here a fortnight, some of the older girls were teasing a younger one. I overheard them and was about to interfere when Elizabeth went up to the oldest, who was a head taller than she, and said, 'Stop it.'"

Katherine shook her head at the memory. "I will never forget it, the force in those words and the expression in her eyes. It was like a sudden burst of fire on a dark night. Once you saw that fire, you realized it was always there—banked, but there." Katherine sighed. "She was a pleasure to teach, too. She always listened, and I knew she would remember all the things I taught her."

"I gather the same could not be said of many of the other girls."

Katherine made a wry little smile. "Unfortunately, you are right. Indeed, sometimes I think most of them will forget everything I've taught them the instant they set foot outside my gates." She shook her head. "It is not easy interesting them in practical matters. All most of them want to think about is men and marriage."

Rafe chuckled. "I've met several knights who could only think about women and wine. The worst of all on that score was Raynard Flambeaux. He seemed to think a title meant women should willingly drop into his bed—not that he would have any idea what to do if they did, I'm sure."

Katherine tried to subdue any and all reaction to the image of a man and woman sharing nocturnal adventures. "You're speaking of Sir Raynard Flambeaux of Castle Beautress?"

"You've met him?"

She laughed softly. "I tried to teach his sister."

"If she's anything like her brother, I don't envy you that. He's as big and slow as an ox."

"She's petite, but oxlike in her own way, and as for the arrogance, I believe she matched him there," Katherine confessed with another laugh that turned into a sigh. "I thought she would never, ever learn how to add even the simplest sum."

"Who was your second-best student?"

Perhaps it was the intimacy of the stable and the golden lantern light, or perhaps it had been too long since she had had someone with which to share her thoughts, or perhaps it was simply that he seemed so keen to listen, but for whatever reason, Katherine answered Rafe's question, and more. She told him things she hadn't told another soul about the joys of teaching the girls, and the heartaches. She smiled as she recounted some of the pranks a few of the braver girls had tried to play on her, and smiled even more when she confessed how she had thwarted their efforts. She sighed over some of their fates, and marveled at the progress of others who had, at first, filled her with despair.

She fell silent when, with a snort and a whinny, Cassius began to get to his feet.

"Oh!" she cried, happy to see the horse so improved. "The calamint has worked."

Rafe also staggered to his feet. He almost fell over, but she hurried to help him.

"Saint Bernard's bones, I'm stiff as a plank," he

muttered as he leaned on her, his arm around her slender shoulder.

"You're cold, that's all," she said. "I should have found you a blanket...."

Her words trailed off as she felt the warmth of his hard, masculine body surround her.

He looked into her eyes, his gaze piercing and yet questioning. "I cannot thank you enough for helping us."

"It was only common courtesy," she whispered, her throat suddenly dry, her heart pounding.

He slowly lowered his elbow, dragging his hand along the back of her neck, and turned to face her. The lantern light made the flesh along the angle of his cheeks glow, while his eyes were deep in shadow. His other hand came to rest lightly on her shoulder. Then he gently pulled her closer and kissed her.

It had been so long, so very, very long, and even then, his kiss was not like any other's. His firm mouth took possession of hers with both surety and gentle query.

He was no selfish, vain young man seeking only another conquest.

He was no old man wanting a young wife to give him children.

Before he kissed her, he had already given her something far more precious than flattery and empty words, or his name. He had given her friendship.

So now she could not resist the invitation in his lips and the question in his eyes. With a low moan, she yielded to the burning need to feel Rafe's mouth upon her own, to taste him, touch him and inhale the masculine scent of him, to remind herself that she was a woman capable of fervent desire.

Their kiss deepened as his arms tightened about her. She eagerly parted her lips for him, and when his tongue entered her willing mouth, she entwined hers with his.

She was young and alive, truly alive, in a way she had not been for years.

In a way she never had.

With a low growl of desire, he tugged off her cap and wimple, and his hands moved through her unbound hair.

This warrior could surely have almost any woman, and he wanted her—the stern, the cold Lady Katherine DuMonde. In his arms she was no longer stern or cold, but vibrant with the thrilling excitement of passionate yearning throbbing in her heart.

A heart that had not given or received love in over fifteen years.

Then something nudged her from behind.

Rafe stopped kissing her and looked over her shoulder, a warning look in his eyes. "Cassius," he chided. "You will be fed soon enough."

Katherine glanced out one of the small windows nearby and was startled to realize that the dawn was breaking over the manor wall.

"I had no idea it was so late!" she cried softly, disengaging herself from Rafe's embrace. "I had best go."

His smile warmed her more than summer sunlight.

"You will come to the hall to break the fast?" she asked, shy in a way she had not been in over fifteen years, either, as she bent down to retrieve her cap and wimple.

His expression grave, save for his merry eyes, he bowed. "I shall be delighted, my lady."

Drawing the cloth of the veil over her head like a scarf, she answered with a smile as she picked up the empty basket and hurried from the stable.

How glorious this morning was, she thought as she made her way across the courtyard through the snow. The air was cold but crisp, the sun glinted off the windows of the hall, the sky was clear and free of clouds.

It was a perfect winter's day, and this year she would have the perfect Christmas. She would order the hall decorated with evergreen boughs and holly and ivy. She would tell the cook to make her finest dishes. She would have the best wine and wassail. She would have music and dancing.

Why, she was so happy she could almost dance now, she thought with a quiet laugh. Indeed, the last time she had felt anything approaching this great joy was the day Frederick had told her he loved her.

She halted in midstep, all thoughts of music and dancing and celebration destroyed as a wall crumbles in an earthquake.

Frederick Delamarch, the man she had loved. Who had told her he loved her and had made love to her, only to callously abandon her afterward. Who had bragged of his conquest to his fellows so that her reputation was in danger, and her only defense to marry the old man her parents found willing to take her.

Frederick, the charming. Frederick, the sly seducer.

What would he be like now?

Very much like Rafe, no doubt, came the dismaying answer.

Suddenly she felt like a fool, and an old fool. For years she had tried to teach her charges to beware of men who spoke of love and promised their eternal devotion. They were surely lying and more likely to be duplicitous, treacherous, selfish creatures interested only in assuaging their own lust. It was better to be alone than used, abandoned, heartbroken and pride shattered.

She, of all people, should remember that.

Glancing around guiltily as she quickened her pace, she hoped none of the servants could see her, or had seen her come out of the stable. What might they think if they had?

That she had spent the night in Rafe's arms, coupling in the straw like a lustful peasant.

TAKING IN DEEP, invigorating breaths of the cold morning air, Rafe energetically swung his arms as he marched across the courtyard. He had washed and made himself as presentable as possible before joining Katherine in the hall. Not only did he have her company and a good meal to look forward to, but Cassius was definitely better.

Even more important, Katherine had kissed him.

And what a kiss! He was not quite so vain as to think it was his personal attributes alone that were responsible for her passionate response. Indeed, he was all but certain that he had guessed aright before. It had been a long time since a man had stoked her fires and, surprising though it may be, he was the first to rekindle the blaze.

But there was more to his happiness than triumph at a potential conquest. He had truly enjoyed their conversation the night before, more so than he would have believed possible. He had experienced a companionship and intimacy with Katherine of a kind he had never known with a woman. In the past, he had spoken to women only to flirt with them, his sole objective being to woo them into his bed.

Walking toward the hall, he suddenly realized that, while he shared her passionate desire and wanted very much to make love with her, his feelings went beyond lust. He wanted to have more long conversations with her. He wanted to hear all about her childhood and her life. He wanted to learn more about her pupils. He wanted to know her secret wishes and regrets.

Most of all, he wanted to make her happy, if he could, because she deserved to be.

"Saint Thomas on a toadstool," he muttered as a new thought assailed him, making his steps slow.

Was this love?

Could this overwhelming need to be near her, even to simply see her face—was that love?

Yet if it was, what could he offer her? He had no home, no land, no wealth. He was nothing more than a vagabond knight who could tell amusing stories, a man past his prime, a man who had accomplished…nothing.

In the cold, harsh light of the winter's morning, he realized he had squandered his life. He had nothing to show for his thirty-two years except a horse, his ancient armor and a change of clothing. He had nothing to offer a woman of Katherine's admirable qualities and accomplishments, nothing at all.

He was a pathetic jester in love with a princess.

Rafe turned on his heel to return to the stable. He and Cassius would leave. At once. He would walk Cassius and carry his gear himself, if need be.

Suddenly he heard a pounding on the gate. He stopped and watched as Dawson came bustling out of the gatehouse and peered out the small window to see who it was.

Then he opened the gate, and a donkey bearing a man wrapped in a dark robe ambled slowly inside.

Katherine had said she had no guests save a priest at Christmas and, as the man dismounted awkwardly, Rafe decided that's who he had to be.

Between his concern for Cassius and his attraction to Katherine, he had completely forgotten about Christmas.

She had given him back Cassius, and he had nothing to give her in return.

He continued toward the stable. Christmas or not, he would soon be on his way and it would be better if he did not linger.

SEATED ON THE DAIS in her hall after hastily changing her attire, Katherine held her breath as the door to the hall opened, then let it slowly out as someone who was not Rafe entered. It was a stranger dressed in the garb of a priest.

Katherine tried to subdue her immature disappointment. It was better for her if Rafe stayed in the stable, even though a sudden dread that his beloved stallion might have worsened nagged at her. She would send Hildegard to ask how the horse fared.

A subtle clearing of the priest's throat made her start and focus her attention on the man coming toward her.

"Greetings on this day before the celebration of our Lord's blessed birth, my lady," the portly man intoned as he approached her and bowed politely. "Father Bartholomew sends his regrets, but he was too ill to come. I have been sent in his place."

"I am sorry to hear that Father Bartholomew is not well. I hope he is not seriously ill, Father...?"

"Coll, my lady. I am Father Coll. No, it is merely a chill. Unfortunately, although the abbey is but a mile away, the weather did not seem auspicious, and it was deemed too risky to his health to travel," the priest replied.

The day was fine, Katherine thought, glancing at the narrow window nearest her. The sunlight was weak, to be sure, but that was to be expected in winter. Then, as if in answer to her questioning look, a howling blast of wind suddenly sounded outside and the sunlight diminished as though the wind had blown the sun out of the sky.

"There is going to be another heavy snowfall, I fear," the priest said.

She turned back to look at him and made a little smile of welcome. "I am even more grateful you made the journey."

"I was also told you set a very good table," he replied with a low chortle.

Katherine wondered what man would next expect her to find life a source of amusement. "Will you join me for some refreshment?"

The priest started slightly. "Before mass?"

Katherine colored. "Of course, we must have mass first," she replied. "If you will give me a moment to fetch my cloak, we shall proceed to the chapel."

After the priest nodded his agreement, Katherine went to her austere chamber as quickly as she could while maintaining a dignified attitude. Once in her bedchamber, she rushed to the window. The formerly clear sky was now filled with dark, ominous clouds. The freezing wind bent the trees, tearing off loose twigs and small branches and sending them whirling about the sky.

No one should travel in this weather. No matter how inconvenient and unsettling, Rafe must stay. She would simply have to be wary of him, that was all. She could keep a cool demeanor toward him.

She had to.

After putting on her cloak, she returned to the waiting priest and led him out of the hall toward the small chapel near the gate. The frigid building was only about ten feet by twelve, with no seating and a plain altar covered in a white cloth. The communion vessels, wine and some bread were already prepared, Katherine was pleased to note. That was one of Hildegard's tasks, and she was glad to see that the servant had remembered it.

Indeed, it seemed Hildegard's memory was surpassing that of her distracted mistress this morning.

Several of the servants, including Hildegard, Dawson, Giles and Egbert, filed into the chapel and took their places behind Lady Katherine. She could hear their teeth chattering, their feet stamping and arms moving to keep themselves warm.

She wished the priest would begin.

"My lady?" Father Coll said softly, coming to stand in front of her.

"Yes?"

"Is this all who are attending today?"

She glanced around. "I believe so. We shall have all the servants tomorrow."

"Have you no guests for the twelve days of Christmas?"

"No."

"I saw a man in the courtyard, a nobleman...?"

"Perhaps he does not care to attend mass."

"Perhaps he does not know we are having it," the priest countered.

Katherine's eyes narrowed ever so slightly. No one had answered her so impudently in years, until Rafe had come. Had his visit somehow altered her external appearance so that this unknown priest would also be comfortable speaking to her in an impertinent fashion? "I think you may proceed."

Apparently unmoved by her glacial tone, the priest said, "I am willing to wait while someone fetches him."

Annoyed at the priest, at Rafe and at all arrogant men in general, Katherine made a small gesture that brought Egbert hastily to her side.

"Go to the stable and ask Sir Rafe to join us for mass," she ordered. "Tell him the priest requests it."

Egbert nodded, then hurried out.

Katherine clasped her hands and assumed a blank expression as she waited, determined to act as if nothing at all were amiss—even though, unlike the rest of the people gathered in that freezing stone building, she was more than a little warm.

Chapter Four

"YOU'RE TO COME TO MASS," Egbert said after he ran into the stable. He skittered to a halt, nearly slipping on the straw, then stared at the knight. "You're not leaving? There's going to be another storm."

"I *am* leaving, so I will not be going to mass."

"But sir, can't you hear the wind? And your horse is still not well!" the boy protested.

Rafe stopped fussing with the leather pouch that held his pitiful belongings and strode past Egbert to look outside. He had heard the wind, of course, but had told himself it was just an occasional gust. Now, however, as he looked at the dark sky, he knew the boy was right. There was going to be a storm, and worse than the one that had brought him here.

Leaving now was impossible, unless he was willing to risk his horse's life because he felt uncomfortable around Lady Katherine.

Uncomfortable? That was a mild way to put the tumultuous conflict she aroused within him.

He forced himself to make a wry grin as he turned back to Egbert. "I see you are quite right. I will have to impose upon your mistress's hospitality for at least another day. Now, about mass?"

"He said you had to come."

"Who said?"

"The priest who arrived this morning. He isn't going to start until you do, and it's perishing cold in that chapel, so won't you please hurry?"

Rafe glanced at Cassius. "My horse—"

"I'll watch 'im."

"You are not the only one who would prefer not to attend mass, Egbert."

The boy blushed and stared at his toe, which he moved in slow circles in the dirt of the stable floor.

"However, since I am a knight, I suppose it is my duty to go, especially when a priest requests it."

The boy looked up eagerly.

"Now you take good care of Cassius. He has been in many a tourney and saved my hide more than once, so he should be treated with deference and respect."

Grinning, Egbert nodded.

"It's freezing in the chapel?"

"Aye, I should say it is!"

Rafe picked up his cloak, noting just how many rents and tears it had. Saint Paul's piety, the next time he had some spare coin, he would buy a new one, he vowed as he resolutely marched from the stables. Unfortunately, this one would have to do for now.

The wind grabbed at his cloak. With a scowl, Rafe held as tight to it as he did to what remained of his self-respect.

The moment he entered the chapel, he knew the boy had not been exaggerating about the temperature. The building was bare as Lady Katherine's hall, and cold as any place he could remember. If he had any doubts, the blue lips, chattering teeth and impatient movements of the servants gathered there would have provided more than enough evidence. Even the priest seemed rather chilled.

In fact, the only person who seemed impervious to the frigid temperature was Katherine.

Although he knew it was a weakness, he couldn't resist the temptation to stand beside her, especially when the servants made way for him. It was folly, of course, because he was only going to torment himself.

Katherine didn't even glance his way.

Well, perhaps that was to be expected, he told himself, when they were in a holy place.

Or perhaps, he thought with growing dismay, she had come to her senses and realized he was not worthy of her affection or desire.

As the mass continued, he struggled to keep his expression calm and unrevealing, even though he dreaded having to speak to her afterward or, what might be worse, still being ignored by her.

When the priest finished, Katherine turned to Rafe and, her expression utterly inscrutable, said, "Because of the weather, Sir Rafe, you must stay another night."

Because of the weather. Not because of any feeling between them. Not even because it was Christmas Eve. "Thank you again for your hospitality, my lady. Cassius and I are most grateful."

As the servants hurried out of the chapel, the priest came to stand beside Katherine and she turned to address him. "Father Coll, this is Sir Rafe Bracton."

Father Coll smiled warmly. "Delighted to meet you, sir," he said. "Are you perchance related to the Bractons of Upper Uxton?"

"My uncle lived in Upper Uxton," Rafe replied with some surprise.

He was even more surprised to see the priest's smile broaden. "A most kind and generous benefactor to the poor."

"Oh yes, he was," Rafe agreed.

In reality, he knew almost nothing of his late uncle save his name and the town where he lived. However, it seemed the man had been worthy of some admiration, and right at the moment, Rafe was desperate for any and all self-esteem he could muster, even willing to cling to that of an unknown, deceased relative.

"Father, Sir Rafe, shall we go to the hall and eat?"

"Since I have been on the road since first light, I am happy to take advantage of your hospitality," Father

Coll replied jovially. "And truth be told, I am most anxious to see if Father Bartholomew was exaggerating when he enumerated your cook's accomplishments."

Katherine made a little smile as she turned to lead the way. "You must tell me if he has."

At the door, they regarded the courtyard with some dismay. Not only was the wind blowing fiercely, but it had started to snow. Mixed with that snow were little pellets of ice which Rafe knew would sting like pebbles if they hit the face. "My lady, please allow me to offer you my protection," he said.

Without waiting for her to speak, Rafe put his arm about her and enfolded her in his cloak as Father Coll hurried out into the courtyard ahead of them. "Come, my lady."

Katherine thought of shrugging off Rafe's protective arm, but his unexpectedly shy, yet definitely intense expression, silenced her. Something was different about him this morning. His manner had been subdued in the chapel, but that might be explained by the necessity of proper behavior in a place of worship.

Perhaps the presence of the priest squelched his natural bonhomie. Or maybe he had stopped acting the merry mortal because he realized she was no longer under the spell of his boisterous charm.

Which was good, of course.

The weather was definitely nasty and she would be foolish to refuse the shelter he offered. Besides, she had mastery of herself now. He was nothing more than an attractive, mature man who had momentarily kindled emotions long buried. She could bury those tumultuous feelings and urges again. She would, once he let go of her.

They proceeded out into the courtyard. The wind caught their cloaks, whipping them about their legs. The snow and ice made it necessary to nearly close their eyes, so their progress was not as swift as it might have been.

Over and above this, however, Katherine was very aware of Rafe's masculine protection. She had relied upon herself for years and would have only herself to rely on when he was gone. Still, she could not help enjoying this momentary and rare sensation of being cherished and safeguarded.

Rafe removed his arm from around her the moment they entered the warm hall. "Saint Mary's mother, that's wicked weather!" he muttered as he took off his tattered cloak and shook it.

Katherine likewise removed her cloak and handed it to the waiting Hildegard. She looked around the room and realized Father Coll was already at his place at the table, as unruffled as if it were a beautiful spring day.

Attempting to emulate him, she went to her place and waited for Rafe to join them on the dais.

"Are we not fortunate to have such a fine hostess?" Father Coll asked as Rafe sat and the servants began to serve the bread and ale.

"Indeed, we are," Rafe agreed.

"I would hate to be caught on the road in such weather. I was afoot in the Alps during a storm once, and I would not care to have the experience repeated."

"That must have been terrible," Katherine agreed.

"Oh, it was. Fortunately, I had a marvelous guide, a fine fellow named Otto. Let me tell you about him."

For the rest of the meal, the priest entertained them with tales of his travels. Katherine was very impressed, and not a little envious. Once again, all the constraints of her life seemed to envelop her.

With Rafe sitting so close, she felt even more trapped.

The stories told by the priest seemed to loosen Rafe's tongue. He began to tell tales of his own adventures, to Father Coll's evident delight.

As Rafe spoke, she noted the difference between the way he had talked to her last night in the stable when they were alone. Then, she had felt she was participating in his memories, with all the joys and frustrations and moments of triumph. Today, the very same yarns were only mildly amusing.

What did that difference mean? Anything at all?

She did not want to have to wonder at Rafe's change of manner. She wanted respect, she wanted dignity, she wanted order and she wanted discipline.

At one time, she had wanted love, but that had proved to be a snare that had ruined her life, so she did not want that anymore.

"If you will excuse me," Katherine said, rising when Hildegard had cleared away the last of the food, "I have my household duties to attend to."

Father Coll smiled. "Of course, my lady, I'm sure the preparations for Christmas celebrations are most time-consuming."

"I do not celebrate the twelve days between Christmas and Epiphany," Katherine explained, wishing Father Bartholomew had saved her the trouble. "We have a special meal on Christmas Day, and that is all."

"What, no decorations? No Yule log? No music or dancing? No games? No gifts for the twelve days?"

Katherine frowned. "We prefer to observe this as a holy time, not an excuse for senseless merriment."

"Then surely you can stay," Father Coll declared, apparently not at all taken aback by her barely disguised reproach. "Sir Rafe was just about to tell me about Arabian horses."

"Sir Rafe is very knowledgeable about horses, and sure to be fascinating," Katherine replied. "However, I must see to your accommodations. Father, Sir Rafe, until later."

"Until later," Father Coll acknowledged genially.

Rafe didn't say anything at all.

THAT CHRISTMAS EVE, at least one person enjoyed Rafe's tale of the knight who lost his boots. Father Coll had laughed and the servants would have, had their mistress not sat stone-faced and grim throughout the entire meal, her eyes darting daggers at anyone other than the priest who had dared to be amused.

After she had gone and he sought solace in his wine, Rafe felt as if last night in the stable, when Katherine had been so companionable and desirable, had been a fantasy that disappeared with the reality of daylight.

Saint Anne's aunt, it was a damned good thing he was leaving just as soon as the weather cleared. He had never met a more confusing woman in his life, and he would be happy if he never met one like her again. He must have been mad to think he was falling in love with her.

As for Father Coll, the man had to be the most unobservant fellow in England not to sense the lady's tension before, and it had not abated a bit when she returned a short while later.

"The storm looks to continue for another day at least," Father Coll noted, breaking the momentary silence.

"There will not be many tenants coming for the service, perhaps," Katherine said. "They will be sorry to miss it."

"Not if they are warm," Rafe muttered, thinking of the shivering servants that morning. "I don't suppose you would consider a brazier or two in there?"

"No. We go to the chapel to worship, not to be comfortable."

Well, if he needed any additional evidence that she was

in no humor to be amused by him, he had just received it. "Perhaps if I had a better cloak, I would agree."

"There is nothing wrong with your cloak that some mending wouldn't fix."

"I daresay that means you were not planning on giving me one for a Christmas present."

She looked shocked, and he was rather fiendishly glad to have gotten any reaction at all from her.

Then she flushed, but not with embarrassment. "The calamint was not enough?" she demanded, anger in her eyes.

Now he flushed, and not with anger. Saint Vincent in a vise, like an ungrateful wretch, he had forgotten that. "Yes, it was."

"I do not believe in giving gifts at Christmas," she explained to the priest. "Sir Rafe's horse was ill, however, so with good Christian charity, I gave him calamint to make a potion to clear his lungs. It seems to have worked."

"I am very glad," Father Coll said. Then he sighed, a far more serious expression on his face than either of them had seen before. "The giving of gifts when none is expected in return is indeed Christian charity."

"Sometimes people cannot afford to give gifts, even if they would like to," Rafe noted with a hint of defiance.

"The most important gifts of all do not cost money," the priest replied, "and if anyone would doubt that—" Father Coll turned his suddenly shrewd gaze onto the knight "—he need only remember the gifts our Lord received on the first Christmas."

"But the Magi brought very fine presents," Rafe pointed out. "Gold and frankincense and myrrh."

Father Coll smiled and pushed his trencher away. "To be sure, they did bring those things, but for me, the important part of the story of our Lord's birth is not what they held in their hands, but the other gift they gave that was far more precious. These important, wealthy and learned men paid homage to a baby in a stable. They gave Him respect, which is something no amount of money can purchase.

"And we must also remember the shepherds, rough men who had come to see their promised messiah. Think of what it must have been like to find not a prince in a palace, but a baby wrapped in simple swaddling clothes, lying in a manger in a humble stable. Yet they still trusted their vision and had faith that this was their future king as they, too, paid him respectful homage. Respect, trust and faith are truly wonderful, precious gifts," Father Coll concluded softly, "for they are the basis of love."

Rafe toyed with the bottom of his goblet for a moment before giving Katherine a sidelong glance. "Would you agree, my lady?" he asked. "Would you say that faith, trust and respect are excellent gifts?"

"Respect, certainly," she answered.

"What of trust?"

She rose. "One can misplace one's trust and live to rue it. I thank you, Father, for your very interesting and unique thoughts. Now it is late, so I must bid you both good-night."

The two men watched her disappear up the stairs leading to her bedchamber.

The priest sighed softly. "I fear a man has wronged our hostess at some time in her life."

Rafe nodded. "Yes. She sounded very bitter."

Father Coll regarded him with a shrewd eye. "She is not the only one sounding bitter tonight."

"Am *I*? It must be the wine," Rafe answered with a laugh. "I'm getting maudlin in my cups."

"No, I don't think that's it."

"I assure you, it's nothing more."

"Would you say too much wine was Lady Katherine's trouble, too?"

"No. I think you have guessed aright. At some time, a man has betrayed her trust."

"And you feel sorry for her?"

"Not sorry. I regret that it happened, but her history means very little to me."

The priest cocked his head. "Do you think me a fool, Sir Rafe?"

Wishing he had been more circumspect, Rafe flushed, then lifted his chin with a show of bravado.

"Why should her past mean anything to me?"

"Because you love her."

"What?" Rafe cried, looking about to see if any of the servants had heard the priest's startling pronouncement.

"You love her. I can see it in your eyes."

"Then you should have a doctor examine them, for you are seeing the impossible."

"Why should that be impossible?"

"Because…because it is!"

"Because you are poor and she is not."

"This is too ludicrous to discuss. I'm going back to the stable," Rafe declared, pushing back his chair.

The priest laid a detaining hand on his arm. "Rafe," he said, his bright eyes intense in his round face, "you and I both know that no matter what has happened to her in the past, there beats a passionate, loving heart inside Katherine DuMonde. I think she wants to love and be loved. Offer her that love, Rafe."

"She would scorn it."

"Why?"

"Because I have nothing to offer her!" he muttered, the truth spilling out. "I have wasted my life. I have lived only for the present, with no thought to the future." He lowered his head and confessed. "How bleak that future looks now. I have no home, no wealth, no family and few possessions. I have managed to hide this truth from myself for a long time, but I cannot any longer. I have nothing. I *am* nothing."

"Look about you, Rafe," Father Coll said softly with an encompassing gesture. "Do you think Katherine needs material goods? Do you think she wants money or power? Don't you think she needs something else, something more precious, something you can give her? She needs love, Rafe, and as you crave respect, she needs to be able to trust again. You can convince her that not all men who love will betray."

"I don't want her respect or her love," Rafe protested.

"So you would like to live out the rest of your days alone, and you would condemn her to do so, too?"

Rafe's chair scraped loudly over the stone floor as he shoved it farther back.

"I know you are afraid, Rafe, but take the risk and tell her how you feel. Offer her your love. Otherwise you may spend the rest of your life regretting that you did not."

Rafe didn't answer. He strode out of the hall, away from this most unusual, troublesome priest and into the storm.

SOMETIME LATER, Katherine crept down to the quiet hall. Unable to sleep, she had decided she should insure that the fire in the hearth had not gone out. Otherwise, the hall would be extremely cold in the morning. She also told herself she might need to put a brazier in the chapel, depending on the temperature of the hall. She did not want to make the chapel overly warm, of course. As she had said to Rafe, they were not there for comfort, but to worship.

She halted on the bottom step and wrapped her

arms around herself, hesitating when she realized Father Coll was still there, sitting on a bench by the hearth. The light of the flames flickered and a piece of wood fell, sending up a small shower of sparks that illuminated his portly shape. Despite the shooting sparks, he must have heard her, for he looked at her over his shoulder and smiled. "Ah, my lady, what brings you to the hall at this hour?"

Katherine approached him. "I wanted to be sure the fire did not go out," she said, gesturing at the hearth. "It is indeed very late, Father. Should you not retire?"

"Oh, I often stay awake for the whole of Christmas Eve," he replied with a smile. "I confess this is my favorite night of the year. I enjoy the quiet of the winter's eve and contemplating how it must have been for those visiting the Holy Child." He patted the bench beside him. "Will you sit, my lady?"

Since she didn't want to return to the barren surroundings of her lonely bedchamber, she did.

"I think Christmas brings you little joy," the priest observed.

"No, it does not."

"Unhappy memories, perhaps?"

"Yes."

"We all have the burdens of our pasts to bear."

"Some apparently bear their burdens more lightly than others."

"Or hide them better."

She gave the priest a wary, sidelong glance. "You find your past burdensome?"

"I was not referring to myself."

"You speak of Sir Rafe, perhaps?"

"And yourself, too, I think. You hide your pain very well."

Katherine stiffened. "I do not know what you mean."

"No?"

"No."

"I gather you think Sir Rafe is little bothered by his history."

"He could not jest about it so if he were."

Father Coll gave her a quizzical look. "Some people hide their pain behind austere dignity, others beneath a jester's hat, but that does not mean they feel nothing. Some would say it takes a great deal of strength to mask one's pain with laughter. In truth, I think Sir Rafe is a very lonely man."

"He seems to have a great many friends."

"I would not say friends. Acquaintances, perhaps. I note that he is not spending Christmas with any of his so-called friends."

"He was caught in the storm."

"I have not heard him mention any invitations."

Katherine realized that Father Coll was quite right. "No, he hasn't."

"So while he is friendly, I think he does not have many friends, and he hides his loneliness. He must sometimes wish for a good friend, especially when he is troubled."

Katherine thought of him in the stable as he tended to Cassius. He had seemed very glad of her company.

Perhaps he was far lonelier than she suspected.

As lonely as she.

"I don't suppose there are many people he trusts, either. The trust that enables us to reveal our vulnerabilities is a rare and great gift, my lady," Father Coll said quietly, "especially from a man like Sir Rafe, who would prefer to hold everyone at bay by making them laugh."

Katherine eyed the priest speculatively. "You believe he amuses people as a defense?"

"Very much so."

Katherine thought of the tales Rafe had told her about his own life and suddenly saw them in a new light. The mistakes he had made, the prizes he had lost, the insults he had borne—he had made her laugh that night in the stable, but now, they were far from funny.

"He wants to be respected, my lady, but if that cannot be—or he believes it impossible—he plays the clown. Better to be laughed at than ignored."

"I respect him," Katherine replied. "He is a knight and my guest, after all."

"But nothing more?"

"He treated his horse's illness with skill," she noted, looking away from the priest into the glowing fire.

"That sounds better. He needs more than respect, though. Like all of us, he wants to be loved."

"I believe he has little trouble in that regard," Katherine replied. "He charms without even trying. My maidservants have been in a dither since he arrived."

"That is not the kind of love he needs, my lady, although perhaps he thinks he deserves no better. He needs the love that sees beyond the banter and tales to the man beneath, the companionable love that will make a woman stay with him during a long, anxious night."

Katherine's mouth fell open in surprise, but Father Coll didn't seem to notice. "He needs a love that is based on respect and trust and faith. He needs *your* respect, your trust, your faith—your love, my lady."

She stood up and faced the priest. "I cannot!" she said firmly, believing it even as her heart ached with loneliness and despair. "I cannot tell you why, but I cannot!"

With a sigh, Father Coll watched her hurry away. Then he returned to his Christmas Eve vigil.

Chapter Five

RAFE PEERED OUT THE DOOR of the stable. Behind him, Cassius breathed easy. Before him, through the gently falling snow, a light shone from the window in the western tower like the Christmas star.

He wondered if Katherine was thinking about the vagrant knight supposedly sleeping in her stable. If she was, she was probably considering him a pathetic example of a life gone awry and looking forward to his departure.

But what if Father Coll was right? What if he could give her something, after all? What if she might miraculously welcome his love?

Doubt assailed him. He could easily envision her scorning him. By all the saints, he would never be able to make an amusing story out of that. Her rejection would be too painful, because he had never in his life wanted anything as much as he wanted Katherine's love. No prize, no reward, no honor he had ever sought could compare to this one—and none had ever been more out of his reach.

Sighing, Rafe turned away and closed the door behind him. "Well, Cassius, it will be you and me again, as always," he murmured. "There's nothing wrong with that, is there? And if I have not the heart to try for prizes anymore, I shall become an apothecary to horses."

He lowered his head and slumped against the wall. "Oh, God," he moaned, despair overwhelming him. He was such a failure, such a useless fellow, undeserving of any woman's regard, and Katherine's most of all.

"It would indeed take a miracle for her to love me, Cassius," he murmured. "A Christmas miracle."

Then Father Coll's words began to sound in his head, about the truly important gifts of Christmas, and the basis of love.

He loved Katherine with all his heart, and he would still love her if she came to him with nothing. She alone was the prize—not her manor, not her wealth, not her title. Just Katherine.

He would not give up. He would not regret the risk not assumed, the chance not taken, the prize not sought. He was many things, but he was not a coward.

He raised his head and pushed himself from the wall. "I have to do it, Cassius," he said fiercely. "I have to risk it, or I shall truly be a shameful failure."

With renewed vigor, Rafe yanked open the stable door and stepped out into the cold air. With equally determined steps, he marched across the crunching snow in the courtyard and into the hall.

Mercifully, no one was there—or at least no one Rafe saw—so he swiftly brushed the snow from his shoulders and continued on his way, up the stairs and toward the lady's chamber.

Once outside her door, he took a deep breath, then knocked softly and walked in without waiting for an answer.

Clad in her shift, her hair loose and flowing, illuminated by a single flickering candle, Katherine peered at him as he stood in the shadows. "Who dares to enter here?" she demanded.

"Rafe," he said softly. Humbly. Like the unworthy petitioner that he was.

She sucked in her breath but didn't move. "What are you doing here?"

"I must talk to you, Katherine," Rafe whispered, stepping out of the darkness and into the pool of light.

She flushed, feeling naked before him. "You must go," she commanded, wrapping her arms around herself protectively.

He didn't leave. Instead, he closed the door behind him.

"You have to leave before you are discovered here!"

"No one comes into your bedchamber. You told me so yourself the other night."

The other night, when he had kissed her with such passion.

"Katherine," he repeated with quiet sincerity, "I must speak with you."

"In my bedchamber in the middle of the night?"

His gaze faltered as if he were a bashful youth. "I couldn't wait. Please do not send me away. I have come...I have come to give you a Christmas present, albeit a poor one." He raised his eyes, went down on his knee and said, "I would give you my love, Katherine, and my heart, if you will take them."

Her gaze softened to one of disbelief. "You love me?"

"Yes."

A tremor went through her, like that of a horse that senses something it should fear. "I have heard vows of love before, but they proved to be meaningless."

"I thought as much." He rose slowly. "Who was he, Katherine?" he asked softly. "Who hurt you?"

She shook her head, unwilling to speak of it even now, for her shame was too great.

"In addition to my love, I would make you a promise, Katherine. If you can find it in your heart to trust me and have faith in my devotion, I will never betray that faith and trust. I give you my solemn vow."

When she did not answer, he felt a despair that was like a physical blow. Then, as he always did, he sought refuge in a jest. "If you require proof, I have been faithful to poor old Cassius for a very long time, and I have never told him I love him."

When she still did not speak, hot tears sprang into his eyes, adding to his humiliation. He quickly turned away and went to the door.

"Rafe, don't go."

Scarcely daring to believe his own ears, he turned back. Katherine took a tentative step toward him.

"I am afraid of you, Rafe," she confessed quietly, studying his face.

"Afraid? Of me?"

"Of the feelings you inspire." She clasped her hands and regarded him steadily. "When I was but fifteen, Frederick Delamarch came to keep Christmas with my family. He was very handsome, and charming, and I was young and vain. I was ready to believe that he could fall in love with me, and when he said that he had, I trusted him without a single qualm. We made love."

Her gaze faltered for an instant, but she bravely raised her eyes to look at him again—and he loved her even more. "Frederick left the next day without so much as a word of farewell. I hurried to the gates and there I heard him laughing and bragging to his companions about what he had done. I had been betrayed, but before that, I had been a fool. I was so ashamed and terrified. What if I was with child? What if my parents found out?"

His heart ached to hear her anguished words, the

pain undiminished by the years. "I did the only thing I could think of to make amends. I agreed to accept marriage to the man my parents had been urging me to wed for months. I explained my sudden change of heart as evidence of a young woman's fickle nature. They were only too pleased to have my agreement and did not press for more of an explanation. We did not know he had gambled away almost all his wealth, so I married Alfred DuMonde, and the rest you know."

"I swear by Saint George's sword," Rafe growled, "if I had known what Delamarch had done, I would have tried harder to kill him."

"Are you making a joke?"

"No," he replied sincerely. "I have met him in melees and tournaments and he would not have been so very hard to kill because he is a stout, slow-moving sot."

"He doesn't matter anymore," she said, feeling the truth of that deep inside. "I respect you, Rafe, because you are a compassionate man. And I want to trust you and be able to have faith in you, because…because I think I love you, too."

"You do?"

She nodded. "If what I feel for you is not love, I have no name for it."

"Oh, Katherine!" he whispered, hurrying toward her and taking her in his arms. "I want so much to believe it is possible."

"I thought it impossible that I should ever love

again." She drew back and smiled. "Now I think I have never been in love before."

He chuckled softly, then kissed her cheeks, her nose, her chin. "Oh, my darling, thank you."

"For loving you?" she murmured as she returned his kisses, thrilled to be in his tender embrace.

"For giving me, little more than a beggar at your gates, the finest prize of all."

"I am the poor beggar, Rafe. Without your love, I am impoverished. I have been trying to convince myself otherwise, but that is the truth."

He caressed her back, then buried his hands in her thick hair. "Katherine, I shall never leave you. I mean that with all my heart."

She smiled tremulously. "I believe you. I trust you. I have faith in you. I love you."

His brow furrowed with puzzlement. "What happened, Katherine? How is it a miracle happened and you love me, a jester, a man who has so little to offer you?"

"You have made me happier than I ever thought I could be, Rafe," she answered softly. Then, to his infinite delight, a sparkle of mischief appeared in her blue eyes. "And perhaps I have been serious too long and am in great need of a jester."

He grinned his wonderful, familiar grin. "My lady, if it is amusement you desire, I am your man."

"You are." She smiled and eyed him speculatively.

"I think I fell in love with you because of your impertinence."

His deep chuckle filled the room as his eyes twinkled with both happiness and something that made her heart race. "What? And after all Father Coll's talk of respect?"

She twined a lock of his hair about her finger. "I did not say I don't want your respect, Rafe."

"As much as I respect you, my lady, there are some rather insolent things I would like to do with you," he muttered as he trailed his lips along her neck.

"And I must confess there is more I desire than amusement," she whispered breathlessly.

"But there is one condition," he murmured as he began to loosen the tie at the neck of her shift.

"What condition?" she gasped, gripping his shoulders as his mouth moved lower.

"The condition is that you agree to make me the happiest man in England and this the best Christmas by consenting to be my wife."

"Yes, oh yes!" she sighed, giving herself over to the pleasure of his kisses and caress.

Now she was no silly girl infatuated and flattered by an admired man's attention. She was a woman who could perceive the honest sincerity of Rafe's heartfelt words and the truth of his feelings for her.

She was a woman who was free again to trust, reborn in Rafe's love.

Her eyes shining, she smiled happily. "I love you, Rafe," she said softly.

He lowered his head, suddenly humbled by her declaration.

She pulled away, then took his hand and led him to her bed.

"Katherine?"

Her gaze faltered, as if she had become a shy maiden again. "You do not want to stay?"

He raised his head, his eyes gleaming in the candlelight with unmistakable passion and desire. "I did not dare to hope for this."

"There is an advantage to finding love at our age," she said in a husky whisper, running her hands up his chest in a bold caress. "I am old enough to know what I want."

Then she hesitated. "Perhaps I am being too undignified...."

"Saint Martha's mouth!" he cried softly, a grin again lighting his features. "I am not complaining." He sat on the bed and pulled her down beside him. "I simply cannot believe my good fortune. But now, my lady, soon to be my wife," he murmured as he slowly took her in his embrace, "I believe you are beginning to convince me."

"What more need I do?"

"That I leave to your own imagination, my lady."

With a throaty, seductive laugh that soon turned into sighs of ardent desire, she found a way.

YAWNING, KATHERINE SLOWLY stretched her arms over her head. The sudden chill of the cool air against her naked skin reminded her of what had happened last night, and she opened her eyes. She was alone in her bed.

She quickly looked around the room, but Rafe was not there. Had she dreamed their passionate lovemaking?

But it was not a dream. They had loved with feverish abandon, whispering endearments to each other, delighting in the sensations each aroused. She knew she had not imagined the weight of his body upon hers, or the thrill of their joining. Nor had she made up the movement of his taut muscles or the feel of his mouth upon hers. She had not dreamed the tension that had filled her or the incredible pleasure of release.

She recalled the moments after their lovemaking, when she lay in his arms, sweat slicked and happy, and they had talked of their future. He would breed and treat horses, since he would no longer be a wandering knight traveling from tournament to tournament to earn a living, while she would continue to teach her girls, if that was what she wanted. Of course it was, although a new, wonderful possibility had also arisen in her mind.

It was not inconceivable that she could bear a child. Rafe's child. What a marvelous gift that would be for both of them! Indeed, that hope filled her with so much joy it was almost too delightful to contemplate.

So where was Rafe now?

It occurred to her that he might have gone to see Cassius. Yes, that was probably it.

And it could be that he didn't want to be discovered in her bed, which was something she really should have considered. What would the parents of her girls think if they heard about that? Why, she would never have another pupil.

Sitting up in the bed, she looked at the sky outside her window. It was still dark, but faint streaks of orange-pink light told her it was dawn and that the snow had stopped.

She reached for her shift, lying discarded at the end of her bed. Shivering in the cold, her teeth started to chatter when her feet touched the stone floor, and she dressed quickly. She began to put on her wimple and cap, then paused. Rafe had whispered many complimentary things about her hair last night. Today, for him, she would not cover it. The servants would talk, but she didn't care. She would rather please Rafe than worry about their opinion.

She was very glad Father Coll was here. Surely he would not object to giving them a marriage blessing. Fortunately, she had no male relative to petition for permission and was not of sufficient rank or wealth that the king would care.

Then she glanced down at the dress she had chosen

without much thought. It was plain and black, like most of her garments.

But this was Christmas Day, and she was in love. She wanted to look beautiful for Rafe.

With a joyous smile, she went to her chest and pulled from its depths a dress she had not worn since before her marriage. In fact, she had never worn it, for once upon a time, she had decided the rich gown of holly-red brocade and samite would be her wedding dress when she married Frederick Delamarch. After he had left her, she had never been able to look at it without mourning his betrayal.

Now, however, all she cared about was that it was a lovely, well-fitting garment whose deep red tones seemed to reflect the happy glow on her cheeks.

She quickly dressed, picked up her cloak and laid it over her arm, then went below.

"Good morning and a merry Christmas to you all," she declared jovially to the servants already working there.

She did not stifle a laugh when she saw the startled looks on their faces, shocking them even more.

As the servants exchanged dubious glances and muttered a subdued Christmas greeting in response, Father Coll appeared. He did not seem at all surprised by her appearance. "A merry Christmas to you, my lady," he called out happily. "Shall we go to the chapel for mass?"

"In a moment, Father." She laid her cloak on a chair and gestured to one of the servants who stood near a brazier. "Light that and take it to the chapel, please."

The man's eyes widened, but he nodded eagerly and quickly did as he was told.

Katherine spotted Hildegard. "Tell the cook to prepare the best feast she can. We will all celebrate today."

"My lady?"

"Come, it is Christmas. Do you not want a feast?" she teased.

Hildegard looked as stunned as it was possible for a human being to be.

Katherine quickly began issuing other orders to be attended to immediately after the celebratory mass, orders intended to prepare the hall for a Christmas celebration the like of which it had not seen in years, if ever. The finest linen was to be taken from the storeroom and laid on the newly cleaned tables. The rushes were to be swept and changed, and herbs generously spread upon them. Other servants were commanded to go to the nearby wood and collect holly, evergreen branches, ivy and mistletoe with which to decorate the hall. There was also to be a blazing fire in the hearth.

It was clear from the confused looks on the servants' faces that they were finding it difficult to believe this was their mistress speaking, and Katherine smiled genially at their befuddlement. She felt young and happy, as if all the barren, lonely Christmases of the past fifteen years were but a bad dream now fading in the daylight.

She spotted Giles standing near the corridor to the kitchen. He clearly thought she had gone mad, and she had to laugh at his suspicious expression. "No, Giles, I assure you I am in my right mind. I have never felt better. Please take word to all the poor you can find and tell them that a Christmas meal awaits them in Lady Katherine's hall tonight. I want everyone to be as happy and content as I am today, and as thankful for God's gifts," she finished with a joyful sigh. "Now, we must go to mass, to give our thanks in worship."

The door to the hall opened and with a smile, Katherine turned to see—Egbert. Not Rafe. The boy glanced about uncertainly when he realized it was indeed Lady Katherine looking at him quizzically.

"Will you ask Sir Rafe to join us in the chapel for Christ's mass?" she asked.

Egbert's gaze faltered and he shifted awkwardly. "I, um, that is, I would if I could, my lady."

"Why can't you?"

"Because, my lady, because he's gone."

"Gone?"

The boy nodded. "Aye, my lady, before dawn, and took his horse with him."

"He took Cassius?"

"Aye."

Father Coll stepped forward. "Did he say when he would be back?"

"No, Father," Egbert replied sadly. "He didn't say nothing. He left when we were asleep."

The priest turned his worried eyes onto Katherine.

"Good," Katherine said briskly. "Then he will be all the more surprised by our preparations when he returns."

The servants exchanged wary looks.

"You think he does intend to return, my lady?" Father Coll asked quietly.

Katherine straightened her shoulders, a defiant gleam in her eyes. "Of course I do. I trust him."

Father Coll sighed with obvious relief. "I am glad to hear it, my lady."

"But he didn't leave his baggage," Egbert protested. "I think he's gone for good—and he took a harness, too."

"I never thought he was a thief," Giles blurted out guiltily, "or I would have set a watch on him."

"He is not a thief, and he must have needed the harness," Katherine said. "He will explain when he returns."

All the servants regarded their mistress as if she were truly deranged. Only Father Coll seemed to find her response satisfactory. She put on her cloak and led her bewildered servants to the small chapel.

They followed her, whispering among themselves, wondering what had happened to their mistress overnight. Some speculated a divine visitation, others an illness, one or two that the creature issuing orders wasn't Lady Katherine at all, but some sort of changeling. Either way, they all agreed, something extraordinary was going on and they didn't think they liked it.

AS THE MASS PROGRESSED, Katherine tried to concentrate on Father Coll and the holy meaning of the ceremony. Unfortunately, every sound from outside made her tense with expectation. Every time the door to the chapel subsequently failed to open and Rafe didn't arrive, she felt an increasing disappointment.

But she would trust that he was not gone away for good. She would believe that no matter why he had gone, he would soon return.

She had to trust and have faith, or the despair, disappointment and hurt would be overwhelming.

Surely she could not have been so callously betrayed twice in her life! Surely, she fervently prayed, the knowledge that she was indeed a dupe and a fool could not be her Christmas gift this year.

The mass ended. The servants quickly dispersed to their tasks, while Katherine lingered long in prayer. Finally she felt Father Coll's gaze and got to her feet.

She managed to smile. "I think I will order a brazier here during the whole of the winter."

The priest nodded, but his bright, black-eyed scrutiny didn't waver. "Are you all right, my lady?"

"I thought I would dress differently for the festivities."

"That is not what I meant."

"I assure you, Father, I am quite well. I am, perhaps, a little anxious over Sir Rafe's continuing absence and curious to know what might have caused him to leave so abruptly. Still, I do not doubt he will return soon and explain."

"You do doubt."

Her gaze wavered under his steadfast regard. "I am trying very hard not to," she admitted quietly. "As you said, trust and faith are the basis of love, and I...I..."

Years of hiding her true feelings made her suddenly reticent.

"You love him."

She clasped her hands together. "I know he will be back soon, and that there is a good reason for his absence."

The priest's smile warmed the chapel more than the brazier. "I do not think your trust misplaced, my lady. I can generally tell who is worthy and who is not."

Suddenly there was a huge thud outside the manor gates. "What is that?" Katherine gasped.

Without waiting for an answer, she dashed into the courtyard, Father Coll right behind her. "What has happened?" she shouted at Dawson, who was peering out the slot in the gate.

"What ho! I come bearing a gift!" a most welcome and familiar male voice shouted on the other side.

"It's Rafe!" Katherine shouted happily, running closer. "Let him in! Let him in!"

Ignoring the curious servants who also rushed into the courtyard, Katherine literally danced with impatience as Dawson hurried to obey. She squeezed through the opening the moment it was large enough and halted, staring incredulously.

Rafe stood between an ox, who bore a harness that was attached to an enormous log and Cassius, whose bridle he held. Behind the log was one of the peasants who lived nearby.

"Is that you, Katherine?" Rafe demanded, a saucy grin on his wonderful face as he ran an admiring gaze over her. "Have you found a potion of eternal youthfulness? If so, you had better share it with your decrepit old admirer."

"It is I, and you are not decrepit or old," she replied. "But what have you been doing? Where did that ox come from?" She noticed the way he kept his weight off one foot. "Are you injured?"

"I have brought you a Yule log, my lady, my love," Rafe said, patting it. "It is not much of a gift, I know, but it was the only one I could think of. I wasn't going to bring Cassius, but he made such a fuss, I feared he would waken everyone. I apologize for my tardiness. I had to find a farmer who would loan me his ox."

The man behind the log tugged his forelock.

"Unfortunately the log rolled and I was not fast

enough on my feet. Or foot, I should say. I suppose I have missed mass, too."

"Oh Rafe!" she cried, hurrying to put her arm under his shoulder to help him and take Cassius's bridle.

"My language was much more colorful," he admitted ruefully.

"Is it very bad?" she asked anxiously, looking at his swollen foot.

"I've had worse wounds in a tournament," he replied, smiling at her, the love shining in his eyes. "And never so lovely a helper."

"You will not be able to dance."

"Dance? I should say not." He paused, then noticed the band of servants carrying greenery. They appeared at the side of the road in single file, like a train of supplicants bearing booty. "What is all this?"

"Decorations for the hall. I decided that this year, we would truly celebrate Christmas." She lowered her voice so that only he could hear. "I have a reason to celebrate this year."

Rafe's delighted smile confirmed that he was pleasantly surprised.

She spotted Giles and Dawson and gestured for them to come closer.

Giles carried Rafe's leather pouch. "We found it under some straw," he explained sheepishly. "And I've shown my son the difference between an ox harness and a horse's harness."

"An old habit. I always hide my belongings, such as they are," Rafe said. "Did you think it was lost?"

"It doesn't matter now," Katherine replied. "Please help Sir Rafe take the Yule log inside the yard," she said.

Gazing warily at the huge length of timber, evidently already trying to figure out how they would maneuver it through the gate and to the hall, they nodded wordlessly. She ordered the other servants to carry on, then turned to Rafe.

"Now lean on me, my love," she ordered. "We should get you inside at once. You must be chilled to the bone."

"I am counting on you to warm me up," he said in her ear. Then he gazed at her askance. "Why, Katherine! I do believe you are blushing like the most modest maiden in Christendom."

"And you enjoy teasing me."

"When my foot is better, I think I shall shout my love for you from yonder wall—"

"Do that, Sir Rafe, and I shall knock you off."

"Is that a threat, my lady?"

"Yes. Now let us get inside."

"I am only too happy to obey. It's very slick underfoot, you might have noticed," Rafe remarked. "We had best take care, or we could both land in an ignominious heap, which would be very undignified."

"I fear I have lost any claim to dignity today," Katherine replied. "Strangely enough, I don't seem to care."

"A merry Christmas, Sir Rafe," Father Coll

declared as they slowly made their way into the courtyard. "Although Lady Katherine kept her faith in you, I was beginning to despair of your return."

Rafe's grip tightened on Katherine's shoulder. "She trusts me," he said, not a little proudly.

"And justly so," the portly priest observed as he joined them.

"I am sorry I have missed mass, Father."

"There should be time for a private celebration in the chapel before the feast is ready," Father Coll replied.

"Excellent! I must say a prayer of thanks." Rafe looked back to Giles and Dawson who were trying to get the ox to move. "I shall leave the rest to you, men," he said jovially. "I fear I would not be much help with this foot anyway. As my lady says, no dancing for me this Christmas," he finished mournfully. "And I am a very fine dancer, too."

His voice dropped to a seductive whisper. "We shall have to think of other ways to amuse ourselves."

"Shh!" Katherine chided, nudging him. "Father Coll!"

Thankfully the priest seemed unaware of Rafe's seductive remark.

They entered the hall, and Rafe halted in stunned surprise. "Why, this is excellent!" he cried softly, surveying the brightly lit, cozily warm hall. Already the servants had it decorated with holly, ivy, evergreen boughs and mistletoe. The scent of hot bread, roasted meat and mulled wine filled his nostrils.

Rafe pulled her close. "Father," he said, addressing the priest without taking his eyes from his beloved, "will you give us a marriage blessing today?"

"Of course, my son!" Father Coll cried, his mouth drawing upward into a smile and his eyes twinkling merrily.

Rafe plucked a sprig of mistletoe from the basket held by a startled Hildegard and held it over Katherine's head as he bent to kiss her. "Merry Christmas, my gift, my prize, my love," he whispered.

"Merry Christmas," she murmured as she lifted her smiling face.

His belly shaking with a delighted chortle, Father Coll placed his finger meditatively beside his nose. "Merry Christmas and may God bless us all," he murmured with happy satisfaction.

SHARI ANTON's husband is convinced she plans holidays around doing historical research, which means visiting every Civil War re-enactment, medieval fair and pioneer cemetery she can find. Shari graciously concedes he might be right, while noticing that he doesn't mind when they can take the Harleys to get there!

When not writing, Shari is usually playing with her grandchildren. She lives in southeastern Wisconsin, is a member of the RWA and WisRWA, and loves to hear from readers. You can write to her at PO Box 510611, New Berlin, WI 53151-0611, USA.

Christmas at Wayfarer Inn

Shari Anton

To the composers of love songs,
especially the medieval troubadours,
whose lyrics are quoted in the story.

Happy holidays!

Chapter One

GRACE BREWER detested the odious chore of chopping wood, but hated the option of freezing to death.

She tossed her woolen cloak on the woodpile, scattering a dusting of snowflakes. With the long-handled ax in hand, she hoped this might be the last time she must split large chunks of wood into hearth-sized pieces.

Her white-haired father steadied her first victim on the chopping block, then shuffled back several paces out of harm's way. Though she'd taken over the chore two years ago, her aim still suffered. One never knew where a shard of wood might fly.

Nay, she'd not miss this chore, nor the other back-straining tasks necessary to keep the Wayfarer Inn open. Still, after selling the inn, she'd miss the only home she'd ever known. 'Twas the best home Watt and Nelda Brewer, her aging parents, had known, too. Both loved the inn they'd purchased shortly after their marriage. Unfortunately, their only offspring didn't possess the vigor to keep up with the work. Nor had she summoned the courage to tell her parents they must sell out, having decided they deserved a last Yuletide in their beloved inn before confronting the inevitable changes to come.

Grace swung the blade in a decent arc. The edge bit too far to the right. A shard shot toward her father, landing at his feet. With his good arm, he picked up the piece fit only for kindling and tossed it into a large basket.

"Your mother ready to go to the ovens yet?" he asked.

Grateful he rarely commented on her poor aim, Grace answered, "Not yet. She was kneading the dough when I came out."

He nodded approval. "Good. We need extra victuals and heat for tonight. Storm coming up. Heavy snow brings guests. Mayhap tonight we will fill all the pallets above stairs."

"Mayhap." Though Grace echoed the sentiment, she knew better than to hope for such a miracle.

She trusted his prediction of snow: the ache in Watt Brewer's knees rarely proved wrong. But she wouldn't bet a copper on filling more than a pallet or two—not, she thought ruefully, that she had a spare coin to wager. Too few travelers stopped these days to sample the fare, quaff a mug of Nelda Brewer's heady ale, or rest weary bones on an upstairs pallet.

Grace knew the lack of patrons was her fault. She

simply wasn't the son her parents should have had late in life—instead of the daughter they'd been given—to care for them in their old age. And not a pretty, sweet-tempered daughter, either, capable of attracting a hardworking, pleasantly disposed husband to take over the business.

She'd been betrothed once, to Rob, the youngest of the blacksmith's sons, thinking him a decent choice until realizing he planned to spend his days in the taproom sampling the ale. When informed she expected him to work, he promptly broke the betrothal and ran off with the miller's daughter. Grace knew it mean-spirited, but she wished them the joy of each other.

She ignored the burn in her arms and sweat on her brow. From down the lane in the village square she heard the merry laughter of children at play. Countering the tykes' laughter, angry geese honked in the butcher's yard, making her heart ache. While she yearned to buy the plumpest goose for Christmas supper, Grace shook off the fanciful wish.

Only five days hence, the holiday would be a meager one. She and her parents would attend Mass, visit with the parish priest and the other villagers, then come home to bowls of thin stew and slices of brown bread and yellow cheese. Soon after, the goat would need milking and the mule want feeding, and that most holy of days would succumb to the patter of any other day at the inn.

Her father bent over to pick up a piece of wood. Grace heard the unmistakable sound of ripping cloth. His breeches. This time not in the seam. She withheld a groan.

"Time to don your new breeches, Father."

"Hellfire." He rubbed at his bared rump where the cloth had given way. "I were saving them for when the weather turned cold."

"'Tis cold enough. Go change."

He gathered up what wood he could carry and grumbled all the way to the door of the taproom. Grace sighed and leaned the ax against the woodpile, her arms weary, her conscience burdened.

Sweet heaven, she loved her parents so very much, but no matter how hard or long she worked, she couldn't keep up. Best for all to sell the inn and purchase a retirement for her parents from Glaxton Abbey. They'd be given a small but comfortable hut and the monks would see to their well-being.

As for herself, perhaps the new owner of the Wayfarer Inn would allow her to stay, serve ale and food in exchange for her pallet on the storeroom floor. If not, then she'd need to find work in another inn, hopefully in a nearby village or town.

"Hail, milady! Have you room for a very hungry, much misused traveler."

Grace spun around to the question asked by a deep, rich male voice. A tall, inordinately handsome man led a magnificent but limping white horse across the inn's yard. Out of habit, she assessed this would-be patron who sauntered toward her.

Wrapped against the weather in a knee-length beaver cloak, he held the reins with black leather riding gloves. Boots to match molded to his calves.

A man of means, she judged him, given the quality of both horse and garments. Not a knight, for he wore no chain mail or sword. Not a noble, for he traveled without escort.

He pushed back his hood, revealing shoulder-skimming hair of sable, a high brow and eyes of sparkling amber. His lush mouth curved upward in an enchanting smile. A charmer.

The warm stirring low in her belly brought her up short and made her frown. Over the years she'd dealt with her share of charmers, rebuffed their advances and managed to escape unscathed. Her father hadn't been so fortunate. Grace quickly squelched the flash of guilt over the incident that had robbed her father of full use of his right arm.

Or perhaps she wasn't being fair. This man might prove of a chivalrous bent, possessed of courtly manners and generous with his coin. One could hope. Either way, she couldn't afford to turn away a paying guest. Perhaps a plump goose for Christmas wasn't beyond reach after all.

"Pallet and a meal costs tuppence." She waved toward the stable. "Another copper to shelter and feed your horse."

He stopped a mere pace before her. His smile faltered. "Ah, therein lies my problem. I have no coin."

The sad state of her purse didn't allow for charity.

"Glaxton Abbey is but two leagues east. The monks will grant you a night of hospitality."

"For myself, I would continue on." He reached down to rub at his horse's leg. "Yseult's injury will not suffer the strain of the walk, I fear. Mayhap we can agree on some other payment."

Against her better judgment, she asked, "Such as?"

His smile returned full force. He bowed low, with a courtly flourish. "I am Alaine, minstrel of some renown. Mayhap you have heard of me."

"Nay." Now she knew why he had no money. Minstrels wandered among the nobles' grand manors and castles, entertaining lords and ladies for the price of a meal and pallet, earning only what coin an appreciative guest might toss his way. A frivolous way to make one's way in the world. Though Alaine must not have done too badly. His horse would bring a fine price.

"Well, then, mayhap you have heard a ballad or two

that I wrote. My music is much sung by other minstrels and courtiers."

"Minstrels and courtiers do not often grace our taproom. I fear your renown has not reached our ears."

He stepped forward and leaned toward her, too close, sending shivers down her spine to the tips of her toes. Sweet heaven, those eyes! Pure amber gems, enticing and mesmerizing, luring her into a sweet befuddlement she didn't dare allow.

"Mayhap 'tis time you heard my songs," he said. "What say I entertain you for my bed and bread this night, with tales of knights brave and ladies fair, and the kisses they steal in the moonlight? Truly, I am very skilled at chansons de geste."

He thought to sing her love songs and steal a kiss, perhaps more, in the moonlight, did he? 'Twas galling Alaine thought her so easily swayed with the promise of a love song, and twice over annoying that she briefly considered the offer.

She needed money, not pretty songs.

"Unless your song has the power to lure a goose into my soup pot, then I must decline."

He gave a resigned sigh. "You turn me away then."

"This is a business, not a charity." To her own ears, she sounded a fishwife, but stood firm. Her parents' needs came first, not those of a wandering minstrel, not even during a season of goodwill.

Alaine gave his horse a gentle pat. "Might I beg favor for Yseult? I promise to return for her, coin due in hand, after Twelfth Night."

Grace thought to say nay, then changed her mind. Father wouldn't mind caring for the horse, nor would the expense be great. And if Alaine didn't return for the mare, she could sell it for a goodly sum of money.

"She may stay. Come, we will put her in a stall."

At the gate, he reached for the latch, to find it broken. He took a long look around him and frowned his disapproval.

Grace hurriedly reassured him. "The building is sturdy, and I will fix the latch anon. Your horse will be safe with us."

He didn't look so much convinced as resigned. "Perhaps I might fix the latch before I leave."

She wasn't about to argue. "If you wish."

Grace fetched a bucket of oats. Alaine led Yseult into the stall and removed his packs from the horse's rump. She assumed one pack held his possessions. The other was oddly shaped, rousing her curiosity.

As if he heard her silent question, Alaine opened the pack and pulled out the most beautifully crafted lute she'd ever set eyes on.

"Shall I play you a song?"

Oh, 'twas tempting to listen to the lute's lovely voice! But she had no time for frivolous pleasures.

"My thanks, but nay. You must be on your way and I have wood to chop."

He removed his cloak, revealing a sapphire woolen tunic that draped lovingly from his broad shoulders. A belt of gold links cinched his trim waist. A fine figure of a man, was Alaine.

Grace didn't want to know what his glittering belt was worth. A gift from a noblewoman, perhaps? She'd heard of how minstrels sometimes dedicated songs to wealthy women and were rewarded in return. Surely no song was worth such a prize.

"A few moments more will not matter." He removed his gloves to expose long-fingered hands, which he then wrapped around the lute's neck. "Just one song?"

She shouldn't give in, but when he plucked at the strings to play a melody so soft and sweet, her resistance weakened. "A short song, perhaps?"

He smiled. "As milady wishes."

The lute's voice filled the stable; the bright melody lightened her heart. Then Alaine sang, his deep, clear voice a pleasing contrast to the lute's lilt.

She didn't understand the words. He sang in French, the language of noble courts and the songs of minstrels. Grace knew enough French phrases to serve the needs of the few nobles who stopped at the inn, but no more. Still she closed her eyes to better absorb the music flowing around her, allowed her spirit to rise at the beauty of it all.

When the last note resonated in the stable's beams, Alaine stated, "Mayhap I pleaded my case badly."

The spell broke abruptly. Prepared for another plea for charity, Grace scolded herself for giving him the chance. "Have you found coins in your pack?"

"Nay, but I believe I offered you the wrong bargain." He waved toward the gate. "The latch needs repair. Several boards in here beg a nail or two. Surely, there are other tasks about the place I can do to earn my bed and bread."

So many she couldn't count. If the minstrel was willing to trade true labor for his supper, she knew exactly the task to give him, which might be worth thinning tonight's stew to stretch for one more person.

"There is wood to chop."

He hesitated for a moment before he said, "Done."

The minstrel propped his lute against the side of the stall before following her outside and over to the woodpile. He picked up the ax, held it out as a knight might test the heft and balance of a sword, then ran a thumb across the blade. The wood on the block yielded easily to his mighty, well-aimed swing. He made it look so easy.

"You have done this before," she commented, unable to hide her chagrin.

He laughed lightly. "Oh, aye, though I admit not for a long time. 'Tis a thing one never forgets how to do."

The wistful note in his voice made her wonder if the chore brought forth some special memory. She'd not ask, though, fearing becoming overly friendly. 'Struth, she'd made too many allowances for him already.

Grace pulled on her cloak and gathered the wood he cut. Within minutes her arms were laden with more than she could cut in an hour.

"Father will come out to help you gather and haul."

Alaine didn't comment, just put another chunk on the block. Grace headed for the taproom.

The mellow odor of ale-soaked oak welcomed her inside. She crossed the dirt floor, winding her way among tables and benches to the far end where her father fed the fire. He tilted his head, listening, confused.

"I hear chopping."

Grace dumped the wood into the hearth-side crate. "We have a guest with no money. He does the chopping in return for bed and bread and to stable his injured horse until after Twelfth Night."

"A fair bargain."

"So I thought. I told him you would come out to help gather what he cuts." She brushed her hands clean. "His name is Alaine, claims to be a minstrel of some renown. He plays a lute and, I must admit, possesses a fair voice."

Her father's eyes narrowed sharply. "You set a lute player to chopping wood? Hellfire, what if he should harm his hands?"

Father scurried out of the inn before she could comment that Alaine didn't seem worried overmuch about his hands.

Grace headed for the kitchen, where brown flour coated most of the worktable and the floor—and Nelda Brewer, who hummed a bawdy drinking song while shaping mounds of dough into round loaves. A wide streak of flour smudged Mother's prominent cheekbone. Tiny and fragile, her mother wasn't neat, but baked the best bread and brewed the heartiest ale in the village.

Deciding she had time to fetch water before the bread was ready to haul to the communal oven, Grace grabbed a bucket. "I am off to the well, Mother. Need you anything from the village?"

"Nay, dearest. Think you we might hang holly when you return? The taproom sorely lacks for color and 'tis nearly Christmas."

Mother tended to hang holly from nearly every beam. Grace couldn't begrudge her mother the pleasure, no matter the work.

"After the bread is baked. Will that serve?"

"Bread first, then holly. 'Tis sensible."

Grace hurried out of the inn. On her way to the village well she glanced toward the woodpile—and stopped.

Alaine and Father engaged in seemingly amused conversation. A few of the village children had gathered to gawk at the stranger. Likely the village maidens would gather, too, when word spread that a handsome bare-chested minstrel chopped wood in the inn's yard.

Sweet mercy, Alaine was glorious to look upon. Sweat glistened on his smooth, wide chest and sinewy arms. A magnificently sculpted male with an enchanting smile. A danger to females everywhere. If Alaine didn't don his tunic soon, she'd have to beat the innocents off with a broom handle until their fathers came to fetch them.

Of course, if the fathers came, they might shoo their daughters home but stay to visit with Watt. And purchase an ale or two. A good thing.

Water bucket swinging at her side, Grace strode up the lane, pausing long enough to inspect the butcher's geese and hope Alaine shunned his tunic for a little while longer.

Chapter Two

THE INNKEEPER'S daughter was named Grace.

While half listening to Watt beg pardon for his daughter's audacity, Alaine watched Grace stroll toward the heart of the village, appreciating the seductive sway of her hips. Always one to mark the finer qualities of a woman's attributes, he freely admitted he'd not seen finer in an age. Lush curves, sapphire eyes, golden hair. The type of woman to whom minstrels paid tribute in the love ballads.

A hard woman, that one, or so she wanted him to believe. But Grace possessed a gentler nature than the straight spine and stoic manner she presented to the world.

In the stable, while he sang, she'd let down her guard. She'd closed her eyes filled with weariness. The thin line of her mouth eased. Beautiful. Exquisitely so.

Then she'd become the inn's caretaker again and set him to chopping wood, a task he hadn't attended to since his days as a squire in his uncle's castle. A squire in need of building muscle and learning discipline.

"Have you a noble house in which to entertain this Christmas?" Watt asked.

Alaine again hefted the ax, determined to cut enough wood so Grace would have no complaint of him when she returned.

"I do. Darby Castle, yet two days north if I must walk, and I suppose I must." A hardship he'd endure to spare his horse. Yseult had proved dependable and loyal, qualities he admired in men as well as horses. "Have you an unguent that might ease the strained muscle in my mare's leg?"

"Nay, but likely the smithy will." Watt waved a hand at the group of lads. "Hail, Thomas! Fetch the smithy for me."

A towheaded boy nodded and sped up the road so rutted that Yseult had misstepped and twisted her leg a few leagues back. If not for the incident, he'd be well along the road to Darby and the comfort of his uncle's grand hall. Instead, he was stranded at the Wayfarer Inn, doing menial work to earn a crust of bread and a likely lice-riddled pallet for the night.

Alaine sliced through a chunk of wood. "I suppose now I must perform some chore for the smithy to pay for the unguent."

Watt scratched his head. "Mayhap not. There be a copper or two in the money box to pay for the unguent."

A copper or two Watt didn't have to spare, judging from the looks of the place. "I wish to cause you no hardship."

Watt smiled brightly. "Lad, you will more than earn your keep tonight with your lute." He glanced at the woodpile where Alaine had tossed his tunic and belt. "How is it you carry no coin? You have done well for yourself. Hellfire, those gold links must be worth a knight's ransom."

Watt overguessed the belt's worth. A knight's ransom cost a suit of chain mail, a horse, a sword and shield. Alaine had both given and received ransom during his tournament days, thankfully now behind him. Of course, if he hadn't fought in the tourneys, then he'd not now have Yseult.

"The belt was a gift of thanks, from a countess whose guests I entertained last Easter." Chagrined, Alaine admitted, "I fear I misjudged upon leaving London. I thought I would have no need of coin, so left my money purse with…a trustworthy friend."

Alaine was relieved he'd caught his wagging tongue. 'Twould be a mistake to tell Watt that he'd left his money with the king's exchequer, a fine, trustworthy fellow he'd known since childhood. Peasants, even

well-to-do peasants, tended to stand off in awe, or re-
vulsion, when they learned of his rank. Best he keep
his nobility to himself.

Watt shrugged a shoulder, his left. The man's right
arm hung limp, rarely moving. Something had
happened to rob Watt of the arm's use. 'Twas why
Grace cut wood and mended latches, usually a man's
work—because her father couldn't.

"A man should always have a coin or two at
hand," Watt mused, "if only to purchase an ale along
his journey."

Alaine chuckled. "Spoken like a true innkeeper."

"Nearly my whole life. Ah, the smithy comes."

Watt shuffled across the yard toward the burly man
coming up the road, patting a youngster on the head
as he passed the children. More of the young ones had
gathered. A group of wide-eyed older girls now stood
near the gate, females much too young to be of any
interest to him. He preferred his female companions
older, more worldly and lushly curved.

The lushly curved innkeeper's daughter hadn't
returned as yet, so he'd best get back to his chore
before she did. Alaine easily swung into the rhythm of
placing a log on the chopping block, splitting it in half,
knocking the pieces off to the side to begin the process
over again.

How much wood need he chop? Were both taproom

and upper floor heated? He hoped so, for that's where his pallet would lie, upstairs in a large room with pallets lining the walls.

At Darby Castle, he'd have a room of his own with a large bed and charcoal brazier. He'd not have to worry about bugs in the straw mattress or wonder if the linens were clean. He'd spend his days catching up on the lives of those he loved there, and his nights strumming his lute for his uncle's guests.

'Twas more than an honor to be invited. Though he'd plied his chosen profession at manors and castles throughout England and France, 'twas the first time the man who'd been like a father to him had issued an invitation to sing at Darby for Christmas.

Matthew of Darby hadn't been pleased when Alaine put down the sword and picked up the lute. Mayhap, on this visit, his uncle would show some acceptance of his nephew's choice. Alaine could think of no other reason he'd been asked to provide the entertainment for the castle's many and highborn Christmas guests. Still, he needed to hear Matthew say the words, or see some sign in his manner, to be sure of the conjecture.

His arm and back muscles began to burn. Sweat trickled from his brow down the side of his face. Not in an age had he worked this hard, for this long. He rarely raised a sweat, not even when sparring sword to sword with the knights of the noble households where he entertained. 'Twould be good to be home, to cross swords with old friends.

However, for tonight he'd rest in a village he knew not the name of, at a place called Wayfarer Inn, with a friendly innkeeper and his comely daughter for company. This eve, his lute would lure patrons into the taproom. Ale would flow and coins pass into Grace's hands. Then, mayhap, she'd realize that his songs were worth more to her than a stack of chopped wood.

She liked the way he sang, though 'twould be more enjoyable for her if she understood the words. He knew a few songs he could sing that Grace might wholly understand. The rowdy drinking songs came to mind naturally. But of ballads, of love songs, there were few which yielded easily to English.

"The Wish of Aucassin," perhaps? Grace had enjoyed the music earlier.

He softly hummed a few lines, swiftly replacing French with English. Settled on the translation, he sang aloud to test the phrasing.

> "In paradise what would I do?
> Therein I'd fain not enter.
> But let me have my Nicolette,
> my fair sweet friend I love so."

Ah, a good match.

'Twas the silence he heard. Alaine let the ax fall to his side and glanced about the inn's yard. A full crowd, male and female, young and old, all stood about quietly listening.

Grace, too. She stood in the inn's shadow, the water bucket at her feet. Had Grace ever been a man's fair sweet friend, as Nicolette had been lover to Aucassin?

Alaine pushed aside the irritating thought of Grace granting favors to any man who might pay the price, as some innkeeper's daughters or serving wenches were wont to do. He couldn't imagine Grace doing so, yet he had no trouble envisioning himself kissing those lips of burgundy, nuzzling in the silken skin of her neck, enjoying the softness of her curves and more.

Grace sauntered toward him. An enticing fantasy sprang full to life and heated his loins, the result of his wayward thoughts bulging in his breeches.

Her eyes widened slightly; a light blush bloomed on her cheeks. She looked her fill, leaving Alaine to wonder if she liked what she saw. Her tongue wetted her lower lip, sending him into throes of agony.

"You sang the same song for me earlier, did you not?" she asked softly.

"Aye," was all he could answer.

She smiled then, warm and full. "You have cut an

abundance of wood, more than I anticipated. Mayhap you should come inside to warm yourself, and rest."

He wasn't cold, basking in her smile.

Resisting the temptation to ask if she'd rest beside him, Alaine measured how much wood lay on the ground against what he'd intended to chop. He'd gone beyond his goal while lost in his thoughts and music. Not unusual. 'Twas easy to lose track of time when the notes and words flowed through his head.

"If you are content that I fulfill my part of our bargain, then I shall be more than pleased to set aside the ax."

"I am content."

He leaned the ax against the woodpile and grabbed his tunic and belt. An audible sigh wafted across the yard. One of the girls near the gate blushed red at the crowd's ensuing laughter.

"You have made an impression," Grace commented, barely containing her amusement.

"'Twas not my intent to impress, at least not this way, and not a willow wisp of a girl." Time to test the waters of Grace's interest. "However, if *you* were to sigh so forthrightly, I might never don the garment again."

She never blinked an eye. "I do not sigh."

"Never?"

"I have not yet found a man worthy of my sighs."

Grace turned her back on him and sauntered toward

the inn, leaving Alaine to wonder if she'd just warned him off or issued a challenge.

Under her mother's direction, Grace hung holly branches. The decorations brightened her mood, as did the outcome of this morn's events in the yard.

As she hoped would happen, several of the village men stayed to visit with her father. They had already downed several mugs of ale while conversing around a trestle table.

Not Alaine, though. He'd come into the inn, hauled his packs up the stairs and donned an obviously older tunic of earthen brown. He now sat off by himself with quill and parchment, busily writing.

Grace dearly wanted to peek over his shoulder to see what he wrote. Her curiosity nagged hard, but she stayed far away, too embarrassed to approach him. 'Struth, she'd been shameless in her inspection of him this morn. She may not have sighed, but her thoughts had drifted decidedly wanton when his lust manifested itself.

Men had looked at her with lust before, become aroused in her presence. A couple had become violent when she rebuffed their advances. Ever since the last miscreant so badly wounded her father, the evidence of a man's randy nature evoked either disgust or fear. Not this morn, not with Alaine. Her body responded in kind, female to male, with an urgency that should scare her witless but didn't in the least.

Alaine wanted the same thing all those other men wanted. A romp on her pallet.

Truly, she hadn't known before this morn how compelling the urge to join bodies could be. She hadn't known the call to mate could muddle one's mind, direct one's tongue. Not until she saw Alaine nearly naked and aroused had she understood how swift and sharp her own response could bloom. She'd gone hot and wet within the space of a breath.

Not good at all.

'Twas because she'd never seen so fine a male body before, she was sure. Alaine's handsome face and enchanting smile only made him more appealing. That his pure, deep voice could lure the fish out of their ponds added to the enticement.

Yet here Alaine sat, fully garbed, deep in quiet thought, and she couldn't look at him without feeling the tug on her innards. Her fingers fair itched to skim those broad shoulders, entangle in his hair. She *wanted* to sit on his lap, his face buried in her bosom, his hands roaming to forbidden places.

"What of over here, Gracie?" her mother called. "Shall we hang some holly on these beams?"

Naturally Mother had drifted to the corner where Alaine sat writing. His head came up when she neared his table, those lovely amber eyes aglitter with…what? Excitement? Amusement? She wasn't sure, but whatever made his eyes light up, she wished it would fade. The flutter in her stomach wasn't from lack of food, she knew, because she'd already eaten two pieces of the freshly baked bread in a vain attempt to quell the hunger.

"I believe I have finished," he said. "Care to hear?"

He'd written a song! "Certes."

"I shall get my lute."

Before she could tell him to just sing, he was up and off toward the stairs. She blew out her impatience and tried to concentrate on the task at hand. Hanging greenery. She took the holly from her mother's outstretched hand.

To hang the holly over the beam, she used the bench Alaine had sat on, proud of herself for not looking at the parchment still on the table. She'd rather hear the words sung.

The bench wasn't all that steady, but then none other in the inn would suit better. Mother had tied three branches together to form a vine. Grace draped the vine around her neck and eased her way up, careful of her balance, then tossed an end of the vine over a beam. To her relief, it caught tight and held.

Alaine's footsteps pounded down the stairs. He stopped in the middle of the room and stared at her, so hard she felt naked, markedly uncomfortable in a room where too many people witnessed his regard.

After too long a moment, she had to ask, "Is something amiss?"

He crossed the room slowly, put his lute on the table.

"I was thinking that every man should have the privilege of watching a beautiful woman hang greenery. You appear an enticing gift all wrapped up in the holly."

Stunned, Grace couldn't think of a thing to say. Her mother had no such trouble.

"Ah, ain't you the gallant one, Alaine. Tsk, must come from all those ballads you know."

Alaine smiled at Nelda. "A gallant knight always takes a moment to pay compliments to a lady's beauty, and to offer his assistance should she be in distress."

To Grace's dismay, he wrapped his large, warm hands around her waist. If he leaned forward, and not too far forward at all, his mouth would touch her breast. She shivered, and knew he felt her tremble.

"Finish your chore so you can come down," he said.

"Truly, I am not in distress." Or hadn't been until he'd put his hands on her. "I need no assistance."

He looked so deep into her eyes he touched her core. "Mayhap not, but I intend to hold fast," he stated, then lowered his voice to just above a whisper.

"I should hate to see you fall and the lovely package I behold become bloodied."

Why did Alaine affect her so? Why this minstrel who made his home wherever he happened to be, who relied upon the fickle generosity of others to make his way in the world? Why had she never felt this incredible pull toward a man better suited to her needs, one who found enjoyment in cutting wood and fixing latches, in settling into a quiet life of home and family?

How terribly unfair!

She hurriedly tossed the holly over the other beam. "You may let go now."

He didn't. "Put your hands on my shoulders."

He meant to help her down. She hesitated.

"You need not fear, Grace. I would not let any harm come to you."

Too late, a small voice within her cried. She placed her hands on the broad shoulders she'd longed to touch. So strong, so sturdy. His eyes darkened when he lifted her as if she were light as thistledown. By the time her feet touched the floor, she could barely breathe. His hands lingered on her waist.

Grace searched for a way to break the tension sizzling between them. "Your song."

He let go of her then and took up his lute. With one foot planted on the bench, Alaine cradled the instrument firmly against him. 'Twas ridiculous to be jealous of a lute.

Her mother settled onto a nearby bench. The men gathered at the trestle table fell silent.

Alaine played the melody now becoming familiar, heard first in the stable then in the yard. He sang of a knight yearning for the favor of his sweet fair friend, of their disapproving fathers, of escape together to a land of adventure, of a long, forced separation. And at the end, of how Aucassin and his Nicolette returned home to find acceptance and happiness, together and forever, the reward due their true love.

Her mother sighed. The men stomped their feet and banged their ale cups on the table. One of them tossed a copper at Alaine, who caught it and graciously bowed his thanks.

Grace wondered what it might be like to be so deeply and thoroughly loved as had been Nicolette by her gallant Aucassin.

Chapter Three

ALAINE sat at the table and listened to the villagers complain about the rents and labor due their overlord. He lightly fingered the lute strings and kept his mouth firmly closed.

He knew well how the system worked. This village was owned by Lord Thorpe, who lived in a manor nearby. From planting time until after harvest, the villagers owed a day or two of work each week in the lord's fields. Alaine had heard complaints from his uncle about how tenants shirked their duties. 'Twas the first time he'd heard the argument firsthand from the other side.

The smithy leaned toward a farmer. "'Struth, John, if you would take a whetstone to that plow of yours, the planting would not be so hard on your ox team, and you would be spared sixpence fine every year."

"I sharpen the blade every winter!"

"Then mayhap you do it wrong."

"And I suppose you could do better?"

The other men at the table groaned. The smithy tossed his hands in the air, giving up the argument. Alaine smiled at the farmer's suddenly chagrined expression. All knew the smithy could do better.

Watt gave John a friendly slap on the back. "Methinks the ale has affected your wits."

"Aye, well, Nelda always did make a heady brew." Alaine strummed the lute.

"A cup of ale, a maiden's kiss, 'twill weaken the mind, but leads to bliss!"

To the sound of the men's appreciative laughter, Alaine glanced toward the kitchen, where a particular maiden had hastened off to after he sang the ballad.

She'd said not a word, simply left the taproom, leaving Alaine to wonder if something in the song offended her, but couldn't for the life of him figure out what. Fascinating creatures, women. Just when a man thought he knew what would please them all, one proved him short of the mark. Of course, Grace wasn't like most women he knew. Her hands bore the redness of labor. She dressed in the drab, rough-weave wool of peasantry, not the colorful, smooth silk of nobility.

What might please a woman who toiled daily to survive? He'd already chopped wood and mended a latch for her. What else could he do? Bah, he was a minstrel, not a woodcutter or carpenter or innkeeper.

He'd have a smile out of Grace tonight with one of his songs or he had no right to call himself a minstrel.

"What say you, smithy? Will I ride on the morrow or walk?"

"Walk. You could probably take the mare with you, but on a lead. Best not put added weight on her leg for several days."

"'Twould be better if I left her in Watt's care, then."

"Aye, especially if Watt's knees foretell the snow rightly."

"My knees never lie," Watt stated. "At least we will not send you on your way with an empty belly, Alaine. I told Grace to sacrifice an old hen, make pies of it."

The smith wagged a finger at Watt. "Blessed you are with such a daughter. If my Rob possessed a dram of sense…"

Watt held up a staying hand. "Quietly, if you will. I do not think Grace has forgiven your son yet."

"Nor have I. Lucky am I she does not hold the son's idiocy against the father." The smith heaved his bulk from the bench. "Time to get the rest o' my chores done so my good wife allows me out tonight to hear your lute again, minstrel. 'Tis rare we have such fine entertainment of a winter's night."

The other men rose and echoed the smith's sentiments. Alaine assured them he'd play again after supper, restraining his curiosity over Grace and the smith's son, wondering if Grace had suffered a hurt of the heart. How recent? How deep?

Watt no more than closed the door behind his friends when Nelda ran into the room, screeching.

"Rats!" Nelda hiked up her skirts and climbed atop a trestle table. "Oh, Watt, there be rats in the kitchen!"

Thwap! Thwap!

"Nelda, come down!" Watt ordered, his attention divided between his terrified wife and sounds of the chase coming from the kitchen.

Alaine laid his lute on the table. "Care for your wife, I will see to Grace."

Grace stood near the worktable, armed with a broom. A mouse darted from beneath a stool, hoping to escape into the taproom.

Thwap!

With the mouse trapped under the broom, Grace looked so proud of herself Alaine had to smile.

"You have done this before." His comment startled her, surprise wiping away her pride. He wished he'd kept quiet.

"Far too many times for my peace of mind." She eased the pressure on the broom. The mouse lay still. "Trouble is, I no more than get rid of one and another finds his way in."

Alaine picked the rodent up by the tail. "Do you know where they come in?"

CHRISTMAS AT WAYFARER INN

"Aye. They burrow their way into the storeroom. They think the grain sacks their private larder."

"Let me get rid of this fellow and we will have a look at his doorway."

Alaine hustled out the back door and tossed the mouse into the shrubbery at the back of the yard. A scoop of snow and quick wipe against his tunic served as a wash for the nonce. When he again entered the kitchen, Grace was plucking chicken feathers.

"My thanks," she said. "I do not mind swatting mice so much as I dislike disposing of them."

"Shall we plug their doorway so you need not swat?"

She glanced at the storeroom. "Later, perhaps. I need to ready this chicken first or we will have a very late supper."

He shrugged a shoulder. "Then show me where it is and I can plug while you pluck."

Her mouth pursed, she pulled out a feather with more force than necessary. "You are a guest, Alaine, have earned your meal by chopping the wood. You need do no more."

True enough. So why did plugging a mouse hole seem a vital task for him to perform?

"Consider the service done in payment for Yseult's stay in the stable tonight."

Grace's shoulders sagged. She glanced at the arch between the kitchen and the taproom. "Father is displeased with me for the bargain we made. He'd be truly disheartened if you should get so much as a sliver in your hand. I will not ask it of you."

Stubborn woman. He crossed the room and laid his hands on her shoulders. A delightful warmth shot through his veins. He struggled to not respond to her shudder, to the sensual glow that brightened her sapphire eyes.

"You do not ask—I offer. My hands will suffer no harm."

She closed her eyes, took a long breath, then wetted her lower lip. What meager possession he retained of his senses prevented him from pulling her against him, kissing a mouth that begged a man's kiss. She opened eyes still bright with the awareness of what little space separated their bodies, of his hands on her shoulders.

"If you insist, then I will show you."

She slipped away. He took a moment before following her into the storeroom, a moment needed to regain his composure.

Grace pointed toward the back wall behind a barrel that, given the odor, held salted fish. "Back there. You can see the hole readily enough. Here, let me get my pallet out of your way."

She grabbed hold of the straw-stuffed sack of heavy linen that served as her bed and pulled it across the room.

Alaine stared at it, realizing that in this room, on

that pallet, Grace stretched out to sleep at the end of her workday. In this tiny room, with the salted fish, a grain sack and various kegs and crates, Grace unbraided her golden hair and stripped down to her chemise to take her rest.

A beautiful lady deserved a maid to attend her, scented oils for her bath and lotions for her hands, should sleep on a down-filled mattress. Grace had none of these, nor could he give them to her. But he'd ensure no more mice disturbed her slumber if he had to build a whole damn wall to do it. And while he was about the work, he'd try to banish the vision of himself stretched out on that pallet beside Grace.

With the evening came the snow her father's knees had foretold. Grace only knew the state of the weather because each person who entered the inn shook snowflakes off an outer garment before settling onto a bench.

She didn't have time to see how much snow had fallen. She barely had time to keep all of the ale cups full.

The inn hadn't seen such a crowd in many a month. Most of the village's men had wandered in to listen to Alaine's music.

The object of their curiosity perched on a tabletop, singing a song about a dairymaid's amorous adventures in a meadow. As minstrels were wont to do, he'd placed a cup on the floor at his feet to collect tributes.

She couldn't begrudge him the coppers tossed into his cup, not when the money box behind the counter now contained enough coins to actually jingle.

Certes, how could she begrudge anything of the man who worked for over an hour to prevent the mice from nibbling on her last sack of grain? The same man who'd eaten two meat pies, proclaimed the simple meal tastier than that he'd been served in an earl's castle. She suspected he overstated, but the compliment stayed with her even now, several hours later.

'Twould be handy to have a man about the place who threw himself into chores with such zeal. 'Twould be nice if the same man could lure patrons into the inn as did the minstrel. And if he could look at her as if she were ripe fruit, ready for devouring, make her tremble with desire...ah, such a fantasy.

The tanner waved his ale cup in the air. Grace grabbed the pitcher off the counter and headed across the room.

The dairymaid cavorted with her knight in a bower of crushed grass and heather, the man vowing to hold the maid precious in his heart. The song ended when the knight abandoned the maid in the grass and rode off, giving no thought to marriage. The men hooted and hollered at the knight's conquest and escape. Grace wondered how much they'd appreciate the knight's lack of honor if the maid in the song were one of their daughters.

She filled the tanner's mug. "There you are, Hugh. A tasty batch, is it not?"

"Aye, and 'tis even better when served by the most beautiful maiden in the village."

She'd heard the phrase uttered before, by nearly every man in the village who hoped for a free mug of ale. They should know better by now.

"Then mayhap I should charge more for an ale when poured by my dainty hand."

The tanner winked at her. "Ah, Grace. Someday some fortunate man will meet your price and pay it gladly. You mark my word."

Grace opened her mouth to ask what he meant, but everyone's attention turned once more on Alaine. From the lilt of the lute and the expression on his face, all knew he began another ballad. No one understood the words; no one cared.

Grace quietly made her way back to the counter and leaned against it, putting the pitcher down without a sound.

She rested her chin on her upraised fist and wished she understood the words of Alaine's song. Then again, 'twas probably best she didn't. 'Twould hurt to hear over and over about a gallant knight and his lovely lady, and of the kisses they stole in the moonlight— only to have the knight desert the lady.

Some man will meet your price.

Had she set her price too high? A man to share the work, to bear the burden of caring for her parents. An honest, decent man to laugh and cry with during the day and converse and make love with at night. Surely 'twas not too much to ask.

As often happened during the ballads, Alaine's gaze wandered her way. She no longer allowed herself to feel flattered or flustered by the attention. She was the only woman in the room besides her aged mother. Naturally, a minstrel would sing a love song to a woman. He meant nothing by it.

Grace heard the inn's door open. Two males, one a man of middling age, the other a lad, stepped inside. Their heavy woolen cloaks and fur hats were burdened with snow. She hustled over to greet the newcomers and ushered them to a table near the hearth.

They eased off their outer garments, revealing long tunics of tightly woven wool in a hue of forest-green. Nobles, Grace realized. For good service and a comfortable pallet, which Grace strove to give every patron, some nobles paid very well.

Softly she asked, "Ale? Or mayhap warm cider?"

The older man looked at her as if she'd offered him nectar from an ancient god's golden flagon. "Cider. And food. The four men of our escort are seeing to our horses. They, too, need feeding." He glanced at the crowd, pausing a longer moment on Alaine. "Have you enough pallets for all of us?"

"Pallets aplenty," she assured him. "I will fetch your cider then see to the rest."

On her way into the kitchen, she stopped to send her father out to the stable to ensure the escorts settled. Within minutes she'd readied enough cider to warm all of the newcomers through. For the nobles she warmed meat pies; to the escort she'd serve soup from the iron kettle hanging in the hearth.

By the time she carried the food and drink out to the nobles, Alaine stood near the nobles' table. The lad's eyes drooped so heavily Grace wondered if he'd stay awake long enough to eat.

The older man laughed lightly at whatever comment Alaine made, then reached for his cider. "My esteemed minstrel, I, too, have eaten at the Earl of Shrewsbury's table. No finer victuals to be found anywhere."

Alaine pointed at the pie. "That pie will change your mind. Grace, you had best heat his lordship another one straight away. He will not be able to resist."

Grace blushed at the praise, wholly unlike her. "If his lordship wishes."

"Likely I will," the man said on a sigh. "We did not stop for nooning for fear of being caught amidst the worst of the storm. Glad I am we go south, not north."

"Deep, is it?" Alaine asked.

"In places. Not impassable, but makes for hard travel."

The villagers, now aware of how bad the weather turned, finished whatever ale remained in their cups and then headed for their homes. Before going up the stairway, the noble gave her two pieces of silver.

"For your good care of us, mistress, and the incomparable meat pie," he said, then herded his son up the stairs.

Soon the inn was quiet, everyone gone to pallets—except Alaine. He strummed the lute and hummed while she wiped down the tables, too exhilarated from tonight's good fortune for sleep. The vision of roasted goose for Christmas had returned, and now she had the funds.

She poured the last of a pitcher of ale into a mug and set it down beside Alaine. He'd entertained the crowd all evening, certainly earning a free ale.

She glanced into the cup at his feet. Several copper coins winked back at her.

"You did all right for yourself."

"Enough to pay you in advance for Yseult's oats until after Twelfth Night, I should think."

A full fortnight away. After the Christmas season.

Grace eased down onto a bench. "Probably, but take the coins with you. Given the weather, you may need to stop at an inn tomorrow night."

"True." He took a sip of ale. "I cannot say I look

forward to two days' walk in the snow. But the morn is still many hours away. What say you to another song?"

"Please, not another dairymaid or shepherdess."

"As my lady wishes," he said, then strummed the lute.

Grace crossed her arms on the table, recognizing the tune. 'Twas one of the love ballads he'd directed her way all evening. Only this time no one raised a mug to distract her. No one entered the taproom to disrupt the magical spell he wove.

His gaze never strayed from her face, as if every word he sang were written for her ears alone. The inflection of his voice, the magnetism of his very presence drew her deeper into the sweet fantasy of being the lovely lady the gallant knight desired, made her vulnerable to the desire in Alaine's eyes. 'Twas both thrilling and terrifying to know her pallet lay in a small but private room only a few steps away, far from prying eyes and ears. If she took Alaine to her pallet, gave him what he wanted, no one but the two of them need ever know.

Dangerous thoughts she had no business thinking, couldn't afford to act upon.

Alaine sang the last verse, knowing he'd somehow lost Grace. The dreamy glaze in her eyes cleared. Her spine straightened.

He inwardly chided his presumption. True, that canzo had touched the hearts of many a noble maid and sometimes led to a night of passion. Grace didn't understand the words, though she'd certainly understood his intent and refused to succumb.

The innkeeper's daughter was made of sterner stuff than he'd reckoned with in a long time. And oddly enough, he wanted Grace more than any woman in memory.

Her beauty rivaled that of any woman he'd ever met. She'd gone about ensuring that a room full of people were content, with the gracious warmth sometimes lacking in women of his rank. Grace quietly went about her business without seeking praise, blushing when he complimented her on her cooking.

For all the copper in his cup, he'd failed dismally tonight. He hadn't made Grace smile.

He strummed the last cord. Grace rose from the bench, walked over to the counter and reached for something behind it.

"A lovely song," she said, coming toward him. "I would be remiss if I did not give you your due." She tossed a silver coin into his cup. "I wish you better fortune at Darby Castle than you have had during your stay here."

Last chance.

"The night is not yet over. We could—"

"Nay, minstrel, we will not."

Chapter Four

GRACE ate her cheese and bread, determined not to join in the argument. 'Struth, she didn't know whose side to take.

Alaine prepared to leave for Darby Castle. Her parents insisted he must wait another day and let other travelers trample the snow on the road first.

"Watt, I appreciate your concern, but I am already a day late."

Her father huffed. "Get yourself deep into a drift and you may not get to Darby Castle at all. You heard his lordship same as I. Snow up to his horse's knees in places. Not a good day for a long walk."

The noble and his son had already left the inn, headed south. Their comments on the road behind them only served to heighten her father's worry. Never had Grace seen him argue so pointedly with a patron's decision to continue a journey, no matter how ill-advised.

"Only in places," Alaine countered.

"Enough places where you might lose the road altogether. Then where will you be?" Father tossed his good hand in the air. "Lost, wet and frozen, that is where. Why take a foolish risk when waiting one more day will make the journey safer?"

Father's argument made sense. The road might prove treacherous. However, after what had almost happened between them last night, Grace wanted Alaine gone.

She still couldn't fathom why she had given him the silver. A penny in his cup would have made the same statement, that all she owed him for his song was payment of the same kind the others gave in tribute. She'd spent a restless night thinking about the silver. Thinking about Alaine.

Once, alone and burning in the dark, she considered going upstairs to fetch him, tell him she had changed her mind. She'd won the battle against temptation when remembering the men of the noble's escort also slept in the common room. In the dark she might very well wake the wrong man!

Best Alaine leave and remove the wanton temptation of his magnificent body and voice. Best he go before he could do her another kindness. Before she must again witness his alluring smile. Before her curiosity and restless body prodded her to lose her common sense.

Alaine swirled the cider in his cup, staring at the amber liquid that nearly matched his eyes. "I suppose a delay of one more day might be wise."

'Twould be agony.

Delighted, Mother applauded the decision. "You will play again tonight, will you not?"

Alaine flashed her a smile. "I might be persuaded."

Mother rested a hand on his forearm. "Might I also persuade you to sing one of the ballads in English, the one that begins *la dossa votz?*"

The song he sang late last night, for Grace alone, the melody and inflection pure seduction.

"Mother, you should not ask so much—"

"Madam asks nothing untoward," Alaine said, interrupting Grace's protest. "If I can find the right words to fit the melody, 'twould be a pleasure to honor her request."

Mother giggled. "How gallant of you, good sir."

Alaine dipped his head and waved his arm in as courtly a bow as she'd ever seen executed while sitting.

The two were actually flirting with each other. Well, if they wanted to trade silly pleasantries for the rest of the day, 'twas fine with her. She picked up her empty cup and tin plate, but hadn't risen from the bench before her father leaned forward.

"Grace, what is the name of the tanner's girl?"

The young lady who'd audibly sighed over

Alaine's bare-chested wielding of the ax yesterday. "Marie. Why?"

"I intend to hire her for tonight, if her folks allow."

Grace inwardly winced, both at her father's choice of hired help and the hit to her pride. Father had never before suggested she fell short when serving patrons. Nor did she want to spend any more of the profits than necessary. She'd already erred badly in giving Alaine the silver. And to have to listen to Marie sighing over Alaine...

"We managed last night, the three of us. Why hire Marie?"

"Because tonight the men will bring their families."

Grace couldn't imagine it. "The women never come into the taproom, much less the children."

"They will tonight. Best be prepared."

Alaine worked on the translation he had promised Nelda, but another verse intruded, the words chasing around in his head.

Usually a melody came to mind first, then the words to fit the rhythm and mood. This time the sentiments, a mixture of angst and joy, begged expression. Knowing what he wanted to say and the best way to say it, however, proved difficult.

He knew damn well to whom he owed the inspiration—Grace, whom he hadn't seen for most of the morning. He supposed she avoided coming into the taproom because he'd taken her father's sensible advice and stayed. She would rather he packed up his lute and left.

He certainly hadn't argued very long or hard this morning, could have been well on his way hours ago. But then he'd not have the chance to bring the smile to Grace's face he'd vowed to have of her last night.

'Twas the other thing he'd craved last night that scared her today, he was sure. His passion. His desire to touch and taste the woman with the sapphire eyes who bedeviled him yet this morn.

So where was the vixen who inspired love songs and tortured his body? Alaine went in search of a fresh dose of inspiration.

He found Grace in the stable, leaning on a pitchfork outside of Yseult's stall. She gave him a tight-lipped smile, then turned her attention back to the stall. From within, the smith's voice soothed the mare, complimenting her fine manners.

"How does she?" Alaine asked.

The smith rose and dusted his hands against each other. "The swelling eases. A few days' rest is all she needs. A prime companion you have here. Must cost you a lot to keep her."

"Aye, but she is worth the expense, and more. I

have gone without mine own supper a time or two so Yseult might have hers."

The smith laughed. "Ah, what we men do to keep the females content. Woman or mare, if treated badly, they become contrary creatures."

Grace patted Yseult's withers. "'Struth, if a female is contrary, 'tis usually some man's fault, is it not?"

Yseult tossed her head and snorted in complete agreement.

The smith lost his smile. "My apologies, Grace. I did not mean to remind you of past hurts."

Grace looked surprised by the remark. "Truly, I spoke only in general. I do believe you more upset over the matter than I."

The smith's fingers curled into his palms. "Mayhap I am. I had not thought my son so foolish."

"Have you had word from Rob?"

"Nay, not in all these months. Upsets his mother."

"So I imagine. Give your wife my greetings."

With that, Grace left the stable.

She may have fooled the smith, but not Alaine. She hurt over whatever the smith's son had done.

'Twas none of his affair. He didn't need to know what the lout of a man had done to Grace. He should let the matter be.

"What happened between Grace and your son?"

The smith gave a long sigh. "They were betrothed

for a time. I thought Rob finally coming into his proper manhood when he asked Grace to marry him. Then he came home one day as angry as a bee denied nectar, said he would not marry Grace if paid a fortune. Refused to say why. Two days later both he and the miller's daughter turned up missing."

Alaine fought his unwarranted anger without success. "Rob broke the betrothal and then ran off with another woman."

"Truth to tell, I think Grace tossed Rob out and he took consolation with Bess." The smith shrugged his shoulders. "No one knows for sure what happened because neither will tell."

Alaine spent his anger by attacking the woodpile. By the time he put the ax down, he'd chopped a month's worth of wood. Still, he doubted that if Rob should appear in the yard he'd be able to restrain his hands from wrapping around the lout's neck.

He gathered up an armful of wood to toss into the taproom's hearth. That done, he followed the sound of a knife hitting the worktable in the kitchen. Mayhap Grace's mother could shed further light on her daughter's failed betrothal. Nelda was nowhere to be found; Grace chopped turnips and wild onions, likely readying them for the always simmering soup pot in the hearth.

Come to think on it, he hadn't seen her parents all

morning, either. The entire family seemed to have disappeared when he began to work on his song.

He snitched a slice of turnip and drew a reproving
glare, Grace's sapphire eyes snapping with annoyance.
A man could drown in those eyes, sometimes calm,
sometimes stormy, too often weary. "Nearly done?"

"Nearly." She glanced at the storeroom. "I should
probably toss in some carrots, too."

"I will get them," he offered, and went into storeroom. Grace had placed her pallet back to where it
belonged, the thick mat large enough for two people.
'Twas far too easy to envision Grace sprawled on the
pallet, her unbound golden hair—

Carrots. He'd come into the storeroom for carrots.

He found a few of them readily enough, then looked
around for more. Surely there must be more in one of
the other crates. He searched, only to peer into one
empty crate after the other, which he'd half noticed yesterday and not given much thought to.

He did now, counted the meager food stores on one
hand. A half a sack of grain, a partial barrel of salted
fish, a quarter round of cheese, a crate of apples, a few
more turnips.

Jesu, with several months of winter left, there wasn't
enough food laid by to see the mice through until
spring, much less three grown people!

It hit him then that the Brewers might have truly sacrificed a hen for last night's meat pies. So why had Grace given him a silver piece last night, coin she could ill afford to part with if needed to purchase food for winter?

He returned to the kitchen and handed her the carrots. "Sparse pickings in there. Hardly enough to feed the mice."

"Thanks to you the mice will feast no more."

"Not near enough food for three grown people to last out the winter."

She began slicing. "We need only enough to last us for a few days past Christmas. With the money you helped bring in last eve, I can buy more grain and cheese. We will not starve."

"And after?"

Grace glanced at the back door, then spoke just above a whisper. "We will no longer be here. By the grace of God we shall have a buyer for the inn and enough money to purchase a retirement for my parents from Glaxton Abbey."

Sell the inn? Alaine couldn't imagine Watt and Nelda Brewer anywhere but here in the Wayfarer Inn, offering up hospitality to villagers and travelers alike.

"A hard decision for your father to make, I imagine."

She took a long breath. "I have not yet discussed it with my parents, so would appreciate your silence. They deserve one last Christmas in their home."

They deserved more, and he could well imagine

Watt refusing to bow to what was apparently Grace's decision—one Alaine found distasteful.

"Why sell?"

She paused in her chopping. "Because there is too much work for one person. My parents help out where they can, bless them, but are hampered by age and frailties. If Father could still do some of the heavy work, we might last awhile longer."

"You could hire someone to help out."

"If I had the money, I would, but I do not. The villagers are willing to help when they can, but they have their own families and work to see to. 'Tis not fair to burden them any longer. I truly have no other choice."

There were always choices. Alaine just didn't know what Grace's choices might be. Zounds, retirements at abbeys didn't come cheaply. Would the inn's sale cover the expense? He didn't know but could only assume Grace did.

"And what of you?" he asked, needing to know.

She shrugged a shoulder and took knife to carrots again. "I will decide after I see to my parents. Ouch!"

Grace stuck the tip of her forefinger in her mouth. A smear of blood marred the knife. He felt the sting as if it were his own finger sliced open.

Alaine held out his hand. "Let me see."

"'Tis nothing, merely a little cut." She turned her hand to show him. "Already the bleeding stops."

So he saw, but he grasped her hand anyway to have a closer look. No dainty miss, Grace Brewer. Her hand was chafed, had likely seen its share of cuts and slivers. A strong, long-fingered hand too accustomed to hard work. The calluses wanted for soothing, the dryness for lotion. 'Twas the most beautiful hand on God's earth.

He kissed her palm.

Her fingers curled. She shivered, wiping his mind clean of everything but the woman who stood close enough to pull into his arms. She didn't resist his tug and melded against him perfectly, igniting a yearning so deep he had to kiss her or go mad.

The light touch of lips wasn't enough. Her lush mouth moved under his, kissing him back, inviting more with a sweet innocence he found utterly enticing. Untouched and untried was the innkeeper's daughter... and a fast learner. Her arms encircled his neck. She pressed so tight against him she must feel his full, hard arousal and pounding heartbeat.

Alaine couldn't remember wanting any other woman as much as he wanted Grace. Slow and lingering or hard and fast, he didn't care. In the storeroom on her pallet or right here on the kitchen worktable, either were fine with him.

Did Grace care? Alaine didn't think so, not if he judged the depth of her desire correctly, a match to his own.

Now, if he could only ensure her parents wouldn't

walk in the kitchen door, or a patron wouldn't enter the taproom and call out to demand an ale.

Reluctantly he broke the kiss, but held her within the circle of his embrace, knowing he must let go soon. With Grace's cheek resting on his chest, he found the inspiration he'd been seeking for the next verse of his song. There could truly be no other. The declaration of love.

How odd that he had sung love songs to most of the highest ranking women in two kingdoms, and only now truly understood how it might actually feel to be in love. The pounding heartbeat, the yearning to hold and be held, to protect. The wish to give one's beloved pleasure in every way.

Tonight, without fail, he would make Grace smile.

Grace couldn't remember the last time she'd worked so hard while having so much fun.

Father had been right about the size of tonight's crowd. Men, women and children alike leaned against the taproom's counter, filled the benches and sat on the floor.

Father had hired Marie, who seemed to be having a good time pouring ale for the patrons. If only the girl wouldn't swoon whenever Alaine sang a ballad. Indeed, most of the women—even the long-married ones—went all dreamy eyed, especially the Widow Tucker. Grace wished the woman wouldn't look at Alaine as if he were honey for her bread.

As for the men, they behaved themselves admirably, drinking but not getting drunk while under the scrutiny of their families. Even the butcher, who normally must be reminded of his manners, seemed content to sip his ale and listen to the music. He'd also vowed to save her his plumpest goose in return for a dance.

Goose for Christmas. Coins aplenty for food. No more mice in the storeroom and enough chopped wood to last for weeks. All because Alaine's horse had suffered an injury, bringing the minstrel to the Wayfarer Inn's door.

And into her kitchen, and into her arms.

The kiss hadn't been a complete surprise. Sweet heaven, how she'd reveled in Alaine's tender hunger. She'd known his kiss would be pleasing, but hadn't expected her knees to weaken or her senses to take flight. If he hadn't possessed the will to pull away, to return to the taproom table where he'd been hard at work before and since, she might well have pulled him to the kitchen floor and insisted on more.

He'd give her more than kisses. Alaine would lie with her if she expressed willingness.

Her body was so willing she thought she might explode. 'Twas the niggling voice of caution that she battled.

Alaine now sang the ballad her mother wished to hear.

"I have heard the sweet voice of the wild nightingale," the song began, then went on to tell of a woman with a fickle heart and the man who suffered her misbehavior. Grace thought the ending unsatisfactory, for the woman hadn't changed her fickle ways or the man's suffering eased.

After the crowd's appreciation waned, from the back of the room a woman called out, "Another dance, kind minstrel."

Alaine laughed lightly. "I do believe I have played every dance you already know. Might I interest you in learning a new one, hardly known outside of France? 'Tis a graceful, courtly dance, the steps easily learned."

Agreement resounded through the taproom.

Alaine put his lute aside and held out his hand. "Grace, would you partner me?"

Her heart thudded against her ribs. She shouldn't. Someone might notice her attraction to Alaine, but she wasn't about to let any other woman seize the opportunity.

Alaine walked her through the steps, sometimes holding hands, others not. Bodies pressed close, then parted. Quick steps and slow, a slide and a bow. Through it all, his gaze locked with hers until she forgot other people occupied the same room.

He began to sing, putting steps and music together. Grace fair floated across the floor, sliding into Alaine's arms and out, barely aware of the other couples sampling the steps. Would that the dance could go on forever, that she might spend the rest of her life in such carefree yet thrilling style. Dancing with Alaine.

Loving Alaine.

She nearly tripped over her own feet. Her common sense screamed a denial even as her heart whispered acceptance.

For the rest of the evening Grace grappled with her wayward heart and wanton thoughts. Was it possible to fall in love so quickly, with a man she knew near to nothing about? Or was she simply as entranced as almost every other woman in the room?

Normally she wasn't swayed by a man's desire. Alaine wanted her, she knew that, but he'd also taken the time to do small kindnesses without being asked. She could talk to him easily, a rarity not to be considered lightly.

Would it be wrong to give herself to Alaine out of love when so many women married and gave themselves to their husbands out of duty? Was it shameful to share one night of bliss with the only man she might ever love and truly want to be with?

By the time the children's eyes drooped and their parents reluctantly took them home, she'd put her doubts to rest.

For one night she would play the lovely lady to Alaine's gallant knight. Falling in love with a wandering minstrel, in the unseemly haste of only a day, might be the biggest mistake of her life. Not seizing the chance to know his passion, to find out if he felt more for her than lust would be the greater regret.

After the last patron ambled off toward home, and her parents climbed the stairs to their room, Grace threw the bolt on the door and put her plan into action before she lost her nerve.

'Struth, she'd spent so many years rebuffing men's advances she'd never given a thought about how to seduce one.

Grace slowly walked toward where Alaine sat on the table that had served as his stage, amazed her outstretched hand didn't tremble or her palm sweat. 'Twas tonight or never.

"Alaine, would you partner me?"

He stood and took hold of her hand, a good beginning to Grace's way of thinking.

"Liked the new dance?" he asked.

"I did, but I do not mean for us to dance. There is…another thing for which I need a partner, if you will have me."

"Another—" His eyes went dark with understanding. "'Tis an offer no man in his right mind could resist. I will, however, if you feel the least doubt. I would not have you suffer regrets come the morn."

Fair warning of his intent to leave her on the morn,

with no obligations or regrets. No future existed for an innkeeper's daughter and a wandering minstrel, just a night of loving.

"No regrets, Alaine," she whispered, then leaned forward for the kiss to seal her fate.

Chapter Five

HE granted her wish with a tender kiss, imbued with the promise of further delight to come. 'Twas more thrilling than she anticipated and yet less than thoroughly satisfying.

Grace sensed Alaine held his passion in tight rein. Without a word he swept her up and carried her into the dark storeroom.

"Have you a candle?" he asked just above a whisper.

"Aye, somewhere." Her legs unsteady, she fetched a short candle. "Will this do?"

"For the nonce."

He left the storeroom. Grace took a long breath, knowing Alaine would come back shortly.

And then what? Sweet mercy, she ached within her woman's places. Aches Alaine would ease, she was sure.

What was taking him so long? She resisted the urge to go out and light the candle herself.

She should do *something* to prepare for his return.

The ladies in Alaine's songs sometimes "made ready" for their lovers, but the songs never said how. Nor had a one of the ladies awaited a lover in so bleak a bower as a storeroom, with only a straw pallet on which to take their pleasure.

Grace took refuge in the ritual of unbraiding her hair, the strands separating to the rake of her fingers.

She heard his footsteps and, when he walked in the door, was glad he held a lighted candle. The flame glimmered in eyes lit with approval and hunger.

Never had she felt more female.

Whatever last doubts she'd harbored over the wisdom of allowing Alaine into the privacy of her room and onto her pallet vanished with the snick of the latch.

He placed the candle on an ale keg. Grace lifted her arms, an invitation he quickly accepted by hefting her up and burying his face in her bosom. She thrilled to the strength that held her in so intimate an embrace, to the warmth of his breath in the valley between her breasts. The tips hardened and tingled, begging for more than the nuzzle of his nose.

"I shall take the greatest care with you, Grace, I swear."

"As a gallant knight cares for his lovely lady."

"Just so."

"Then I shall be content."

"Oh, more than content."

The statement intrigued her. "More than?"

The sensuous slide down his long, lean body drove her nearly witless, especially when the vee between her legs encountered the hard bulge in his breeches. With her feet on the floor, she reached for the ties of her gown.

"Not yet," he said, clasping her hands at the back of her neck. "'Tis one of the pleasures I intend to partake of slowly, peeling your garments off. 'Twill ensure I see and taste every inch of you."

Grace struggled for patience, her imagination taking flight over where he wanted to look, what part of her he wished to taste. He dipped his head for another kiss.

She clutched fistfuls of his tunic, glorying in the sensation of floating, leaving behind her cares and worries. For the next little while her world consisted of only her and Alaine in a softly lit storeroom that seemed more and more a scented bower with each passing moment.

Her innocence enticed him.

Grace might lack skill, but her enthusiasm flourished. She responded with abandon to deeper kisses. Her slight start of surprise at the touch of tongue to tongue sent a jolt of need to his already aching loins.

He fumbled with the ties at the nape of her neck; she deftly unbuckled his leather belt and let it drop to the floor.

Alaine gathered fistfuls of her gown, easing the skirt

upward. Grace did the same to his tunic, slowly raising the hem until able to sneak her hands beneath. Her fingertips skimmed the bare skin along the tops of his breeches until she halted at the lacing.

His control coming undone, Alaine sucked in his breath, willing Grace to tug on the string and free him. Her hesitancy reminded him that she'd likely never undressed a man. Would the sight of him please Grace or frighten her?

'Struth, he'd die a slow, painful death if fright overcame her and she asked him to halt. But halt he would, if she asked.

Reluctantly he broke the kiss. He saw no reserve in her expression, only an unasked question.

"Your gown first," he said.

She raised her arms, giving a permission he immediately took, until Grace stood before him in only her shift—a sheer white veil that hid nothing.

The dark circles at the tips of her breasts drew his hands like iron to lodestone. Within moments both her shift and his tunic lay on the floor, next to the pallet where he and Grace pressed flesh to naked flesh.

Grace didn't think there was any finer place to be than molded against Alaine, his hands stroking her side, his lips tasting the hollow of her throat.

Grace now knew the full meaning of wanton.

She tried to lie still, allow Alaine to do as he pleased

without interference. 'Twas near impossible. Her hands simply wouldn't be still, not when his broad shoulders begged a caress.

Soft skin covered unyielding muscle. This man she lay with played a lute and sang as sweetly as a lark, yet his body spoke of physical labor. A puzzle, was Alaine, and she had only tonight to sort out and fit together the pieces.

Then he rolled her over and lowered his mouth to her breast. His rough tongue licked a sensitive nub and sent her reeling. His hand slid downward, over her hip, then inward, over her thigh, until his palm rested between her legs, over the ache she most wanted eased.

"There, Alaine. Oh, please."

"Here?" His palm pressed against her need.

Grace's sharp intake of breath shot straight to Alaine's heart. Would that he could pierce her without causing pain and drawing blood. Impossible. Unavoidable. Best to do the deed swiftly and thoroughly.

He slid his finger into her wet, tight place. Her body rose up to meet him. He stroked her velvet sheath, heightening her arousal, readying her for his entry.

First he had to get his breeches down. He rolled, reached for his lacing and ended up pinned to the pallet.

Grace wasted no time on pleasantries. She did to him as he'd done to her—spread light kisses over his chest, having her own sweet way with his body.

She slid downward. He held his breath. Then the minx slipped her tongue into his navel and he damn near lost his wits.

"Have mercy, Grace."

Her head came up. She smiled wickedly.

"Do you hurt, too, Alaine?"

"The most delicious hurt you can imagine."

She placed her palm on the bulge in his breeches. No amount of fabric could shield the heat, certainly not the layer of wool between her hand and his male parts. Then she untied the lacing and freed him to the open air and her gaze.

She stared at his staff with widened eyes, driving him wild. Tentatively, with the tip of her forefinger, she touched the head. "You are bigger than I expected."

Through the sizzle of heat and boost to his pride, he heard her hint of worry, and wondered who she compared him to.

He raised up on his elbows. "Expected?"

A rosy hue bloomed on her cheeks. "Sometimes, when the men drink too much ale, they…talk."

Knowing how men bragged when in their cups, Alaine could imagine what Grace might have overheard, likely in bawdy terms.

"Did their talk frighten you?"

"Nay, merely made me curious."

"And is your curiosity satisfied?"

"Not entirely."

She tugged on his breeches. He lifted his hips, then lay still as she removed his garment and boots. Shamelessly she ran her hands up his legs, along his inner thighs, but stopped short of putting her hands where he most wanted them.

"I will not object if you satisfy your curiosity entirely."

She grasped him gently, her cool fingers enclosing him. He lay back and fought for control.

"'Tis as velvet over steel," she whispered, then grew bolder, becoming more skilled with every movement of her increasingly busy hand. He let her fondle him as long as he dared, then pulled her up atop him.

No other woman had ever fitted against him this perfectly. Her soft curves melded along him in singular unity as if designed for him alone. Even as he took pleasure in the joy of skin against skin, in the kisses and caresses that led them ever closer to the physical coupling, Alaine couldn't ignore the stirring deep within his soul.

This woman, Grace, touched him in places no other woman had begun to reach.

Over the years he'd bedded other women, high- and lowborn alike, and generally enjoyed the experience. He'd given and taken pleasure with no other goal in mind but to assuage his lusty urgings.

Tonight, with Grace, he craved more.

He had no right, yet he yearned to possess her so completely she'd never want to couple with any another man. He had no right to her heart, yet he yearned for her love.

'Twas unfair to Grace to wish her eternally bound to a minstrel who roamed the kingdom, to a man she might see but a few times a year. 'Twas against both human nature and common sense for Grace to remain unwed—and to keep herself celibate, except for during his visits.

She'd not be satisfied with such a life.

While his wishes battled with what couldn't be, Alaine rolled Grace to her back and worshiped her beautiful body and bold spirit with the ritual older than time, fresher than spring.

Grace wondered at the sudden urgency of Alaine's loving, but couldn't give complaint. Never had her spirit soared so high. Each brush of his skin against hers focused her needs more acutely. Even as she writhed beneath Alaine's caresses, Grace yearned for the relief she sensed just out of her reach.

The candle sputtered. Grace feared losing the light, wanting to witness every moment until the end, in whatever form that might take.

"Alaine. The candle."

"Have you another?"

"Not in here."

He nudged her legs apart and rose up on his knees. A fingertip to her wet woman's place raised her hips off the pallet.

"This may hurt a bit, but not for long."

Beyond caring, she could only whisper, "Then hurry."

He placed his hands on her hips, lifted her to meet him, then slid inside. His entry caused a sharp pang, quickly over with, replaced by the wonder of his full possession.

Just as she became accustomed to the joining, he braced his hands on the pallet and leaned forward, causing an entirely new sensation Grace considered divine.

Alaine maintained complete control until Grace moved. She rose to meet his rhythm, taking him in deeper with each stroke. She fitted around him like a scabbard especially made for a sword—tightly yet gently, fully, with no room to spare. On the verge of release, from somewhere deep within, he drew will-power he didn't know he possessed, then thanked the Fates when the woman he wanted to pleasure burst apart in glorious fashion.

She went over the edge with her head tilted back, her expression a mixture of pain and bliss. The tremors of her inner tumult caressed him in intimate waves, lapping at the edges of his control until he plunged to the depths and succumbed.

When had a woman ever responded to him so readily with such hunger? Never. Had he ever been more willing to delay his own pleasure for a woman's sake? Not in memory.

In the aftermath of the grandest lovemaking he'd ever known, Alaine realized he must move soon.

Then a sweet smile captured Grace's lips and he didn't think he could bear to budge for the rest of the night.

She stroked the side of his face. "Now I understand why the ladies in your songs take such risks to be with their lovers."

Lovers. Aye, he and Grace were lovers, yet the word rang shallow, wholly inadequate for what they'd shared. Nor did he wish to be compared to the knights who loved their ladies and then left them for months on end, sometimes never to return. But wasn't that what he would do come morn? Leave the Wayfarer Inn and Grace until after Twelfth Night.

And after, what then? Where would she go and what would she do after she sold the inn?

Alaine rolled onto the pallet, bringing the object of his concern with him, unwilling to put any space between them just yet. He held her close and listened to her breathe, unable to imagine Grace in any place other than Wayfarer Inn.

"Grace, what would it take for you to keep the inn?"

She sighed softly. "A miracle."

He'd never performed a great feat, much less a miracle. "I should like to help, if I can."

Her head shifted on his shoulder. She kissed his cheek. "You have. I now have enough coin to purchase a goose for Christmas and hire a village boy to chop the rest of the wood. We will be warm and decently fed until I can find a buyer, even if after Twelfth Night. You are very good for business, Sir Minstrel, and I thank you."

Good enough to thank him by giving herself to him? He couldn't bear the thought that she'd made love with him out of a twisted sense of returning payment.

Nay, not Grace. She'd be more forthright, give him coin. What had happened between them was the result of undeniable physical attraction. She'd desired the coupling as much as he.

"Have you enough to purchase the retirement for your parents?"

"Nay. For that I need to sell the inn. Must we talk about this now?"

Alaine wanted to, but acknowledged that tonight should be spent loving, not talking. Time enough in the morning to find out how much money Grace needed to fix up the inn so she could stay in business. He'd return the silver she'd given him, knowing it not enough to make a big difference but enough to give her a few more days in her home, where she belonged, where he'd know where she was, where he knew her to be safe.

Her hand skimmed his belly. His loins stirred. The need to possess her again overcame him.

This time he didn't need light. He knew her body intimately, had learned where she liked most to be touched and kissed to bring her to bliss. He could see her in the dark as well as if a candle burned bright. Never would the vision of her pleasured smile leave him, burned as it was into his memory forever.

Chapter Six

GRACE woke alone, the room dark but for a wisp of daylight seeping in from under the door. She closed her eyes and lay motionless, still replete and full of wonder.

Alaine made love as grandly as he sang. While her flesh yet hummed from the stroke of his fingers, she recalled the sweet love words he'd whispered in the dark. She knew her lips didn't taste like honeysuckle. Nor was her skin as smooth as rose petals or her hair as sleek as the finest silk. She didn't possess a fragile or dainty bone in her whole body, yet Alaine had likened her to a vessel fashioned of porcelain, to be cherished and handled with delicacy.

If only her lover weren't leaving this morn.

Grace swallowed hard to hold back useless tears. She'd known all along her minstrel must leave for Darby Castle to entertain for the Christmas season.

My minstrel. An unwarranted claim of possession. Alaine belonged to no one, owed no loyalty to anyone but himself—and his music, his greatest love, his very soul.

No regrets, she'd promised him, and truly couldn't say she sorrowed over the decision to lay with Alaine, though she'd rather not have to tell him fare-thee-well this morn.

Grace flung back the coverlet—and groaned.

Sweet mercy, her body ached from the vigorous activity in which they'd engaged, especially those muscles deep within her that had yearned for Alaine's invasion and now protested because he had. A smear of blood stained her inner thighs and the bed linens, evidence of her loss of virginity, proof that she'd yielded to Alaine. Without question, she'd do so again, if he was of a mind, when he returned after Twelfth Night.

'Twas the surety of his return that kept her tears at bay while she dressed. Alaine intended to come back to fetch his horse when finished entertaining at Darby Castle.

'Twas a minstrel's life Alaine led, going from place to place to play his lute and sing his songs. He was good at and enjoyed how he made his way in the world.

Still, mightn't the time come when he wished to settle in one place? Make a home and take a wife. Sire children.

Grace sighed and chided her imagination for embarking on such a foolish flight. She had nothing to offer him as enticement. No dowry, certainly. Soon she'd not even have the inn, which might interest a man used to long hours of sometimes arduous work. She couldn't imagine a man of Alaine's ilk trading a carefree life for one of chopping wood and mending mouse holes.

Too much to hope for.

Or was it? He hadn't minded chopping wood overmuch. He surely possessed a body designed for laborious tasks.

Grappling with the vision of a life spent watching Alaine chop wood, Grace opened the door and stepped into the kitchen.

"Good morn, Grace!" Her mother stood near the worktable on which was spread a variety of food. "I was about to wake you. We have more visitors!"

"So early?"

"'Tis nearly midmorning. You slept overlong."

Midmorning? She'd never slept so late! Grace knew why. Did her mother? Hopefully not!

She glanced at the door, her heart falling.

"Has Alaine left?"

"Not as yet. He converses with the newly come travelers while I fix him a food packet."

Grace tossed on her cloak. "From where are the travelers?"

"London, I believe. Alaine knows them."

Then the travelers were likely headed north, in the same direction as Alaine. How nice 'twould be if he could make his journey in familiar company. Safer, too.

"How odd that he should meet up with acquaintances."

"Oh, more than acquaintances, I would say. Noble, too. Have a good look at his lordship's conveyance. A right fancy wagon if you ask me."

Her curiosity high, Grace went out the kitchen door.

This noble traveled in style, with a large contingent of horse-borne guards and several oxen-drawn wagons. 'Twas easy to pick out the lord. Richly garbed, gold winking from several fingers, he stood near a high-wheeled wagon. Atop the wagon bed loomed a red velvet canopy from which hung matching heavy drapes. Whoever rode inside would stay warm and dry. A right fancy wagon, indeed!

Grace glanced about for Alaine and saw him coming out of the stable—with Yseult on a lead, making his way toward the noble's fancy wagon.

If Alaine took his mare with him, then he had no compelling reason to return.

Alaine tied Yseult to the back of the wagon. "My thanks, Henry. You are sure she will not slow your progress overmuch?"

The noble gave Alaine a friendly cuff on the shoulder. "No more than this damn snow. Truly, 'tis the least I can do to see you *and* your horse home safely."

Alaine had a home? He'd not mentioned one. And wasn't he on his way to Darby Castle?

"Aye, my uncle spares no expense during the season, and Yseult will be glad of the pampering from the stable lads. My thanks for your kind offer."

"'Twas kind of your uncle to invite us to celebrate the season at Darby. 'Struth, 'twill be a grand Christmas."

Grace groped for answers, and could come up with only one stunning conclusion. Alaine journeyed to Darby Castle, and from the sound of it, his uncle was the castle's lord.

Noble blood flowed through Alaine's veins.

The velvet curtain parted to a female hand. "Father, are we nearly ready?"

"Aye, dearest, nearly."

The curtain parted farther, revealing a lovely young woman. She smiled at Alaine.

"Do remember to bring your lute, Alaine."

He gave her a gracious bow. "Lady Constance. Since you are so good as to share your wagon with me, I shall certainly strive to be good company."

"And my ladies and I shall strive to be your most ardent admirers, will we not, ladies?"

From within the wagon came female laughter, and a chorus of agreement.

Nearly overwhelmed, Grace wanted to run back into the storeroom, throw herself on her pallet and pull the coverlet over her head. She couldn't move.

For the first time she saw Alaine as he truly was—

a noble playing at being a minstrel—instead of the wandering entertainer she'd wanted him to be.

She should have guessed Alaine's rank the moment she'd set eyes on Yseult, a much too expensive and quality horse for anyone but of knightly or noble class.

He's not coming back.

Grace tried to breathe, to cope with the onslaught. With her world tilted badly askew, she barely heard Alaine call her name.

She stared at the man she'd thought the most marvelous being in the world. Whom she had led to her pallet and then dreamed of a life with.

Nobles dallied with innkeeper's daughters. They married women of their own rank. Ladies with dowries, soft hands and sweet-smelling bowers.

Mercy, how foolish she'd been.

The urge to scream at Alaine for misleading her nearly won out. Except he hadn't made her any promises, indeed, hadn't been the one who initiated their love play last night. He even, quite honorably, suggested she might have regrets.

All illusions shattered, Grace gathered up the shards of her pride and answered Alaine's summons. With each step toward him, she gained further control over the tears she refused to shed. Alaine mustn't see how badly she hurt.

Grace dipped into a curtsy before Henry, a gesture every noble expected from a peasant.

"Henry, this is Grace Brewer, the innkeeper's daughter," Alaine said. "She assists her parents in the running of the Wayfarer Inn."

Henry gave her the barest nod of acknowledgment.

Forcefully reminded of her position, Grace sought refuge in her role as caretaker of the Wayfarer Inn.

"Greetings, my lord," she mumbled, then turned to Alaine with what she hoped a stoic expression. "My mother prepares your food packet and will bring it out anon. Is there aught else you require of us before you depart?"

Alaine's eyes narrowed. She chose not to wonder what he was thinking, for it no longer mattered. Within minutes he'd be gone and life would go on as if he'd never been here.

"Nay. I believe I have everything I need."

"Then I shall bid you all good journey."

More than ready to escape, Grace took her leave. She got no farther than three steps when Alaine appeared in her path. Though tempted to walk around him, she halted.

"A rather terse farewell," he commented, bewildered.

What did he expect? The embrace and parting kiss of a lover? One night of bliss didn't make them lovers, only a man and woman who'd shared a pallet. He was about to walk out of her life without remorse. She owed him nothing in return.

"I beg pardon if I offended, my lord. I did ask if there was aught else you required."

His hand rose as if to touch her. She stepped back, knowing she couldn't bear it. His fingers clenched before his hand fell back to his side. If it was sorrow that flashed in his eyes, it was quickly gone.

"You gave no offense. Indeed, my stay here has been amiable. I would recommend the inn to any traveler requiring a good meal and soft pallet."

She wanted to scratch his eyes out.

"Your kindness is appreciated. Do mention the inn to all and sundry, minstrels in particular, who will be welcomed most warmly. I have learned they are very good for business."

Christmas day dawned cloudy and gray, but nothing could stop the revelers in the great hall from feasting, drinking and generally having a grand time. Seated in a high-backed chair on the dais, Alaine sipped at an after-supper goblet of fine wine, watching a group of small boys try to imitate—without much success—the feats of the acrobats who had performed last eve.

Holly and colorful silk banners decorated the hall. An enormous Yule log crackled in the hearth.

Guests had robed themselves in their finest

garments, most in jewel-hued velvet. Fingers glittered gold and silver in the firelight.

Uncle Matthew had begrudgingly admitted that Alaine might have made a good choice in trading sword for lute, a gift Alaine always hoped for but never dared expect. A bit later he'd pick up the lute, lead the guests through the traditional carols and, perhaps, sing them the song he'd finally finished this morn.

A perfect Christmas, or it would be if he could shake his bad humor.

Good for business.

Grace had as much as admitted she'd slept with him as payment for his entertainment, and wouldn't mind the company of another minstrel she could welcome most warmly.

He'd expected an affectionate parting and received a brusque send-off. Even after two days of pondering, he wasn't sure how the woman who'd been so warm and giving could turn so cold and contrary.

Regrets? Possibly. Or mayhap he'd said or done something to offend her—though he had no notion what that might be.

Just as he'd always remember the pleasured smile on Grace's face, 'twould now be marred by the bluntness of her rejection.

And why was he wallowing in melancholy over a rebuff by a woman he'd now never see again? What sense was there in going back to the Wayfarer Inn to see a woman who welcomed him only for his value to her in coin?

Why, in a grand hall filled with cheerful people, did he feel so damn alone?

"Alaine? Where are you?" From beside him, Aunt Faye leaned over to put a hand on his forearm. "You sit here beside me yet seem so far away."

He managed a smile for the woman who'd been like a mother to him and done her utmost to make his homecoming joyful.

"Not so far that I do not hear you."

"'Tis not like you to be so quiet or still. You have not been gone so long that I do not know you as well as I did from the day you came to us. Give over, Alaine."

Well he remembered the day he'd arrived at Darby, grieving for his parents, who'd succumbed to severe fever, unsure of his welcome. Matthew and Faye, his only living relations, had given him a true home without reservation. As a child, he'd wept on Faye's shoulder. As a man, he'd not burden her with a tale of woe on a day meant for joy.

"Mayhap I mellow in my advancing age."

"And mayhap you think my wits grow dull in mine."

"Never." He kissed her cheek. "I merely need a distraction from my own thoughts, is all."

"Hmm. Well, be closedmouthed if you wish, but I

will have the truth from you yet, mark my words. In the meantime, tell me, do you intend to sing us your new song this night?"

He'd told no one of the song. "What makes you believe I have prepared a new song?"

Faye flashed a wicked smile. "When I passed your door last night, I heard you playing. Since I did not recognize the tune, I assumed you prepared a new song. Am I right?"

Alaine inwardly sighed. "Right, as always."

She tilted her head. "Is it the song that troubles you? Does it not flow as you wish it to?"

'Twas his finest work yet.

"I believe the song good, but you must judge for yourself."

"I can barely wait to hear."

She turned back to her meal. Alaine glanced around the hall, noting the whereabouts of several men he wished to speak to about buying the Wayfarer Inn, a few of whom he'd already approached. All of them had the means.

Grace had dismissed his wish to help her, but then, she hadn't been truly aware of his ability to help. Nobles were always looking for ways to increase their fortunes. He needed to convince only one of these men to purchase the inn and let Grace and her parents remain as caretakers.

How were the Brewers celebrating Christmas? Had Grace bought the goose for their meal? Had she noticed that he'd placed the silver coin—as well as all the coppers the villagers had placed in his cup—in her money box?

Uncle Matthew rose from his chair, a signal to all that the feast was done and the evening's revelry should begin. Alaine reached to the floor for his lute and a silver bucket.

Carols soon echoed from the holly-decorated rafters. Wine and ale flowed freely. Alaine lost count of the number of toasts offered to Matthew and Faye's good health. Gold and silver coins overflowed the bucket at his feet.

Toward the end of the evening, when Faye's stares became more expectant, Alaine strummed a loud, discordant flourish that never failed to silence a room.

Into the ensuing hush he plucked bright tones and began the as yet untitled song of the lovely lady and the knight who loved her. He'd chosen the style of an *alba*—a song of impending dawn—in five verses, each a mingling of praise for the beloved and curses against the coming of morn when lovers must part.

He sang first in the expected French, letting the music and the words course through him, then began again in English.

Alaine envisioned Grace, her loving hands roaming his flesh, the smile of pleasure curving her lips. He missed the sound of her voice, the spark of mischief glittering in her eyes, the scent of woman that belonged to Grace alone.

> "Of that sweet wind that comes from far away
> Have I drunk deep of my beloved's breath
> Yea, that of my Love so dear and gay
> Ah God! that dawn should come so soon!"

Would that the end had not come so soon. Would that he could return to the inn and he and Grace could begin again.

Would that he knew what had gone amiss.

The last tones reverberated through the hall. Alaine put his lute aside, his heart heavy and emotions drained. The sound of a woman's teary sniff turned his head. Indeed, several of the women's eyes were red rimmed.

The hall erupted in a cacophony of shouts, banging cups and stomping feet. Alaine stood to accept the accolade, his pride boosted by the volume and length of their appreciation. Yet, 'twas a hollow accomplishment, for the woman he wanted to play the song for, who'd inspired him, would never hear it.

Faye approached him, wiping away a tear. "Now I know why you are so morose. You must love and miss her very much."

She might have punched him in the gut, her words hit so hard. Miss Grace? Aye, more than he could say.

Love?

Was it love that befuddled one's mind when beholding a woman of such rare beauty that only he seemed to see it? Did love make a heart yearn for a touch, a kind word, a smile? Had love goaded him to hurry home—not so much to see his family but to find a buyer for the inn?

He'd been singing of love for years, and only now truly knew the emotion firsthand.

"I suppose I do," he told his aunt, and a strange, not unpleasant, quiet settled in his soul.

"Then why did you not bring her home with you?"

Would Grace have come if he'd asked? Likely not. She saw her duty as clear—care for her parents. She'd not have left Watt and Nelda alone at Christmas. 'Struth, she mightn't have accepted an invitation anyway, given her mood the morn he left.

"I do not believe my love returned."

"Fool woman."

Her ire on his behalf made him smile. "Grace is no fool."

"A lovely name, Grace." Faye tilted her head. "Alaine, have you told her of your love?"

A lump formed in his throat, unsure if he could ever tell Grace for fear she'd either not believe him or, worse, not care. He shook his head.

"Fool man."

His aunt flounced off in a huff, leaving him standing alone with his lute and bucket of coins. Not a fortune, but a hell of a lot of money.

Enough to buy an inn?

He bent down to finger the coins. What if he bought the Wayfarer Inn? Grace and her parents could hire the help they needed to have the place fixed up. Buy whitewash, nails and latches. Planks for the fences. Patching for mouse holes.

And Grace? If he eased her burden to so great a degree, might she smile at him once more, mayhap grow to love him, even marry him?

Dare he ask for so much in this season of miracles?

More snow had fallen. However, several horses in his uncle's stable were more than capable of enduring a harsh trip to the inn. His aunt and uncle wouldn't be happy about his leaving before the Twelfth Night celebration, but his aunt might understand, and perhaps he could bring Grace back with him.

Alaine hurriedly scooped up the coins, then went to find his uncle, planning to leave on the first morn he thought it safe for both man and beast.

Chapter Seven

GRACE placed the largest of the three meat pies on her father's trencher. The last scraps of the Christmas goose, drowning in thick, spicy gravy, wrapped in flaky yet sturdy crust, was a shameless attempt to improve his humor.

She'd already endured his silence—after his short, pointed tirade—all morning, ever since she dared utter the word *retirement*. If he didn't start talking to her during nooning, the remainder of the day would be very long, indeed.

While Mother hadn't been talkative, she hadn't lapsed into furious silence. Grace knew that if she won her father over then her mother would follow his lead.

Intent on returning to normalcy, she sat down to her own meal. The pie tasted like dust, went down her throat in a lump and hit her stomach like a rock. She ate half before she pushed it aside.

"You cannot ignore me forever, Father. Pretending

a problem does not exist will not make it go away. I know you do not care for my solution, but neither have you suggested another."

"The inn is our home. I will not leave," he muttered, then took another bite of pie.

She'd heard the exact sentiment this morn, just before he'd stomped out the door. He may not have softened his position, but at least he wasn't shouting.

"I know the thought of leaving distresses you."

"Then we will not leave."

"We cannot afford to stay."

Mother crossed herself. "The Lord will provide. He sent Alaine to us, did he not?"

A blessing and a curse. One could argue that a darker power had arranged for his horse to stumble and twist her leg. Without Alaine's visit, Grace couldn't have afforded the Christmas goose. Because of Alaine's visit, her parents considered the money box a treasure chest.

They'd been innkeepers most of their lives. Surely they knew the extra money only a reprieve, not their salvation—just as she now knew her time with Alaine only a bright moment of joy, not a prelude to future happiness.

She'd come to peace over their difference in rank, and realized his music was his first and all-encompassing love. She had yet to forgive herself for her brusque manner the morning they'd parted. He'd done nothing to deserve her anger and waspish tongue. Alaine must think her a harridan, but there was nothing she could do about it now, no way to ask his forgiveness.

"Alaine's visit filled the money box, but the funds will dwindle over winter. I doubt the Lord has arranged for another minstrel to come our way anytime soon." She leaned forward. "That is why I want to make arrangements for you with the abbot now, while we still have the extra funds."

Father dusted crust crumbs from his hands. "Better to spend the money on whitewash and nails."

"And who will spread the whitewash and pound the nails?"

"I will help you, so will your mother."

Grace bit her bottom lip to keep from blurting out that neither one of them had the strength or energy for heavy or grueling work.

"So we spread whitewash and put in a few nails. What good would it do? Business has not been good for the past two years, ever since…your wounding. I see no reason to think 'twill be better next year." She sighed. "I accept that the dire state of the inn and lack of patrons is my fault—"

"Not so!" His ferocity set her back. He glanced at the arm wounded when protecting Grace from an attacker. "'Tis that blasted noble's fault, damn his hide. He was not satisfied with my blood. He threatened to ruin us, to spread the tale to all and sundry of how we ill-treated guests."

Grace gasped. "A lie!"

"True, but he thought himself ill-treated because I would not allow him his way with you. He considered a wench to warm his pallet as part of the service due him, and believed I should order you to bend to his wishes. When I did not, he decided to teach us a lesson on how to serve our betters."

Grace felt the blood drain from her face. "Why did you not tell me this?"

"You had already left the taproom in tears. I saw no reason to upset you further. We were prepared for a lull in business, Grace. Perhaps not this long or this harsh, but 'twas expected."

"And you expected your arm to fully recover, did you not?"

"I did," he admitted. "But when I finally accepted the loss, you had already taken over so many of the chores that I thought 'twould not matter, that we could still wait out the lull. I believe we still can."

"I believe he is right, dear," Mother injected. "And now we have an ally in Alaine."

Confused, Grace asked, "What can Alaine do now that he is gone?"

"He can help us rebuild our reputation. He enjoyed his stay here, he told me so. If he recommends us to his friends, especially his minstrel friends, we could be prosperous again come spring."

'Twas too much to hope that a good word from Alaine would lead patrons to the inn's door. She also doubted her parents knew she'd given him a less than warm fare-thee-well.

Truly, he'd made her no promises, done all one could expect a man to do to ensure she'd have no regrets. And she hadn't, not until realizing Alaine's noble birth, a circumstance neither of them could change, placed him far out of her reach.

What was done was done. He'd gone back to the world in which he belonged, one of privilege and comfort and music. She expected nothing of him, and neither should her parents.

"'Tis a fragile string on which to tie our future. We could starve before Alaine thinks to mention the inn to any of his friends, longer still before they pass our way in their travels."

"So we give up?" Father asked. "Do we let the bastard who set out to ruin us win? Nay, Grace. We have not held out this long to give up now."

His pride had suffered so severely she hated to deal it another blow, but if 'twas what it took to make him see the reality of their situation, then strike she would.

"Who is truly the winner if the inn falls down atop our heads, or we end up in early graves? Mother will fall first, then you, if I do not precede you by working to exhaustion. Is that winning, Father?"

His eyes narrowed. "You so blithely consign us to graves if we stay. 'Struth, Grace, you make it sound as if finding a buyer will be so easy. Just where, in the dead of winter, with the inn in disrepair, do you intend to find someone willing to purchase and fix everything that needs repair?"

A very valid question, one to which she'd given much thought.

"I will go to the abbot. If he does not wish to purchase the inn, then he may know of someone who does. I may even be able to convince him to barter the inn's ownership for your retirement."

Father opened his mouth, closed it again.

"What of you, Grace?" Mother asked. "You have said nothing of your plans."

"'Tis my hope the new owner will let me stay on, serve ale in trade for bed and bread. If not, I shall have to look for work elsewhere. Heaven knows, I have the experience to manage an inn, not just serve ale."

Her parents exchanged a look she knew well—one of concern over their child's well-being.

"You must not worry over me," she said firmly. "I am young and healthy and capable. I can care for myself. What I can no longer do is provide for the two people I love most, in the manner they deserve. If I know you two are sheltered and fed, within calling distance of the monks' aid if it is needed, 'twill give me peace of mind."

Father shook his head.

Grace pressed onward. "Would it not be nice to rest for a change? Enjoy your remaining days without the hardship of rising early and working till the sun sets?"

"'Tis what I have done all of my life, Grace. Without something to do, what sense rising?"

Grace thought hard and fast. "Then work in the abbey, with the monks who oversee the abbey's hospitality. Surely they would welcome the aid of a man who knows how to treat guests. And Mother might lend a hand in the brewery, or the kitchen. You need not be idle, simply work at a more leisurely pace."

Both were silent for a long time. Mother finally asked in a small voice, "If the abbot sees fit to purchase the inn, might he let us all stay as caretakers?"

Grace had no notion. 'Twas not the way things were usually done. The hope on her mother's face was painful to behold.

"I can but ask. Father, what say you? The weather has turned mild again. I could go to Glaxton Abbey and be back within the space of a day."

He glanced from her to her mother and back again. His chest rose and fell twice before he answered. "Ask."

* * *

Seeing no one in the yard, Alaine dismounted in front of the Wayfarer Inn, dropped the reins of the battle-trained horse to the ground and sped into the taproom.

Watt and Nelda sat at the trestle table nearest the hearth, so forlorn neither uttered a greeting, merely stared at him. On the verge of tears, Nelda's bottom lip trembled. Something horrible had happened. His heart thudded against his chest.

"Where is Grace?"

Watt cleared his throat. "She left several hours ago for Glaxton Abbey, to see the abbot."

His knees nearly gave way with relief that Grace was alive and well. Then he realized why she'd gone to the abbey, to purchase the retirement. She couldn't have sold the inn so quickly! But apparently she had, somehow, if she was off to purchase the retirement. Hellfire and damnation, he'd arrived too late with a sack of money in his pack and a much rehearsed marriage proposal on his lips.

Grace didn't need his money, his help—him. She'd done well enough all on her own.

Alaine eased onto the bench beside Nelda. She gave him a wan smile.

"What brings you back so soon?" Watt asked.

Love of Grace. Misguided belief in miracles.

"I had hoped to purchase the inn."

Watt's eyes narrowed. "Grace told you of her plans?"

Alaine understood her father's anger. "Only in passing, and only because I pressed her. To whom did she sell?"

"She has not—yet. She goes to bargain with the abbot."

His stomach flipped. Hope welled up as he bolted from the bench. Chances were she'd already arrived at the abbey. Chances were she'd talked the abbot into the purchase. Did he have a chance in hell of catching Grace before it was too late?

"Watt, come get my lute."

Alaine was out the door and had his belongings unstrapped from the horse's back before Watt shuffled out the door. He handed the lute over, then pulled down the heavy pack containing a few pieces of dry clothing sprinkled generously with coins.

"Alaine, what are you about?"

Alaine led the way into the inn. "Off to catch Grace before she sells the inn." He dumped the pack into the corner. "Wish me good fortune and pray Grace is a bad bargainer."

"What would a minstrel want with an inn?"

"I want Grace. The inn just happens to come with her."

Nelda finally smiled. "Good fortune, Alaine."

Watt frowned. "Grace always makes a good bargain."

"Then hope I catch her before she has the chance." Alaine hurried toward the door, then stopped. "I assume the abbot will somehow know she has permission to negotiate on your behalf."

"She carries a parchment. Grace wrote it out, and I put my mark to it."

Damn.

The road to Glaxton Abbey proved little better than a well-worn path to the east. For the entire two leagues, Alaine pushed the horse as fast as he dared over the snow-slicked ground. A set of footprints marched along the path, leading him steadily eastward.

Grace's footprints.

He noted where she rested, saw where she must have slipped and fallen, and prayed as hard as he'd ever prayed that she wasn't hurt, but that her journey proved so taxing she walked slowly.

What if she arrived in good time? Abbots were busy people, especially during Christmas. Perhaps the abbot wouldn't grant Grace an audience right away, would make her wait until his schedule allowed—perhaps tomorrow.

Alaine doubted his luck would run so much in his favor.

The horse withstood the rigors of the ride. Within sight of the abbey, Alaine urged the beast to a gallop across the wide expanse of cleared land surrounding the imposing stone buildings.

The gate stood open. He passed through and

brought the horse to a halt just within, then bore down on the first monk he spotted.

"I seek a young woman who came here this morning to see the abbot. Where might I find her?"

"Likely the abbot's office." He pointed. "Through that door, up the stairway. You will find the abbot's secretary at the top."

"My thanks, good monk."

"May the joy of this most holy season be with you, my son."

Joy of the season. Alaine held the good wish close as he again ground-reined the horse and sped up the stairway.

He'd visited enough abbeys in his travels that the wealth of the Church no longer awed him. He ignored the gold-gilt frames surrounding paintings of saints and deceased bishops. The bright tapestries held no interest. Only the round-faced, tonsured monk sitting behind a desk of dark, richly carved wood could help him find his own treasure.

"I seek Grace Brewer. Is she here?"

The monk rose from his chair and waved a hand toward the huge, ornate doors to his right. "She is speaking with the abbot. If I might inquire—halt! You may not—"

Alaine stepped through the doorway and quickly closed the door behind him.

Grace stood before the most ostentatious desk Alaine had ever seen, her hand outstretched, holding a piece of parchment.

"Grace. Wait. You need not sell the inn."

She spun around. Her eyes went wide. "Alaine?"

He crossed the room quickly. "One and the same."

The abbot, garbed in the full regalia of a man in high position in the Church, rose from his thronelike chair. "Who are you, young man?" he huffed. "How dare you enter my chamber both uninvited and unannounced?"

Alaine did him the courtesy of a courtly bow. "Alaine of Darby, Your Grace. Forgive the intrusion, but I must speak with Mistress Brewer forthwith." He snatched the parchment and grabbed hold of Grace's hand. "The Wayfarer Inn is no longer for sale. Come, I will take you home."

He tugged. She resisted. He should have known this wouldn't be so easy.

"What do you mean the inn is no longer for sale?"

He couldn't envision making explanations and begging Grace's beautiful hand in marriage in the presence of an abbot. 'Twould be hard enough in private. So he took the easy way out.

"Your father has changed his mind." A small lie, and Watt would certainly do so later. After all, there was enough money in his pack to buy the inn four times over, or so Uncle Matthew had assured him.

Her brow furrowed in confusion. "But—"

"Give the abbot his due, my dear, then we shall be on our way and the abbot can return to his prayers."

The abbot came around his desk, his mouth pursed. "Unhand the girl."

Alaine never hesitated. "I think not."

"Alaine of Darby, you say?" he asked, the question a threat.

"Sir Alaine of Darby, nephew of Lord Matthew, dear friend of Lord John of Gaunt."

The mention of John deflated the abbot, as Alaine knew it would. He'd have to apologize to John for invoking his name, but guessed his friend wouldn't mind when given the reason. This time, when Alaine tugged Grace's hand, she dipped a small curtsy and followed him out the door.

Too confused for rational thought, Grace grabbed hold of one of the many questions racing through her head.

"Who is John of Gaunt?"

"The king's exchequer."

"The king's—" Grace halted at the top of the stairway, pulling Alaine up short. "You are a friend of the king's exchequer?"

"Actually, I am the king's favorite fencing partner and the queen's favorite minstrel. May we go now?"

"Nay. Hold a moment." Grace willed her composure into obedience as best she could, having been dragged from the abbot's chamber by a minstrel who refused to let go of her hand.

Well, she was holding on rather tightly, too, had no intention of letting go unless she must.

What was Alaine doing here? He'd planned to stay at Darby Castle until after Twelfth Night. He must have gone to the inn and talked to her parents, who'd told him where to look for her or, more likely, sent him after her. The utter grief on their faces upon her departure this morning still haunted her.

"Father changed his mind?"

He smiled, like a little boy caught in mischief. "Come, I will explain everything on the way home."

At the bottom of the stairway stood a large, mean-looking black stallion. Alaine dropped Grace's hand to pick up the reins. Once mounted, he reached for her hand again.

"Think you can swing up behind me?"

Grace looked at the great height and shook her head.

Alaine chuckled. "Then give me both hands, use my foot for a boost."

'Twas an awkward mounting, but she soon sat crossways on his lap, his arms around her for support. A cozy seat, or would be if she weren't up so high. She turned her face into his shoulder until her stomach settled. The horse's gait was smooth, and Alaine's body warm. Lulled into contentment, she wished the inn more than two leagues away.

She hated to disturb the quiet peace of riding through the countryside snuggled up to Alaine, but those questions returned to nag at her.

"You said you would explain."

She felt him sigh.

"I suppose I should first tell you that your father has not truly changed his mind, not yet. He will, however, when I tell him about the buyer I found for the inn."

Grace stiffened. "You lied to the abbot? What buyer?"

He took a long time to answer. "Me."

She sat up straighter, the better to look at his set jaw, to vent her disbelief and growing ire.

"Alaine, you chopped wood to earn your supper that first night. Now you ask me to believe you have enough coin to buy the inn?"

"I do. 'Tis at the inn, in my pack."

Alaine braced for the tirade he felt and saw coming. Then a single tear trickled down her cheek.

"We have no need of charity, Sir Alaine. Set me down and I will go back and see if the abbot is yet agreeable."

Sir Alaine? He halted the horse. "I do not purchase the inn out of charity. I do so because…because…"

Jesu, he'd never stumbled over words before. 'Twas how he made his livelihood. He'd so carefully planned exactly what he would say to her, and now that single tear tied his tongue in knots.

No words seemed the right ones, not even the song he'd written for her.

"Because I want you, Grace. The inn and taking care of your parents just happen to come with you."

She pursed her lips. "Me?"

"If you will have me. Marry me and we shall raise a whole new brood of innkeepers."

Her anger eased, but not her reservations, apparently.

"Knights do not marry innkeepers' daughters."

"Aye, well, someone once told me I could not become a minstrel, either, and I did so anyway."

"Oh, Alaine." She wrapped her arms around his neck.

He liked the feeling, but not the tone of her voice. Very aware she hadn't given him an answer, he hugged her hard, nuzzled into her neck, seeking her scent to give him courage.

"I love you, Grace, cannot imagine my life without you. The money is yours to do with as you please. Fix up the Wayfarer. Buy another inn in some other town. Toss the money into a river, for all I care. Just let me share your life, let me wake beside you every morning."

She backed away, eyes wet, her smile heartbreakingly sad.

"I love you, too, Alaine. I would marry you in an instant if I knew you wouldn't grow to hate me for it."

He opened his mouth to object; she placed a finger on his lips.

"Alaine, what of your music? It is your soul. You would die inside if you must give up being a renowned minstrel for chopping wood and mending mouse holes."

Granted, he'd miss the traveling, the excitement, even the money. But the music? How did he make her understand?

He kissed the finger at his lips, removed her hand.

"The music never leaves me. I can make people happy or bring them to tears. It used to be enough, but not anymore, not since you entered my heart and became a part of the music."

She didn't look convinced. "Could you truly be happy singing only in the taproom of an inn?"

"Should I feel a pressing need to entertain a larger crowd, we can go up to Darby Castle and I can sing my fill. My uncle would be delighted. In fact, if I do not take you there within days my aunt may never speak to me again."

"Surely not."

"On my honor." He brushed a long strand of her golden hair back from cheeks beginning to dry, a mouth touched with a true smile. "I swear, my love, if I had to choose one over the other...well, I could be happy just singing you love songs every night. You inspired one, you know."

"Did I? Sing it for me."

"Tonight, just before dawn."

She sighed and curled up into him again. 'Twas nice, but she hadn't yet given him an answer.

"Grace, you do mean to marry me."

She smiled up at him, her eyes shining with love, giving him the answer he craved without words, setting them both on a path to forever and ever.

"I should be a fool not to marry you," she said wryly. "Have you not heard how very good minstrels are for business?"

This time the words held no sting, only humor. Minx.

Alaine set the stallion to a comfortable pace, the words to a new song coming together. One about a minstrel, an innkeeper's daughter and miracles.

* * * * *

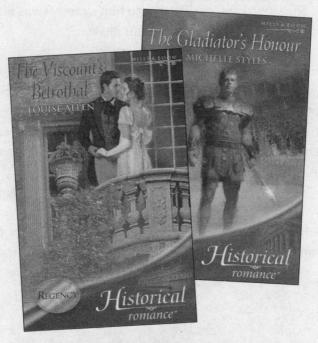

1206/04a V2

MILLS & BOON®

Live the emotion

Historical
romance™

NOT QUITE A LADY *by Louise Allen*

Miss Lily France has launched herself upon the Marriage
Mart in style! The wealthy and beautiful heiress is
determined to honour her much-loved father's last wish
– and trade her vulgar new money for marriage to a
man with an ancient and respected title. Then she meets
untitled, irresistible and very unsuitable Jack Lovell – but
he is the one man she *cannot* buy!

THE DEFIANT DEBUTANTE
by Helen Dickson

Eligible, attractive, Alex Montgomery, Earl of Arlington,
is adored by society ladies and a string of mistresses
warm his bed. He's yet to meet a woman who could
refuse him… Then he is introduced to the strikingly
unconventional Miss Angelina Hamilton, and Alex
makes up his mind to tame this headstrong girl! But
Miss Hamilton has plans of her own – and they don't
include marriage to a rake!

REGENCY

On sale 5th January 2007

*Available at WHSmith, Tesco, ASDA, Borders, Eason,
Sainsbury's and most bookshops*

www.millsandboon.co.uk

MILLS & BOON®

Live the emotion

1206/04b V2

Historical
romance™

THE BRIDE SHIP *by Deborah Hale*

A ship *full* of women could only cause trouble! Of *that*
Governor Sir Robert Kerr was certain, just by considering
their chaperon! Though a widow, Mrs Jocelyn Finch was
young, vivacious and utterly determined to have her
own way – especially with him! Maybe her challenging
the governor to a duel was less than ladylike, but
someone had to show this strait-laced man that there was
more to life than doing one's duty!

A NOBLE CAPTIVE *by Michelle Styles*

Strong, proud and honourable – Roman soldier Marcus
Livius Tullio embodied the values of Rome. Captured and
brought to the Temple of Kybele, he was drawn towards
the woman who gave him refuge. Fierce, beautiful and
determined – pagan priestess Helena despised all that
Rome stood for. She knew she must not be tempted by this
handsome soldier, because to succumb to her desires would
be to betray all her people...

THE BACHELOR *by Kate Bridges*

Diana Campbell knew even a brief relationship with
Officer Mitch Reid, her bachelor auction 'prize', could only
lead to heartbreak for her. A lonely outsider in town, Diana
couldn't help but want this commanding man. Mitch had
returned to Calgary wanting to forget the errors of his past.
He had neither time nor desire for romance – until
Diana won his services for a day!

On sale 5th January 2007

THE STEEPWOOD

Scandals

Regency drama, intrigue, mischief…
and marriage

VOLUME THREE

A Most Improper Proposal by Gail Whitiker

When Desirée Nash is propositioned by Viscount
Buckworth, she is outraged. A year later impossible
circumstances force Desirée shamefully to agree to
become Sebastian's mistress…

A Noble Man by Anne Ashley

To discourage the pampered men her father would have
her marry, Sophia puts out a rumour that she is looking
for a husband outside her class! Could a duke disguised
as a groom change her mind?

On sale 5th January 2007

Available at WHSmith, ASDA, Tesco
and all good bookshops

A young woman disappears.
A husband is suspected of murder.
Stirring times for all the neighbourhood in

THE STEEPWOOD

Scandals

Volume 1 – November 2006
Lord Ravensden's Marriage by Anne Herries
An Innocent Miss by Elizabeth Bailey

Volume 2 – December 2006
The Reluctant Bride by Meg Alexander
A Companion of Quality by Nicola Cornick

Volume 3 – January 2007
A Most Improper Proposal by Gail Whitiker
A Noble Man by Anne Ashley

Volume 4 – February 2007
An Unreasonable Match by Sylvia Andrew
An Unconventional Duenna by Paula Marshall